Reviewers love
New York Times **bestselling author**
SUSAN ANDERSEN

"A hot, sexy, yet touching story."
—*Kirkus Reviews* on *Some Like It Hot*

"This warm summer contemporary melts hearts with the simultaneous blossoming of familial and romantic love."
—*Publishers Weekly* on *That Thing Called Love*

"A smart, arousing, spirited escapade that is graced with a gentle mystery, a vulnerable, resilient heroine, and a worthy, wounded hero and served up with empathy and a humorous flair."
—*Library Journal* on *Burning Up*

"This start of Andersen's new series has fun and interesting characters, solid action and a hot and sexy romance."
—*RT Book Reviews* on *Cutting Loose*

"Snappy and sexy… Upbeat and fun, with a touch of danger and passion, this is a great summer read."
—*RT Book Reviews* on *Coming Undone*

"Lovers of romance, passion and laughs should go all in for this one."
—*Publishers Weekly* on *Just for Kicks*

"Andersen again injects magic into a story that would be clichéd in another's hands, delivering warm, vulnerable characters in a touching yet suspenseful read."
—*Publishers Weekly* starred review on *Skintight*

"A classic plotline receives a fresh, fun treatment…. Well-developed secondary characters add depth to this zesty novel, placing it a level beyond most of its competition."
—*Publishers Weekly* on *Hot & Bothered*

Susan Andersen

Running Wild

HQN™

HQN™

ISBN-13: 978-0-373-78846-0

Running Wild

This edition published by arrangement with Harlequin Books S.A.

For questions and comments about the quality of this book,
please contact us at CustomerService@Harlequin.com.

www.HQNBooks.com

Printed in U.S.A.

Dear Reader,

Some years back, I had a trilogy I called the Sisterhood Diaries. In the first book, *Cutting Loose*, the hero's brother Finn Kavanagh featured quite prominently. Then he grabbed himself another role in *Playing Dirty* (book three). I gotta admit, from the time he began coming to life for me on a manuscript page, I wanted to make him the hero of his own story. And readers apparently agreed, for in the interim between the beginning of that series and now, I've received an astounding amount of email asking when Finn would get his own book.

The answer, of course, is "It's *heeerrrre*!" I'm so excited that the stars finally aligned and the perfect heroine for Finn at last presented herself to me. Heaven knows she took her sweet time. But Magdalene Deluca was worth waiting for as well, because from the moment Finn intervened when a drug cartel soldier tries to kidnap her at gunpoint outside a little South American cantina, the sparks they generate caught even me by surprise.

I hope you enjoy reading their story as much as I did writing it. And my wish, for those of you who took time out of your schedules to drop me a note asking for Finn's book, is that I did him justice in your eyes.

Happy reading!

Susan

This is dedicated, with love
to
Lois Faye Dyer,
who is one of my favorite people.
Thanks so much for brainstorming this story with me—
and all our years of you/me/and Stef lunches,
even if we sometimes have to go to another state
before we find the time to get together.

To
Stefanie (Hargreaves) Sloan.
You're as big a sweetie as yo' mama, and I treasure my
times with you every bit as much as the ones with her.

And
last but not least,
to
Margo Lipschultz,
for years of kickass editing and friendship.
You always make my books better.
And have you noticed that when we get on the phone,
we don't get off in under an hour?

You guys rock.

Susan

CHAPTER ONE

Santa Rosa, El Tigre—South America

THE BLONDE STRODE into the cantina as if she owned the joint, instantly snagging Finn Kavanagh's attention. The afternoon had been laden with impulses and he congratulated himself on following the one that had brought him here.

He'd only arrived in the capital city of this tiny South American country some forty-five minutes ago. After the usual long day of travel frustrations, he'd fully intended to head straight to the hostel that a Kavanagh Construction vendor had recommended. But when the always-in-motion network of overhead gondolas caught his attention, he'd hitched his backpack over one shoulder and tracked down the nearest Metrocable station instead.

As he'd ridden toward the crest of the crazy-steep hill to the north, he'd enjoyed the hell out of the bird's-eye view of the sprawling, bustling city in the valley below. Mountain views from every angle and a river that cleaved the town in two took an already amazing vista and turned it into something flat-out spectacular, sending him reaching for his camera. The higher the gondola had risen on its steep climb to the destination station, however, the more run-down the area below had become. Shanties stood cheek-to-jowl on the flats and if the patchwork roofs were anything to go by, the places were made from whatever materials the dweller could scrounge. More rickety dwellings supported by fragile-looking stilts rose out of the verdant green foliage of the hillside. From Finn's overhead perspective, the area looked big-time poverty-stricken.

The woman who pushed through the door, on the other hand, looked like a million bucks. He frowned, because that wasn't quite right. The vibe she projected wasn't even close to rich girl. But she was sure as hell easy on the eyes.

Real easy.

Not that he could put an exact finger on what it was about her that so captured his attention. She was pretty, yes, but not at all his usual type. Okay, he didn't really have a type. But he could honestly say he'd never gone for the punk girls.

And this chick was definitely that, with those sleek blond sidewalls and the longer, shaggier top that ended in bangs bisecting her eyebrows in edgy points. It was far from a look he was ordinarily drawn to, yet something about her was setting off serious sparkage.

And he honest-to-God didn't understand why.

She was a medium-tall, blue-eyed blonde but, hell, he was thirty-four years old; he'd met an abundance of those. He couldn't claim to have seen many blondes since arriving in this part of the world, but then he'd been here less than an hour. They held no novelty in

Seattle, however, the city he'd called home since birth. And while she had a fine body, again it wasn't Vegas-showgirl material.

Maybe it was the energy she projected so strongly that it practically generated a red aura around her. Or her general vibe, which hinted she not only knew the score, but had maybe even invented it. Hey, a man could hardly ask for more than that, right? Sipping the cold brew he'd ordered, he lounged back in his chair and watched as she strode up to the bar. He made no bones about eavesdropping when she ordered up a drink.

Not that it did him a helluva lot of good. She spoke in liquid, rapid-fire Spanish.

Okay, language barrier. That was kind of deflating. He didn't know why he'd gotten the impression she was American. Maybe it was the fair skin and light hair in a room full of dark-complexioned, dark-haired people. Or the cargo shorts and double tank tops, or that shoulders-squared, tits-out posture with a 'tude. Whatever it was, her Spanish was fluid and sounded like no American-accented version he'd ever heard. He was hardly an expert, but he'd bet it was her first, and quite possibly only, language.

Damn.

The unexpected disappointment had him straightening in his chair. *No*. It was just as well. He'd come to El Tigre for a vacation, partly because he just plain needed one—and partly because lately he'd begun questioning the choices he'd made. Choices that until recently he'd found perfectly satisfying.

He laid the blame for the current rise in second-guessing himself squarely on his brother's shoulders. Of the seven Kavanagh siblings, he was closest to Devlin in both age and shared interests—and last year Dev had gone and gotten himself hitched. The guy was so moon-faced in love with his wife, Jane, that Finn was kind of embarrassed for him.

Yet he found himself surprisingly envious as well. And *that* tipped so far to the left of normal he could hardly wrap his mind around it.

Despite—or more likely partly because of—Aunt Eileen's constant harping about how it was time he traded in his bachelor ways for the love of a good woman, he'd always reveled in his single status. He'd sure as hell never harbored a burning desire to change from a *me* to a *we*. He got enough of that crap working side by side with his brothers every day. So when he'd suddenly begun questioning why he'd been patting himself on the back simply because he'd dodged having a special woman in his life for longer than a night or the occasional weekend, it had stirred up a never-before-encountered restlessness. An itchy sensation that had reached epic proportions when he'd started to wonder if maybe it wasn't time he joined the ranks of the committed-to-one-relationship grown-ups.

So, hell, *yeah*, he was jumpy. His thoughts had never trekked that particular trail before. And he could honestly say he wasn't all that thrilled to have them trekking it now.

That he was even thinking about settling down, however, had driven home how much he needed to get away and see if this was something he actually wanted—if maybe it *was* time he grew up and joined the marriage brigade that was an integral part of his large, extended family.

Or if he had simply been brainwashed by all the happy-happy shit that seemed to surround him these days.

His gut told him it was the latter, but with these chick-type thoughts popping into his head lately, who was to say his gut wasn't overcompensating?

In any event, he didn't have to figure out everything right this minute. All he really needed to do this evening was drink his beer, check out the pretty girl and contemplate which route in this part of the Andes he most wanted to hike. And relax. Yeah, especially that.

Above all else he'd come here to relax.

THIS WAS THE WORST damn birthday Magdalene Deluca could ever remember. God knew, a few back in her early teens had been pretty crappy, but that happened when a girl's parents shipped her off to boarding school in order to free up more time to pour their missionary fervor into other people's kids. Gazing at the shot of tequila the bartender had just given her, she was sorely tempted to toss it back where she stood and hold out the empty for a refill. Hey, she liked to party as much as the next woman and if she got a little buzzed…well, there was no one here she had to be accountable to for her behavior.

A bitter laugh escaped her. *No shit.*

All the same, she walked away from the bar, took a seat at a nearby table and simply stared for a moment into the pale amber liquor. Then she picked up a wedge of lime, bit into it and tossed back the shot of tequila. She shuddered as warmth flowed down her throat and spread through her veins. Yet it didn't touch the coldness in the pit of her stomach. But that was her own fault. Because, dammit, would she never learn?

She'd taken a leave of absence from her life in California to come running down here. The last two letters from her mother had detailed Nancy Deluca's distress with the way the Munoz cartel, over her frequent, clearly stated objections, kept trying to recruit some of the barely teenaged boys and girls the Delucas mentored. It wasn't the letters alone that had brought Mags to El Tigre, however, although those had certainly set up a niggling in the pit of her stomach. It was the way all communication from her mom suddenly ceased after she'd received them. *That* had really made her get her butt in gear.

The abrupt lack of communication had given her a very bad feeling. Because while both the United States and the relatively newer, kinder El Tigre regime had worked to clean up the proliferation of drug cartels down here, plenty of crime syndicates still existed. So did the violence that accompanied them. And despite a bombardment of government-sponsored aerial herbicide spraying, illegal coca crops hadn't been wiped out. Some of the minor grow farms had disappeared, but the larger cartels had merely scaled down their operations and redistributed them to a few smaller, harder-to-reach plots.

Mags hadn't seen her parents in years. But she

didn't think for a minute that her very vocal mother had changed during their time apart. Nancy had never been shy about stating her disapproval over anything she considered wrong.

Mags worried that very fact might have put her parents in danger.

Well, fool me once, right? Because, it turned out she was a chump. No, hell, why be so modest?

She was the freakin' *queen* of chumps.

She had dropped everything and wiped out her meager savings. Worse, she'd given up a prime makeup-artist position on a space epic that would have *rocked* and for which she had campaigned for over a year. All in order to run to the rescue.

God, wasn't that rich? Considering she'd been informed by her parents' landlord when she arrived at their place that the missionaries had gone back to the States on a sabbatical.

They'd just up and left. Without mentioning a word to her about it.

She knew it shouldn't come as a shock, or feel like such a betrayal. Heck, she'd learned five months, two weeks and three days after her thirteenth birthday that not only wasn't she a priority in her parents' lives, but she was an obstruction to their accomplishing everything they'd come to El Tigre to get done. So if they didn't feel the need to let her know that they'd be in the States for a while, well…fine, then. It was nothing new. And she frankly didn't give a rat's ass.

Or not much of one, anyhow.

Mags straightened in her seat. Why was she even

thinking about this anyway? Families were what they were; whining about it was pointless. Looking around for something to distract her from her thoughts, she caught a guy checking her out.

Great. That was what she needed—some local lounge lizard looking to score. And yet...

Locking eyes when his lazy gaze reached her face, she found herself unable to look away. For one thing, she was wrong. His coloring might fit with the locals, but he was definitely American. It was clear in the clothing and excellent dentistry.

Brown hair flopped in deep-set bittersweet chocolate-colored eyes and it took some effort to tear her gaze away. But given the way the rest of her day had gone, gawking instead at the wide shoulders that topped what she could see of a lean, muscular frame probably wasn't an improvement, so she went back to admiring that face.

Its flesh was close to the bone and, coupled with his long bony nose, gave him the austere look of a Trappist monk. Yet when she met his dark-eyed gaze again, she encountered a world of heat.

And for a single tempting instant she considered going over to his table and starting something up. She had a boatload of aggression she'd just love to work off.

But...no. She was going to collect the beater car she'd left down in the valley, where the economically depressed barrio that had been her folks' most recent stomping grounds gave way to a neighborhood a bit more affluent. Or where she'd at least had less fear that she'd come back to find the car sitting on its axles, stripped of its few amenities. With a final regretful look at the hot monk guy, she picked up her huge purse and headed for the door, pulling the tote's long strap over her head and settling the bag cross body as she walked.

The cantina had hardly been what anyone would call a bastion of silence, but the wall of sound that came off the streets the moment Mags pushed through the doors rocked her back on her heels. The engine of a high-end SUV roared as it started up and equally noisy motorcycles wove in and out of the ubiquitous old Volkswagens clogging the narrow avenue. Young men and women laughed and talked and called to each other as they made their way between bars and restaurants. A little girl on a big bicycle pedaled within an inch of Mags's toes.

After dancing out of the kid's way, she stopped at a donkey-drawn cart full of mangoes to escape the crush long enough to reset her mental compass. She bought two of the green-and-blush-colored fruits and dropped them into her purse, then made a beeline toward the street that would take her back to the route she'd used earlier to come up from the valley.

After learning her folks had bailed without so much as a forwarding address, she'd had a potent urge to burn off the overload of furious energy that made her nerves jump and her heart pound so furiously. But had she collected her rental car like a smart person would have and gotten her butt to the airport to catch the first plane out of here? Oh, no. She'd thought climbing the steep hills to this neighborhood was a good idea.

It didn't make sense to her right now, but at the time it had struck her as a good way to work off her agitation.

And to some extent it had been.

Except now she was in no mood to navigate her way back down to the valley. Still, the sooner she got herself down the cliff-like hill, the sooner she could get her ass back to California. Clearly she wasn't needed in El Tigre. And since it had only been late yesterday that she'd had to say thanks, but no thanks to the position on the film, maybe there was a slim chance she could still get in on the production.

Here's hoping. Because she knew exactly what an enormous boost the gig would give her career. At the very least it would allow her to give up her other job.

And creating aliens with paints and putties would be a fabulous stress-buster. She could use that about now.

She walked several blocks before it occurred to her that she'd seen a cable station earlier when she'd been searching for a place to park the car. She couldn't remember precisely where, and she had zero familiarity with Santa Rosa. In her golden pre-boarding-school days, she and her folks had lived first in rough-and-tumble Tacna, further south, then in a small township in the northern Amazon region.

But the Metrocable ran north and south, so even if it was a long walk between the station and her car, it would be on level ground. And that beat picking her way down the near-vertical hills.

Content to have a plan, she about-faced and started back the way she'd come.

She'd reached the main street and had just come to the opposite end of the block from the cantina where she'd had her drink when a man suddenly materialized

SUSAN ANDERSEN 19

out of nowhere and shoved her up against the brick
building. Heart slamming up against the wall of her
chest, she sucked in a deep breath, prepared to scream
her head off.

Before she could, however, a rough, dry-skinned
hand covered her mouth. The man, who wasn't much
taller than she—and was a good ten years younger—
shoved his face close to hers. "I'll take my hand away
if you agree not to scream," he said in colloquial Spanish. "I don't want to hurt you, but I will if you make a
fuss. *Comprende?*"

Not really, but she nodded her head.

"Good," he said, dropping his hand and taking a
short step back. "You're coming with me. Victor Munoz
wants to talk to you."

YAWNING, FINN PAUSED on the street outside the cantina
and looked around to get his bearings. The long day's
travel was catching up with him and he was ready to
go find that hostel.

Even knowing the Metrocable station was to the left,
his gaze automatically went right. And he shook his
head. "Huh. You again."

The same punk-rocker blonde who'd grabbed his attention by the short hairs in the cantina reached out
long metaphoric fingers to latch onto them again. He
still didn't get why she had such a pull on him, but he
couldn't look away from her and a guy who looked
barely out of his teens as they stood nose-to-nose a
short distance away.

He frowned. The kid might be young, but something

about him looked menacing. Maybe it was the way he had Blondie crowded against a wall, or maybe it was the gangbanger vibe of his clothing. The reason didn't matter. Blondie didn't look happy, and although Finn couldn't hear their conversation he got the distinct impression they were arguing.

And that was before he saw the thug grip her arm when she slapped her hands to his chest and shoved him back. Finn started walking in their direction.

He heard the quick patois of their exchange as he drew near and was mere feet away when he saw the blonde suddenly freeze. Then she jerked her arm free. Instead of shoving the youth back again, however, she thrust her nose right up under his.

"What?" Her voice rose in incredulity, but if something the guy had said blindsided her, it didn't prevent her from drilling his chest with a fierce finger. "Let's hear it, Speedy Gonzales," she said with a you-*will*-tell-me authority that Finn would've had a hard time ignoring—and he was accustomed to dealing with customers a lot tougher than this chick.

The thug just pokered up. "My name is not *Speedy*," he spat, clearly insulted—and the fact he got bent out of shape not because she'd challenged his authority, but had assigned him a less-than-macho moniker, reinforced Finn's impression of the young man's youth. The kid thumped a fist off his chest. "I am *Joaquin*."

"You could be Jesus Himself," she snapped, "and I'd ask the same thing—my folks are *where*?"

That's when it kicked in that she was speaking American English. Yet even as the reason for his sudden ability to comprehend the conversation registered, she snapped what he could only assume were the same questions in Spanish.

Finn didn't have a clue what this Joaquin character had said to precipitate the full-metal-jacket questions she shot at him like an unceasing barrage of bullets from a semiautomatic. But from the look on his face, the kid realized he'd made a major mistake.

And that could be bad, because guys that age already harbored a serious need to prove their machismo at every turn. Throw in the possible gangbanger element and things could turn ugly fast.

Sure enough, even as Finn watched, Joaquin's hand reached for the small of his back. The other male stood in profile to him, so he saw the butt of a gun as Joaquin fumbled beneath the hem of his shirt.

Finn was on the move before the weapon cleared the little shit's waistband. With no time to consciously think the matter through, he simply yanked off his backpack and took the final Mother-may-I-worthy giant step that brought him within range. Then, gripping his pack by its straps, he swung it at the young man's head.

It connected with a solid *thwack* and knocked the punk to his knees. The gun dropped from Joaquin's hand and skittered a few feet away. Finn lunged for it, his only thought to keep it out of the other guy's hands. But before he could get his own hand around the pistol grip, the blade of a monstrous knife slashed down, aiming for his fingers.

Swearing a blue streak, Finn jerked them out of range. Jesus. The kid must have a head made of iron—

wood if he'd recovered that fast. And Joaquin clearly had no intention of letting Finn get his hands on the weapon. Not without drawing blood, anyhow.

With no other real option in sight, Finn kicked the gun as far away from both of them as he could.

"Go, go, go!" The blonde's voice was insistent as she grabbed him by his free hand and they took off at a dead run in the direction of the Metrocable.

The woman could move and they covered the distance to the station in no time. She danced in place like a toddler in need of a bathroom as she dug a fistful of El-TIPs—the country's official pesos—out of her pocket, taking quick glances over her shoulder the whole while.

Then she abruptly stilled. "Shit! He's coming after us." She looked around wildly. "Where the hell is help when you really need it?" she demanded, turning back and shoveling pesos into the ticket machine. "I was told these stations are lousy with security." She punched buttons at a dizzying rate.

The machine spit out two tickets and she grabbed his hand again. "C'mon, let's go!"

They went through the turnstiles and onto the platform as a gondola swung around the turnabout and slowed to a crawl a few feet away. It disgorged its passengers in front of them, and since they were the only ones currently waiting they climbed aboard. As one, they turned to watch Joaquin as the young man raced up to a ticket machine, shoving a woman about to use it out of his way.

"Nice guy," Finn muttered. "I'm surprised he didn't

just jump the turnstile." It wasn't like the asshole was your basic law-and-order type.

"Security might not've been around for us to report Joaquin's gun, but according to my mother they're on jumpers like white on rice."

The door to the gondola doors hissed closed and, with the slightest of jerks, the car picked up its pace once again. Finn took his first deep breath since this business began and slowly expelled it. Finally having a second that didn't feel fraught with danger, he shrugged on his pack and adjusted its straps.

Then he turned his attention on the blonde. The girl had soft, seriously pretty lips, great skin and a slight dent in her chin, but right at this moment he couldn't summon up a good goddamn about any of that. Instead he looked her dead in her pretty blue eyes.

And snapped, "Who *are* you, lady? And what the fuck is going on here?"

CHAPTER TWO

MAGS'S ADRENALINE SPIKE hit the skids and she sagged against the wall of the gondola, small tremors quaking every muscle in her body. She stared at the man who had come to her rescue.

"I'm Mags Deluca," she said in response to his question. "Thanks for the intervention." She didn't know anyone else who would have stepped in to help her the way he had and that fact had her chin lifting in pure reflex. "Not that I couldn't have taken care of the matter myself." *Maybe.*

"Yeah, I could see how well that was working for you."

Tempted as she was to dig in and keep defending her not particularly defensible position, honesty compelled her to admit, "Not many people would've involved themselves in a stranger's problems, especially when it meant going up against a guy bristling with guns and knives."

He hitched a broad shoulder. "I have three sisters, a mom, two grandmothers and a boatload of aunts and girl cousins," he said. "It's been drilled into me from *birth* to involve myself if I see a chick in trouble." His voice hardened. "But I'd like to know what the hell I just got myself into."

"Ohmigawd," she breathed in awe, totally diverted. "You have three sisters?"

"And three brothers." He gave her a level look. "Which doesn't answer my question."

"I know, I'm sorry," she said and, with the wave of her hand, knocked away the envy that surged at the thought of having not just one sibling you could call your own, which would be awesome enough, but *six* of them. Just the idea had made her forget for a moment how shaky her grasp on her courage was, but meeting his hard-eyed will-you-get-to-the-*point* stare, she shoved the distraction aside and wrestled herself back on track.

"My parents are missionaries," she said and brought him up-to-date on the noise her mother had been making about the Munoz cartel's recruitment of teens and the abrupt silence following Nancy's letters.

When she fell silent, Finn said, "People still write letters? It's the twenty-first century—I thought everyone and their brother emailed."

"*That's* your big takeaway from what I just told you? That my mother doesn't email?" You would've thought she'd said Nancy sent telegraphs, and she gave her shoulder an infinitesimal hitch. "My folks have spent their entire adult lives ministering to the poor. And while there likely are computers and internet available even in the most poverty-stricken barrios, my mother would consider the time it took to learn to use them a frivolous waste when she can just as easily grab a sheet of paper and slap a stamp on an envelope." Then she waved the interruption away and explained how, when she'd arrived at her parents' apartment this afternoon, she'd been told they'd returned to the States.

"But when Joaquin had me against the wall, he said Victor Munoz wanted to talk to me. He's the cartel leader." Was that right? Suddenly it seemed supremely important that she have the correct terminology. "Or don or whatever you call the head guy who runs a cartel."

Unlike her, he stuck to the point. "Try to stay on track here. Why did he want to talk to you?"

Another stray thought popped into her head and she blurted, "I don't know your name."

"What?" But he blinked dense, inky lashes over those dark eyes and shook his head as if to negate the question. "It's Finn. Finn Kavanagh."

Good name. But this time she knew better than to get sidetracked. "Unfortunately, Finn Kavanagh, he refused to answer that very question. He just kept saying I'd find out from Senor Munoz himself. But Joaquin's clearly not the brightest bulb in the tanning bed because even as he was detailing all the dire things that could happen to me if I *didn't come quietly*, he let slip that my parents are being held on the Munoz grow farm."

"And your first reaction was to let him know you'd caught that?" He shook his head as if he couldn't believe anyone could have such a blonde moment.

"Hey!" Indignant, she shoved away from the gondola wall. "Excuse the heck out of me if I was rattled. I was already reeling from learning my parents had gone back to the States without saying word one to me about it. And then he tells me they're being held prisoner by a drug lord? Hah!" She pointed at him. "*That's* the job description I was looking for." She promptly shook her head, however, because that was hardly the point and, in truth letting on that she'd caught Joaquin's slipup *hadn't* been her smartest move. "*An-n-nd* that's so not important." Looking Finn up and down, she had to admit that, unlike her, he practically oozed competency. "I'm sure you could have handled it much better."

To her surprise, he flashed her a wry smile and said, "Probably not. I would've been rattled, too, if it involved my family. So what's the plan? You want me to go with you when you take it to the cops?"

"I can't go to the police."

He jerked upright. "Are you shitting me? You have to report this!"

"It's not that I don't want to, Finn—I literally can't. My mother devoted an entire letter to the way Munoz bragged about his favorite cousin, who's in the Policía Nacional de El Tigre." She could have added that 99 percent of her mother's correspondence had to do with her and Brian's ministry and their impatience and frustration with anything that interfered with it. But she didn't, of course, because, truly, why should Finn Kavanagh care about her dysfunctional family relationships?

Still, it cheered her up to a surprising degree when he strung an impressive number of truly obscene words together, even though she knew it was in response to her comment, not her situation.

"My thoughts precisely," she agreed. Looking past

him, she tried to see into the gondolas behind them to determine which one Joaquin had caught. It was a fruitless endeavor, however; she could see nothing more than shadows. So she pulled a big, brilliantly colored scarf out of her voluminous tote and turned her attention back to Finn.

"Look, I'm sorry I dragged you into my mess," she said, taking her hair out of the tight French twist she'd worn, with its fanned tail ratted and brushed forward to give her a short-haired punk/goth look. Finger-combing it until she could gather it all in one hand, she then tied it into a loose knot atop her head. "I've got a car down in the valley, so when we get to the station after next I'm going to do my best to bail without Joaquin seeing me. I honestly don't believe he'll be expecting me to get off this soon, since a smart person would choose the main station, where help is more readily available and where you can disappear into any one of a half-dozen regular Metro lines." She wrapped, twisted and tied the scarf around her hair to disguise its color.

Finn cocked an eyebrow at her. "The crapshoot here being that Joaquin's not all that smart."

"Yeah. There is that. Still, I'm hoping someone drummed the idea into his head, because I think it's my best chance to shake him." She blew out an impatient breath. "But this is just a long-winded way around saying thank you for saving my butt. And that I hope you enjoy the rest of your time in El Tigre. It's a great country." Studying him, she tried to imagine him as a big nightclub kind of guy or wine enthusiast, both of which Santa Rosa offered. Somehow, though, he struck her as a bit too earthy to be either. "What brought you down here, anyhow?"

"The prospect of hiking this part of the Andes and maybe seeing a little of the Amazon."

"Hiking, huh? That's your idea of a vacation? Busting your butt, breathing thin air and sweating like a pony?"

His teeth flashed white. "Darlin', that's my idea of pure heaven. And one of the biggest perks? Not once in the wild have I gotten tangled up in a female's problems."

"Wow. You're just an all-around silver-tongued devil, aren'tcha?" She sank to sit cross-legged on the floor and fished the pared-down version of her professional makeup kit out of her tote, then looked up to raise an eyebrow at him. "I bet people tell you that all the time." Still, as they slowed to enter the first station she had to admit that if she was any example, he might have a point. Considering the only thing she'd contributed to his day so far was the prospect of getting shot or stabbed. Not to mention, until they were free and clear, the target she'd painted on his back.

"You should change your shirt," she said. "And if you have a hat, it wouldn't hurt to put that on, either."

She half expected him to thump his chest in a me-big-man macho display, but he merely reached over his shoulders and grabbed two fistfuls of his Rat City Rollergirls T-shirt and hauled it off over his head.

Whoa! All the moisture in Mags's mouth dried up as she stared up at his *very* nice, *very* buff upper torso. Honestly, a woman could light candles to that body.

The door swished open to display a couple of locals standing ready to board. When they saw her and Finn, however, they moved to the next car and a moment later, the door closed again. The gondola glided out of the station.

She was peering into a mirror, sponging foundation that was several shades deeper than her natural coloring onto her face, neck and hands, when the gondola jerked slightly as it approached her station. Nerves jittered through Mags's stomach but she feigned calm while applying a coral lipstick that went with the scarf.

Fake it till you make it, that was her motto.

She threaded big silver hoops through her ears and returned the kit to her bag. After pulling out and donning her long-sleeved SPF shirt, she climbed to her feet.

As their car swung around the turnabout toward the debarkation point, she followed an impulse she knew she'd be smarter to suppress. She turned and crossed the short distance between her and Finn. Reaching up, she wrapped her palms around the back of his warm-skinned neck, curling her fingers to hold him in place. For one suspended moment, she looked into his eyes, which were now shaded by the bill of a faded Mariners cap. Then, rising onto her toes, she kissed him.

She'd intended something swift and sweet—a thank-you of sorts. But the instant their mouths touched, electric shock–like impulses hurtled through her veins and all she could think was *gimme*. And before she knew what was what, her lips had parted and she was kissing the bejeebers out of a man whose name she hadn't even known a half hour ago.

Not that Finn was exactly a slouch when it came to getting with the program. Big-palmed hands slid down her back to grip her rear as he slanted his mouth over hers.

It took every drop of willpower she had to lower her heels back onto the floor, but she did so, breaking their connection. Stepping back, she touched a knuckle to her still-tingling lips. Then she slung the strap of her bag back over her head and, in an attempt to minimize anything that might set off recognition from Joaquin, positioned its bulk on the opposite side from where she usually wore it and slid on a pair of shades.

The doors whooshed open and she met Finn's eyes. "Thanks again, Finn Kavanagh," she said in a voice that sounded rusty. "You did your mama, three sisters, two grandmothers and boatload of aunts and girl cousins proud."

Stepping out onto the platform, she slid on her iPod earphones. Then, pretending to move in time to music she hadn't turned on, she carved a path for herself through the thankfully crowded station.

FINN STEPPED INTO the car's open doorway to watch Mags salsa her way through the throng waiting to board. He ignored the people clumped up in front of the gondola even as they surged forward the second Mags cleared it. He was bumped and jostled but refused to budge. Instead, he did his best to keep Mags's brightly patterned head-cover thing in view as his gondola inched along in one direction while she moved in and out of view in the opposite.

He was happy as a monkey with a peanut machine to have his vacation back, but he had to admit that while the past he-didn't-know-how-many minutes had been far from relaxing, which, face it, was his chief goal for the next two weeks, they had sure as hell gotten his blood pumping. And as he'd watched her sit on the floor and transform herself with the help of only a few items, he'd found himself downright mesmerized.

And then there was the three-hundred-pound gorilla in the car. Her kiss.

Man. He hadn't been expecting that and it had knocked his socks off.

Licking his bottom lip as if a ghost taste might have survived, he felt the cabin door trying to close against his side and stepped out onto the platform. He could always catch another car. But before he went whistling on his merry way, he intended to make sure Mags made a clean getaway.

His gondola glided away, then out through the turn-about and he crossed to one of the center pillars to get out of the flow of still fairly heavy foot traffic. With coloring closer to the El Tigrians, he didn't stand out in the crowd the way Mags had before she'd worked her magic with the scarf and her face paints. Yet even so, he was an obvious gringo. So he found a spot in the shadow of a column that at least partially concealed him as he kept an eye on the two remaining cars that had entered the terminal behind his. Best-case scenario, Joaquin had caught the car still approaching. If that were the case Mags would be in the wind before the guy cleared his gondola.

But, of course, that would've been too easy, and even as Finn watched, Joaquin pushed past an elderly couple who were exiting the furthermost gondola, then stopped dead to survey the crowd. The cabin's remaining few occupants split to flow around him like a stream circling a boulder.

The cartel enforcer, or whatever the hell he was, stood silently as seconds stretched into eternity. His gaze intent, he appeared to be sectioning the area into quadrants and scrutinizing each closely. After several moments that felt like hours to Finn, Joaquin turned back as if he planned to catch the next group of gondolas already entering the station.

Finn breathed a silent sigh of relief.

Prematurely, as it turned out, because Joaquin suddenly spun around, then leaped up onto a bench against the inside wall and stood on his toes, obviously craning to see something. Seconds later, he leaped down from the bench and sprinted for the down escalator.

"Son of a *bitch*!" Clipping together his backpack's belt to keep it from bouncing, Finn took off after him. Chasing an armed-to-the-teeth maniac was *not* how he'd intended to spend his vacation.

Yet how would he live with himself if he walked away and Baby Psycho hurt Mags?

Or worse. Because *hurt* was probably putting a pretty face on things. God knew Joaquin hadn't seemed the least bit averse to shooting her or stabbing him.

Mags had done a good job of disguising herself, so how the hell had the kid recognized her? He understood Joaquin exiting the car at the station. Subjecting each station to at least a cursory check was just good business sense, and the way the cars crept through the station with a new gondola always less than a minute behind, it wasn't as if the guy would have missed his ride if he failed to spot her. But that was the logic of a mature mind and the boy had struck Finn as a whole lot more reactionary than a logical thinker.

So maybe someone coached him. But how had he recognized Mags?

The streets around the station were busy when he burst through the exit a few minutes later and he moved to the side of the door to get his bearings.

At first all he could see was the kaleidoscope of people moving up and down a long narrow avenue made of multicolored pavers. But taking a page from Joaquin's playbook, he climbed onto a bulkhead that separated a restaurant's outdoor tables from the sidewalk traffic and sectioned the area into quadrants. He started with the one dead ahead of him.

And spotted Mags by the color of her headgear a couple of blocks ahead of him. When he shortened his focus to the area between them, he located Joaquin as well. And the other man was a helluva lot closer to her than Finn was.

Determined to eliminate that distance, he set off at a dead run.

He was closing in on Joaquin when Mags stopped at an ancient car that looked as though it was held together by spit and rubber bands. He also saw Joaquin stop. The young man pulled that damn gun from the back of his pants and took a serious-looking shooting stance.

But then Joaquin seemed to hesitate. His heart crowding his throat, Finn put on an additional burst of speed just as the other man called, "Magdalene?"

With a whole lot less certainty in his voice than Finn had heard before.

So he *wasn't* sure it was her. If Mags played her cards right, she'd ignore Joaquin, get in her car and take off as if his insistent shout had nothing to do with her. It wasn't like the kid could follow her on foot.

She clearly wasn't a card player, however, for she whipped around just as Finn came up behind Joaquin.

And as if sensing an impending threat, the cartel soldier started to turn, but Finn, who had several inches on him, drove his elbow into the vein he saw throbbing on the side of Joaquin's neck, then snapped the back of his fist into the side of the thug's face.

"Ow! Jesus!" He cupped his hand to his chest, feeling like he'd fractured his knuckles on the kid's hard head. But at least Joaquin dropped like a stone. Once again his gun clattered away, but this time with a better outcome since Finn was able to snatch it up and shove it into the front of his own waistband. He didn't have time to check that the safety was on. But he did cross himself and say a quick prayer that he didn't shoot his dick off.

Because *there* was an outcome that didn't bear thinking about.

Although, looking on the damn bright side, it at least would put an end to all this bullshit agonizing over should he or shouldn't he be thinking about settling down.

He heard the whine of an overworked car engine reversing faster than sounded wise and looked up from using one hand to relieve Joaquin of his knife and feeling for a pulse with the other to see Mags's junker. At the same time, he felt a thump beneath his fingertips—and had mixed feelings. He'd give a bundle not to have to spend the entire time he was down here looking over his shoulder. But neither did he want anyone's blood on his hands.

Shelving the dilemma when the car screeched to a stop alongside him so abruptly its chassis rocked on its axles, he pushed back from where he was crouched over Joaquin's unconscious body.

Mags leaned toward the passenger window. "Get in!"

He climbed to his feet and got in. She burned rubber the ancient tires couldn't afford to lose getting out of there and Finn retrieved the gun from its precarious hiding place and leaned forward to slide it under his seat.

Without taking her gaze from the road, she reached across the seat and gripped his wrist. *"Thank you,"* she said fervently, her palm warm against his skin. "Again." She gave him a quick glance before turning her attention back to the road. "I made that necessary twice in one day. It was dumb of me to answer when he called my name."

"That's how we learn." He watched as her long, narrow fingers slipped away. Then he raised his eyes to study her face. "So. Magdalene, huh?"

She scowled. "Nobody calls me that but my parents."

He didn't understand why, since he thought it was a prettier name than Mags, if not as hipster cool. But he merely shrugged. "Where you heading?"

"As far away from here as I can. Then I need to get to a phone. I know my mother mentioned the Munoz grow farm in one of her letters but I kind of skimmed the part that said where it was. *If* it actually did say." She took her gaze off the road long enough to give him a quick grimace. "It didn't seem important at the time so I don't really remember."

She flapped a hand at him. "In any case, I'll call my neighbor to see if she'll go over to my place and try to find the reference in one of my letters. It wasn't that many mailings ago."

"Are you kidding me?" Not being hampered by anything so modern as a seat belt, he turned in his seat to stare at her. "Your big idea is to head right into the heart of a cartel?"

"I plan to get my folks away from one, yes."

"Are you undercover DEA?"

She snorted. "Do I *look* like a drug enforcement agent?"

"Ah, the always popular answer-a-question-with-a-question ploy—I'll take that as a no. You trained in special ops, then?"

She sighed. "I'm guessing you know I'm not that, either."

"Then I suggest you get back on your meds, darlin', because you clearly have suicidal tendencies if you're self-aware enough to know you lack said training, yet intend to tackle an organized syndicate, anyhow."

"I do *not* have suicidal tendencies! I didn't say I was going in there with guns blazing—supposing I even had a gun. But if I can pinpoint the farm, then I can take that information to the nearest US embassy. *They* should know which agency to contact to get my folks out."

"Let the cops pinpoint the farm!"

"You think they haven't tried, Finn?" For the first time he heard frustration in her voice and realized that up until now she'd actually been damn calm about all the violence aimed her way. "The government's been aerial spraying the crap out of every grow spot they hear about, so if Munoz's operation is still intact, the way Joaquin made it sound, it's because the cops don't have a clue where it's located." Making a face, she turned off the main street. "With the possible exception of his cousin, that is. But for all we know, they could have a don't-ask-don't-tell policy. And even if they *don't*...well, clearly he isn't talking."

She turned two more corners before glancing over at him again. "In any case, it's not your problem. Where do you want me to drop you off?"

His teeth clenched so tight he felt muscles jump in his temples and jaw. "Not my problem?" he said in a low, quiet voice that would have had his siblings backing away. "You don't think it's a bit of a problem that if I wanna stick around Santa Rosa I'd better be prepared to keep a constant eye peeled for a homicidal maniac who probably hasn't even seen his twenty-first birthday? Because, sister, that boy's gonna be gunning for my ass."

She shot him a stricken glance but he wasn't feeling particularly charitable at the moment. "Much as I sympathize with your plight, lady, you're not the only one who got sucked into this mess." He twisted around to look behind them, then blew out a breath and settled forward again when he saw the road was empty.

Then he looked over at Mags. Her face was set in determined concentration and her hands held the wheel so tightly her knuckles were white beneath her skin. She hadn't asked for this any more than he had, and he knew he oughta cut her some slack.

But his temper, always slow to rise, was equally poky to cool back down once it had. So, even as he regretted the flatness in his voice, he said, "Whataya say we just drive the hell away from here until we put some distance between us and this cartel that thinks it's copacetic to try to kill us? Once we get that part down pat I'll be happy to explore the issue of where to drop me."

CHAPTER THREE

JOAQUIN DRUMMED IMPATIENT fingertips against his thigh as he waited to be admitted to Victor Munoz's inner sanctum. He'd been cooling his heels for twenty minutes and was tired of waiting. Yet the moment the door opened, he braced himself, suddenly wishing he had more time to prepare. Because while his boss was mostly a reasonable man, during those times when he wasn't, he was *really* not. As in, psycho not.

And there was no predicting which reaction you'd get.

But the one thing Joaquin could be certain he'd always get was El Tigre's most powerful drug lord. Standing now in the doorway of his plush office, dressed in pristine white linen, Munoz looked at him with a hooded gaze. "It is done?" he demanded in the English he insisted upon whenever he met Joaquin in his office. "You have brought her to me?"

Easing out his breath, Joaquin collected himself, then shook his head. "I'm sorry, Boss. They got away."

For a second Munoz's expression was noncommittal. Then his eyes turned to obsidian ice. "Define *they*."

"Deluca's daughter and some gringo who interfered both times that I had her. I don't know if they knew each other beforehand or if he's merely a do-gooder who just can't stop himself from sticking his nose in my business. They weren't actually together either time, but were definitely in the same areas."

He couldn't bring himself to admit that one or the other of the North Americans had relieved him of his gun and his knife. Not that it was hard to get his hands on any weapon he desired—he could replace what was stolen from him with the snap of his fingers. Retaining his boss's good opinion, on the other hand—

Well, that might not be as easily achieved.

Munoz swore creatively, but as quickly as his anger surfaced it disappeared behind a calm facade again. This was because Munoz was a businessman. And temper, as his boss was fond of saying so frequently, had "no place in business."

Cold comfort, Joaquin thought, to the man he'd seen Munoz gun down while still in the grip of this temper that had no place.

But that had no bearing on the here and now. He shoved the memory into a shadowy corner of his mind as the older man stood aside and indicated he should step into his office.

"The fault is not entirely yours," Munoz said in a rare near-apologetic tone as he rounded his desk to take his seat. He waved Joaquin into one of the two guest chairs. "As it turns out, the blame in this instance can be laid at my *madre's* feet."

Joaquin shivered and surreptitiously crossed himself. He had no idea how old the venerable Augustina Munoz was. If he were to judge by her thick, sturdy shoes, eye-liftingly tight bun and perpetual black, head-to-toe clothing, he'd say she must be closing in on the hundred-year mark. Yet considering how surprised he'd be if Victor had reached his fiftieth birthday, that probably wasn't so. Unless, of course, she had her son late in life.

But he was once again veering from the track. He'd only wondered about her age because Senora Munoz wasn't even five feet tall and she was a scrawny little thing. He doubted she'd tip the scales at a hundred pounds if she was soaking wet and had a concrete block tied to one ankle.

But the woman was crazy scary. He licked lips gone dry at the mere thought of what she could do and whispered the unthinkable aloud. "She threatened you with the *mal de ojo,* didn't she?"

Anyone who had half a brain knew not to displease Mama Munoz. She'd lock you in the crosshairs of her evil eye in a heartbeat and your cojones would shrivel up and fall off.

And *that* was only if she was feeling charitable.

All the same...

"But, no," he said, shaking his head as he answered his own question. "A mother would never do that to her own son."

"Mine would," Munoz disagreed. "And she did. She has strong opinions, my *mamita.*" To Joaquin's surprise, the older man sounded proud of the fact. But the pleasure in his eyes faded as he focused on Joaquin.

"You know as well as I do," Victor said, "that the Deluca woman has been a thorn in my side for some time now with her constant interference in my business. I speak, of course, of the missionary, not the daughter you failed to bring me." Annoyance snapped in Victor's eyes and his voice grew clipped with the unnecessary clarification, causing Joaquin's blood to cool considerably.

But then the older man seemed to forget his pique as he selected a cigarillo from the ornate humidor on his desk. He didn't bother offering Joaquin one, but Joaquin was perfectly happy to be ignored when he saw how, in the wake of lighting the small cigar with a gold lighter, Munoz seemed to wave his spurt of displeasure away along with the perfect blue smoke ring he blew out. Then the drug lord turned his attention back to the subject under discussion.

"I was through having my new recruits tell me they couldn't run drugs because Senora Deluca said it was wrong. But when I said to my lieutenant in the privacy of this office that the mouthy Deluca needs to be silenced once and for all, my mama, who is studying her Bible two floors away, she sends for me and says no killing of the missionary. The woman has the ears of a ghost bat and she insists that even though the Deluca is a Baptist and not one of the True Faith, she is a woman who does good works and makes our people's lives better." He fixed his gaze on Joaquin. "So I expect you to find Deluca's daughter and bring her to me. She's my leverage to make the missionary toe the line."

"I'm not sure where she is," Joaquin admitted. "The man, he knocked me out so I didn't see which way she leaves. All I know for certain is she is driving a—how do you say it?—a ruin of a rental car."

"A wreck?"

"*Sí*. This."

Munoz pinned him in his sights. "Then track this rental car down—it's a place to start." Shrugging, he swung his heels atop his desk and blew a stream of smoke at the ceiling. "At least we have in our favor the fact that she thinks her parents are in the States and doesn't realize they're being held at the farm."

Joaquin opened his mouth to correct Munoz's mistaken assumption, but then snapped it shut without revealing what he'd done. He didn't plan to end up like the last hombre who had displeased the boss, staring with fixed, sightless eyes at this very ceiling while his blood pooled on the tiles beneath his body.

So he forced a smile. "*Sí,*" he agreed as strongly as he could. "At least she doesn't know that."

MAGS STARED AT the water dripping from the rental car's radiator hose onto the potholed macadam and felt her frustration grow. When it came to most things mechanical, she was hopelessly unqualified. Still, needing to do something, she gave the nearest tire a hard kick.

And oh, crap. That *hurt*.

Determined not to let her travel companion see the result of her childish fit of temper she turned her head away so that even if he looked, which he didn't show any actual sign of doing, he wouldn't see the tears that rose in her eyes.

She blinked rapidly to help speed their retreat. But the tears kept mounting because she couldn't ignore the fact that she and Finn Kavanagh were in the middle of nowhere. Admittedly, that wasn't unusual in this country where most of the population centered around a handful of cities, but they were still who *knew* how many miles from even the smallest township. With a dead car.

"Worthless piece of crap," she muttered.

"That's not necessarily true." Finn, squatting on the road in front of the car's raised hood, quit pawing through his backpack to look up at her.

Strictly to disagree, of course. They'd only known each other a few hours and already she understood that they looked at darn few things through the same spectrum. Turning away, she hastily wiped away her stupid, stubborn tears.

"This car's actually in better shape than she looks," he said with an irritating good cheer that made her want to kick another tire. She turned back to see him once again digging through his bag. A second later, he made a satisfied noise deep in his throat and pulled out a roll of red tape. "This oughta fix her," he said and surged easily to his feet.

"What? Really?" Her tears evaporating along with her foul mood, she stepped forward to see. Not that she had the first idea what was so magical about the tape that it could restore function to their rental—and probably wouldn't even if it came with detailed instructions.

"Yep. Here, hold this." He handed her the roll. "Put your fingers through the spool like so." He touched his index fingertips together to demonstrate.

She did as directed and, standing this close, gained an unwelcome awareness of the clean scent of his skin. To keep herself from staring at the damp cotton that banded his biceps and stretched across his strong chest, she looked down at the roll slowly rotating around her finger bridge as he unspooled a length. It had some kind of plasticky substance that kept the layers from touching. "What is this stuff?"

"Silicone tape," he said as he separated a good foot of it from the roll. "Best invention ever. It tolerates high temperatures and sticks to itself. That adhering part's no small deal, because it eliminates the need for clamps." He looked around and, with a jut of his jaw, indicated the knife he'd liberated from Joaquin. "Hand me that, will ya?"

Sliding one hand free of the roll, she reached for the knife and passed it to him. Finn sliced off the length he needed, then turned back and bent over the engine compartment. Mags leaned to watch over his shoulder as he peeled the plastic strip from the tape a few inches at a time, wrapped the revealed silicone tape around the damaged hose and repeated the process, meticulously overlapping each rotation around the tube.

To distract herself from the display of muscle that shifted beneath his skin with every flick of his wrists, she said, "You always bring an emergency roll of tape on your vacations?"

"If I'm going hiking, I do." He gave her a dark-eyed glance over his shoulder. "Which was my intention, you might recall."

It was difficult to forget, since guilt over the way she'd dragged him into her mess still made her squirm. But she'd said she was sorry umpteen times since they'd gotten away from Joaquin, so she bit back the fresh apology rising her throat. She had to keep reminding herself that she hadn't deliberately drawn him in to her mess, that he'd actually inserted himself. Working to let go of her tendency to make it all her fault, she merely said, "Yes." But she couldn't resist giving his shoulder a commiserating little there-there pat.

It was unyielding but hot under the damp cloth beneath her fingers and she whipped her hand away. Because, really, it was one thing that she'd kissed the man when she believed she'd never see him again. But now that they were practically living in each other's pocket, she'd be wise to keep her hands to herself. She cleared her throat and forced lightness into her voice when she said truthfully, if with a slightly sarcastic tone, "You're a handy guy."

"I am that, darlin'. There!" He straightened.

She was still hovering over him and his shoulder blades made contact with her boobs, flattening them against the wall of her chest. She took a hasty step back.

And almost fell on her butt when the molded rubber heel of her Tevas caught in a divot in the optimistically termed highway.

Long, work-roughened fingers closed around her upper arm to halt her backward momentum. "Easy there." He pulled her upright and gave her a comprehensive once-over before he turned her loose.

"Thank you. But I could've—"

"Done it your own self," he said sardonically before she could complete her sentence. "Yeah, yeah. Been there, heard that."

She huffed out a put-upon sigh and rubbed a hand

over her lips with enough vigor to shift them about as
though they were made of Silly Putty. The feel of them
beneath her fingers reminded her of what she could do
to features with her tool kit of tricks. That in turn reminded her of what she was good at—and what she
wasn't. She dropped her hand to her side.

"Yeah," she sighed. "I do like doing things myself."
A girl was much less likely to be disappointed if she
didn't allow herself to become dependent on others.
"But, much as I hate to admit it, I would've fallen on
my keister without your help. So thanks again."

He looked down at her, his dark eyebrows drawing
together. "Dammit, I wish you'd stop doing that."

"What? What did I do wrong this time?"

"Acted reasonable."

She felt her mouth drop open and snapped it shut.
"And that's a bad thing?"

"It is when it messes with my conviction that you're
a thoughtless, spoiled brat."

"Excuse me?" Her hands hit her hips. "I'll cop to
being thoughtless at times. But I'm here to tell you I've
never been spoiled in my life."

"Uh-huh." He gave her a quick up and down perusal.
"You're an only child, right?"

"Yes." She narrowed her eyes. "But how did you
know that?"

"It's a no-brainer, darlin'—you were way too awe-
struck by the number of my siblings." He made a rude
sound. "Only someone who's never dealt with a brother
or sister of her own would have that reaction."

"Maybe I was just astounded that your folks would continue having kids after they rolled you off the production line. No, wait." She narrowed her eyes at him. "You must be the baby of the family. Otherwise, they surely wouldn't have risked having more like you."

To her surprise he laughed. "Good one. I'll have to remember that for Kate." He met her gaze. "The actual baby of the family. But getting back to you, you had your parents' undivided attention and you want me to believe you weren't spoiled rotten?"

It was her turn to snort. "This may come as a shock to you, Kavanagh, but I don't particularly care what you believe. But as for Nancy and Brian's undivided attention—my ass, I had that. They shipped me off to boarding school in the States when I was thirteen so they could concentrate on other people's kids."

"Whoa." He stared at her, and for a second she felt a hint of vindication. She knew playing the unwanted-kid card was not cool and, yes, probably smacked of juvenile gamesmanship. She usually put a much better face on things so people wouldn't realize how much it had destroyed her to learn her parents' love had come with an expiration date. But he was just so darn smug that it had slipped out.

Apparently she'd misread what she'd taken for sympathy, however. He merely raised those expressive brows and gave her a cool look from his dark, heavily lashed eyes. "And you're complaining about that? I *wish* I'd been sent to boarding school. I had to share a bedroom with three brothers."

"Oh, poor you." She had to swallow a hot ball of rage at his lack of appreciation for something she'd have given everything she had to possess. "It must have been hell having to put up with companionship and always having someone on your side."

"Hey, you live in a twelve-by-twelve-foot room with a bunch of big slobs, then we'll talk." He thrust a forefinger at her ever-present tote. "You got a bottle of water in that thing?"

She pulled one out and barely resisted throwing it at his head. She did shove it a little harder than necessary into his stomach and took her satisfaction where she could when a quiet "Oof!" burst from his throat.

That contentment died an abrupt death when he lifted his shirt, studied the rock-hard abs he'd exposed and said, "Sure hope that doesn't bruise my delicate skin."

Damn him.

It didn't help that he was Mr. Self-Possessed while she felt like a cartoon character about to have steam explode from her ears with a strident end-of-shift whistle from the sheer overload of bottled-up frustration.

And, fine, lust as well.

But she would cut her tongue out before she'd give him the satisfaction of knowing he was getting to her. Watching him turn away to pour the water into the radiator, she acknowledged that it was too late to unsee the hard ridges of his abdomen and the silky stripe of dark hair that bisected it. She could, however, shove it into a far, dark corner of her mind. And act like the adult she'd been since striking out on her own at eighteen.

But, good Lord. If she behaved this Maggie-middle-school over spying a little man skin, she'd clearly gone far too long without getting any.

She was going to have to do something about that when she got back home.

CHAPTER FOUR

WHAT THE HELL are you doing, Kavanagh?

It was an excellent question, but Finn shrugged it aside in favor of transporting his backpack and an old beat-up carry-on suitcase Mags had retrieved from the trunk of the car into the tiny room they'd rented for the night in an El Tigre version of a B and B.

He gave the place a cursory glance. *Boardinghouse* was probably a more accurate description and he gazed over his shoulder, curious to see Mags's reaction to their accommodations.

She didn't even seem to notice. She looked worn-out and discouraged as she trudged behind him, that big ol' purse of hers, which she'd been hauling around with such panache, all but dragging on the floor.

Something about the discouragement her posture conveyed made his gut clench.

Not that her expression lasted once she noticed him looking at her. Because the instant she did, her slightly cleft chin jutted skyward.

Masking the involuntary smile wanting to spread across his face, he dropped his pack and the suitcase to one side of the doorway just inside the cramped ac-commodations. Then he took one look at the narrow bed and any inclination to smile was wiped away. "I'll take the floor."

Given a choice, he'd have taken a different *room*. But of the three townships they'd come across during the hours spent driving south toward the Amazon, this was the only one that had offered a place with rooms to let. And this room had been the sole vacancy.

"Don't be silly," Mags said. "You *paid* for the room—you oughta sleep in the bed."

"I'm a hiker, darlin'." He tapped his backpack with the side of his foot. "I have everything I need right here."

Looking around, he gave the room a closer inspection. The bedspread was threadbare but immaculate, and not so much as a fleck of dust marred the small scarred dresser next to the bed or the carved crucifix hanging above it. The only other amenity to grace the tiny room, a sturdy wooden chair, held two neatly folded towels and washcloths. All four were thin in texture but blindingly white beneath the light from the dresser lamp.

He turned back to Mags. Her I-don't-need-your-stinking-help attitude, which seemed to blink on and off like a light in a defective socket, was nowhere to be found at the moment. During a stop a couple of hours back—the last one just before the sun went down with such startling speed—she'd washed off the dark makeup she'd applied in the gondola. And sometime between then and now her fair skin had lost its natural glow, her cheeks their wash of pink.

Squatting in front of his pack, he pulled his ultralight sleep pad out of the deep pouch on the pack's side and unfastened the straps that attached the sleeping bag to the rucksack's bottom. He carried both to a spot as far removed from the bed as he could manage and unrolled them. In less than a minute he had his nest prepared and, giving it a pat, he glanced up at Magdalene.

Only to see her sitting on the side of the bed, staring vacantly down at the long, pale fingers she'd threaded together in her lap.

"Hey," he said softly, rising to his feet. He reached to stroke soothing fingertips to her shoulder, making her jerk and her gaze lock with his. He stroked his thumb over the spot he'd touched. "Didn't the lady at the desk say something about a bathing room?"

She nodded. "Down the hall."

"Why don't you go grab a shower and I'll see about getting us some food."

For a moment she simply looked at him, then visibly gathered herself. "You speak Spanish?"

"Sure." When she merely looked at him, he admitted, "A smidge, anyhow. I understand more than I speak—provided it's not too rapid-fire."

Her lips tipped up in a slight smile. "Unfortunately, it requires more than a smidgen in most of these out-of-the-way villages. The people who live in them tend not to travel far from home, so they don't have the same familiarity working with tourists that their city counterparts do. Add to that how late it is and—" She rose to her feet. "You take the first shower and I'll go talk to Senora Guerrero about where we can buy some food. I didn't realize until you brought it up, but I'm starving."

He watched as she walked from the room and wondered where this weird urge to comfort her, or cheer her up had come from. Hell, he'd grown up with sisters who could manipulate like nobody's business to get what they wanted. Consequently, his more usual first response when presented with a female who looked at him with big, sad eyes would be to question if he was being played. Not to feel an urge to fix what ailed her.

So why the hell had he wanted to fix things for Magdalene?

He shrugged and let it go. She wasn't his sister and she'd spent most of their time together bending over backward trying to get him to step *away* from her problems, not take care of them for her. Besides, offering her the shower had led to her assigning herself a task. And if nothing else, that seemed to give her back some of her energy.

So his job here was done.

He rummaged through his pack for a bar of soap and cautiously sniffed his T-shirt's underarms to see if he dared put it on again after his shower. Fortunately, his deodorant had held up, but the shirt was limp and still slightly damp. Santa Rosa had been warmly springlike, cradled as it was in the foothills of the Andes. But with every foot of elevation lost and each mile farther south that they'd driven, it had become hotter—until sweat had pretty much been the order of the day. And looking at his watch, Finn saw that although it had just turned ten, even with the small room's louvered window open, the night was hot and still.

But not quiet. There was a cantina on the corner and

the sounds of guitars and merriment were a faint rhythm in the air. At the window insects clicked and whirred as they threw themselves against the thin screen. And somewhere among the cacophony of crickets out in the darkness, frogs croaked and an unidentified creature occasionally barked in a tone eerily seal-like.

He dug through his pack again to retrieve the Rat City Rollergirls T-shirt he'd changed out of in the gondola, then picked a towel up off the chair and headed down the hall. He washed his clammy shirt in the sink, wrung it out as best he could and carefully spread it over the basin. Then he stepped into the shower.

The space was narrow, the water pressure weak, and regardless of how cautious he tried to be, he couldn't avoid bumping his shoulders or occasionally knocking an elbow against the enclosure walls. The water, however, was wonderfully cool. And when he stepped out several moments later, he felt refreshed.

But he still didn't have a clue what he was doing here. He and Mags had stopped in a small town below Santa Rosa so she could call her neighbor from a landline. Her cell phone was low-tech and didn't support international calls. Not that his smartphone was appreciably better. Coverage was spotty everywhere except in cities and more well-populated towns.

On the bright side the woman had been home, but it had taken her a while to find the correct letter from Magdalene's mother and get back to them with the general location where Nancy Deluca had believed the grow farm to be.

At no time during their wait and the several additional hours they'd driven had there been any sign of Joaquin. So Finn could probably let her take it from here and get back to his vacation.

Except he couldn't quite shake the feeling that the minute he turned his back, Joaquin or someone like him would track her down. And the thought of leaving Magdalene on her own to twist in the wind chafed against every behavior he'd been raised to adhere to when it came to women. So he was sticking until she found the grow farm. And if his decision didn't exactly thrill him?

It was still accompanied by a strange feeling of relief.

THE MERE SCENT of the rice and beans and the two fat shellfish-filled empanadas on the tray Mags carried cheered her up. She'd expected to be directed to the cantina for such a late meal, but Senora Guerrero had happily insisted on heating up leftovers for her and Finn.

The thought of the generously poured glasses of wine the older lady had included didn't hurt her vastly improved outlook. The woman was a love. During their chat as the senora assembled the meal, Mags had admitted how exhausted, yet wired, she felt. Mrs. G. had promptly splashed some rich red wine into a glass for her, then poured the rest into the additional two goblets to add to the serving tray.

Mags acknowledged she was running on fumes. She'd rolled out of her cushy pillow-top bed in LA at zero-dark-thirty this morning and felt as if she'd been awake for a straight two days rather than the nineteen or so hours it had actually been. And the minute, the very *instant*, she finished eating, she planned to grab that shower, then tumble into bed.

What she *didn't* intend to do was turn herself inside out any longer stressing over Finn's involvement in her mama's drama. He seemed okay with it—at least for the most part. She'd simply have to find a way to be so as well.

Arriving back at their shared room, she balanced the tray on one hip and freed a hand to turn the doorknob. After taking the platter in both hands once more, she used her left hip to push the door all the way open, then backed into the room, turning as the tray cleared the opening. She spotted Finn over by the chair, spreading a wet T-shirt atop his damp towel over the chair's back. "You ready to eat?"

"Oh, hell, yeah." He inhaled deeply through his nose. "Man, that smells good." Finger-combing his hair back, he came over to her and took the tray. "Oh, God, you even scored us some wine. You are a *goddess*."

"I know, right?" She shot him a grin. "About the wine, that is, not the goddess part. Give me hot food and a nice glass of red and for this moment, at least, life is good."

He looked down at the platter in his hands. "Where do you want this?"

She liberated a plate, balanced her cutlery atop it and sank to sit cross-legged on the floor in front of the bed. She patted the tile next to her hip. "Right here is fine."

"Works for me." He handed her a glass of wine and sat down next to her with his own food and drink. For the next several minutes the only sound in the room was the clink of silverware against the brightly patterned crockery and the slight tap of their glasses when they set them back on the tile floor between sips of wine.

After scraping up the last of his empanada, Finn set his fork on his plate and the plate on the tray and rested his head back against the side of the bed. "I'm beat," he said. "I'll take the dishes downstairs while you take your shower, then I've gotta hit the sack. I've been up since three a.m."

"You just came in today, too?"

"Yeah. You?"

"Yes. And I only had a half hour's more sleep than you." She climbed to her feet and started gathering her towel and a few toiletries together. "I'll be back in five minutes."

It wasn't much longer than that when she returned to the room, but Finn was already sound asleep, an occasional snore erupting between deep, regular breaths.

She couldn't prevent herself from staring at him as she towel-dried her hair. He hadn't bothered unzipping his sleeping bag and he sprawled atop it in a posture that combined side and stomach sleeping. She knew it was hot in the room, but she found it hard to ignore the fact that he wore nothing but a pair of black-waistbanded, gray boxer briefs.

One muscular up-drawn leg stuck out to the side and his head was cradled atop biceps that looked much too hard to be comfortable. His back was an art-class study in wide shoulders, long, supple spine and the hard, rounded curve of a butt that gave way to yard-long, leanly muscled legs. And all that bare skin gleamed with good health beneath the lamplight he'd left on for her.

Pulling off the shorts she'd donned to traverse the hallway, she folded them atop her suitcase, then applied lotion to her arms and legs. Dressed in only her undies and a tank top, she quickly braided her damp hair, turned off the lamp and, tossing back the spread, slid between the sheets.

She fell asleep the instant her head hit the pillow.

IT FELT LIKE five minutes later when someone shook her shoulder. Trying to shrug the irritant aside, she rolled onto her side.

But the touch returned with even more insistence, and she cracked an eye open. "Mmmph?"

"Wake up, senorita," Senora G. said in an adamant whisper. "You have to leave."

Mags pushed up onto one elbow and blinked up at the older woman, trying to make out her features in the dark room. "Leave?" she repeated in confusion. "Why?"

"I walked over to the cantina to have a drink with my neighbors and a man came in demanding to know if we'd seen a couple answering to your and Senor Finn's description."

A cold dose of water to the face couldn't have worked better to wake her fully. "A young man?"

"Sí. I did not like his looks." A slight displacement of air against Mags's face suggested Mrs. G. waved her hand. "Not his looks," she amended. "His…manner."

"If he's who I think he is, you're right to be leery of him. His name is Joaquin and he works for a dangerous drug lord." Hearing a rustling, she raised her voice slightly. "Finn, are you awake?"

"Yeah. Did I hear Joaquin's name?"

"Yes. We gotta get out of here." She relayed the senora's news.

He was a shadowy figure sliding off his sleeping bag, and she rose onto her knees to turn on the lamp. Blinking against the sudden light, she saw him crouched in front of his bedroll, readying its two pieces with swift efficiency for a return to their respective places on his pack.

He glanced at her over his shoulder. "Tell Mrs. G. that when Joaquin shows up here she needs to tell him the truth—that she rented us a room. And for her own safety, she should try to act surprised when he finds us gone."

Mags interpreted for Senora Guerrero as she scrambled into her clothing, then translated Mrs. G.'s reciprocal warning to be as quiet as possible because Hector down the hall was both a light sleeper and an incorrigible gossip. Looking at her watch, Mags saw she'd slept longer than it had felt like. It was almost 1:00 a.m.

Finn finished dressing before her, and the instant he had his shoes tied, he carried his gear over to the backpack. After storing it, he glanced over at Mags's suitcase, then turned those dark eyes on her. For a single brief, hot moment his gaze slipped over her still bare legs before rising to meet her eyes.

"We might not be able to get to the car and if that turns out to be the case it's gonna be difficult to move fast hauling a suitcase. I have a little room in my pack

for some of your stuff. You think maybe you can fit part
of it into your purse?"

She nodded and grabbed a change of clothing, a
sweater in case the evenings grew cooler than tonight,
clean undies, socks, a pair of shoes to supplement her
sandals and, after a brief internal debate, her performance gear. She handed a share of it to Finn and stuffed
the rest into her tote. She pinned up her braid, tied another scarf around her head to disguise her hair color
and used a pencil to quickly darken her eyebrows and
draw a beauty mark next to her upper lip.

Finn swung the rucksack onto his back and came
over to the senora. *"Muchas gracias,"* he said with palpable heartfelt appreciation and bent to press a fleeting
kiss upon the older woman's forehead. Then he turned
to Mags.

"Let's move," he said briskly, and headed with long-
legged strides for the door.

She followed in his wake.

The senora was right behind her. "Leave through the
kitchen," she said in a low voice.

Finn had already entered the room before Mags could
finish speculating how much she dared raise her voice
to translate Senora Guerrero's instruction. He made a
beeline for the back door, but Mrs. G. raced to place
herself between him and the exit. She put a hand on
his chest and pointed first to herself, then out the door.

Stepping back, he nodded, and the senora grabbed
a lidded earthenware pot from the counter, turned off
the kitchen light and opened the back door. She carried
the pot over to a compost heap and emptied the kitchen

waste onto it, glancing casually around the small yard as she did so. Straightening, she made a small, close-to-her-body hand gesture to indicate they should come out.

She and Finn had no sooner stepped into the yard when a pounding commenced on the front door and for a second Mags thought her heart had stopped. Then it thundered in her chest with such force she was surprised the entire neighborhood didn't start yelling for her to keep it down out there. Mrs. G. scuttled past them into the kitchen and quietly closed the door behind her. Mags jumped when Finn's work-roughened fingers suddenly wrapped around her wrist.

He placed the knife he'd liberated from Joaquin in her hand, and she saw that he'd retrieved the gun as well.

"Come on," he breathed and edged around the corner of the house.

For a second she stared down at the knife in horror. Then she gave herself a mental shake and took a giant step to catch up.

He put a hand back to halt her when they reached the front corner of the house and cautiously he craned his head to look around its edge. Almost immediately, he pulled back and lowered his mouth to her ear. "There's a guy keeping an eye on our car," he said. "And there's an SUV in front of it that's too shiny and new to belong to anyone but city guys." He hesitated, then asked, "What are your thoughts on distracting him while I disable it?"

Her stomach went queasy and she wanted to say, "Are you out of your freaking mind?" Instead, she whispered, "No problem," and handed him back the knife.

She yanked her tank top down to showcase some cleavage and tucked it into her shorts to keep it low and tight. "I'd better cut through the neighbors' yards, though. Coming out of this one won't help our cause."

"Wait." He gripped her arm. "I don't know what I was thinking." His voice was surprisingly fierce for a tone so low-pitched. "Because on second thought, putting you in danger doesn't seem like such a hot idea."

No shit, Sherlock, her mind agreed, so relieved she wanted to break into a dance. Because it really was a lousy idea. But her big mouth said, "And yet, it's the only idea we have. And I really like the thought of you disabling their car. Otherwise, they'll be right on our tushies, and if that's the case I don't think we'll have a prayer of shaking them."

He was quiet for a moment. "Here, then." He thrust the gun at her. "Take this."

Her hands flew back, palms out, in repudiation. "I'm not going to shoot the guy!"

"Then use it like a hammer if you need to," he said in a hard whisper. "Because, baby, if it comes down to you or him, better that you're the one who walks away."

True. But still—

"I've never handled a gun in my life, Finn. He's more likely to take it away and use it against me."

"Then, here." He held out the knife. "Take this back."

"No. It's too big and the same thing applies. Plus, you might need it to disable the car."

He studied her for a nanosecond, then nodded. "Okay. You have anything small and sharp in that behemoth purse?"

"Yes!" She dug out a pair of pointy little manicure scissors and immediately felt better to have some kind of weapon she could easily hide.

Finn looked less than impressed with her choice, but he didn't say anything. Instead, he bent down and pressed the same kind of kiss to her forehead that he'd given Senora Guerrero. She felt surprisingly strengthened by it.

Then he stepped back. "Good luck, Magdalene."

"Mags," she insisted.

"Mags," he agreed and repeated, "Good luck. And be careful."

"You, too." She turned and went to the back of the yard before crossing to the one next door, then slipped through that and a couple more fenceless adjoining yards. As she crept along the side of a little house several down from Senora Guerrero's, she pulled out a richly pigmented lipstick and dabbed some on her mouth, rubbed her lips to give her what she hoped was a just-been-thoroughly-kissed look, then massaged the color that had transferred to her fingertips into the apples of her cheeks.

She waited until the man standing guard over their rental car turned his back, then stepped out onto the narrow concrete sidewalk bordering the packed-dirt road that ran through the village. She was only two buildings away from the cantina and as she began walking back toward the boardinghouse, she drew in a calming breath, then slowly eased it out.

She could do this. She'd spent practically every Saturday since she was nineteen years old performing on the streets. Of course it was more posing than true acting.

She swallowed a snort. Because she'd been acting, one way or another, since five months, two weeks and three days after her thirteenth birthday. This was simply more of the same, only with more physical risk at stake. So she shook out her hands.

And called out in friendly, faintly slurred Spanish, "See you tomorrow, Rosita!"

CHAPTER FIVE

AT THE SOUND of Mags's voice, the man guarding their rental car whirled to face her. He had the excessively developed muscularity of a weight lifter lacking an enough-is-enough gene. He also looked like a guy who could turn mean as a snake with very little provocation, and that had her second- and third-guessing herself in the suspended seconds he stared at her through narrowed eyes.

Then it apparently sank in that she was a lone woman with weapon-free hands and the tension in his burly shoulders eased. He slipped the gun held close to his side into the back of his waistband.

Flashing him a loose, friendly smile, Mags pretended not to notice. But she thought, *Gotcha*, when she saw his chest puff out.

"Hola." Adding a swing to her hips and the occasional faint stagger to her stride, she made her way toward him with the exaggerated care of a drunk. "I know every one in town," she said as she reached the trunk of the rental and eased her tote down her arm and onto the packed dirt road, "And have since birth, so I know you're not from around here. I'm Benita." She pulled back her shoulders a bit. "Who are you?"

"Frederico." He seemed to be speaking directly to her breasts, and even though her aim had been precisely that—to utilize whatever assets she had to distract him—she couldn't help but wish she hadn't showcased her boobs quite so effectively.

Not that she could do anything about it now. She tilted her head toward the boardinghouse. "Are you staying at Senora Guerrero's?"

"No. We're just here to see if someone we know stopped for the night."

She made a derisive sound deep in her throat and doodled a design in the dirt that covered the rental's trunk. Its hood was only feet behind the cargo hatch of Frederico's sleek black SUV and he stood next to the rental's passenger-side door. He stared at her, not even pretending he wasn't checking her out. It was creepy, but luring him down here so Finn could work whatever magic he planned on the SUV shouldn't be too difficult.

Despite the thug's definite awareness, however, her near snort had his brows drawing together. "Are you mocking me?"

"What? No." She managed not to sigh, but she'd forgotten about the Latino machismo. "It's just that, other than you, *no* one of interest has stopped in this town for a very long time." She waved a hand, staggered as if the action had thrown her off balance, then slapped her hand down on the trunk to catch herself. "Well, I did hear in the cantina that a couple of *americanos* are spending the night here, but I didn't actually meet them." She shrugged. "Not that I would've been able to talk to them anyway—*americanos* never bother to learn our language, you know?"

His expression said he agreed wholeheartedly, but he merely nodded.

She licked her lips. "You're very handsome. Where are you from?"

He left his post next to the passenger door and swaggered down to her end. "Santa Rosa."

"Ay! You are so lucky! I would *love* to see Santa Rosa someday!"

"You have never been?"

"No. It is far away and I have no car." Out of the corner of her eye she saw Finn slide out of the shadows. "But hopefully someday." She turned to lean her rear against the back of the vehicle and patted the fender next to her hip.

"Still," she said, tilting her head to look up as if she didn't care one way or the other if he joined her, "I bet you don't have a view in the city that can rival our sky."

It was certainly like nothing *she* had seen for far too many years. Yet as if her first thirteen years in El Tigre had imprinted it in her DNA, it was a sight she'd carried with her wherever she went. Even in the dead of night—or in this case, earliest morning—the sky was a deep midnight blue strewn with a million stars. Many shimmered dimly and looked every bit the hundreds of light-years away that they were. Others burned brightly and seemed close enough to reach up and gather by the fistful.

Frederico merely shrugged, however, unimpressed. "Give me the bright lights of the city any day," he

said, leaning against the trunk next to her. He turned
to give her a smoldering once-over. "I like looking at
you, though."

She brought a hand up to brush back her hair and
maybe buy herself a few moments' reprieve from the
intent she saw building in his expression. Just in time
she remembered the elaborate head wrap she'd created
to disguise the fact she was a blonde. But the action
brought her hand into her line of sight and even in the
dim light she was sidetracked by how dirty her index
finger had gotten from writing on the trunk. Without
thought, she popped it in her mouth and sucked.

An unfortunate impulse, as it turned out, and one
she regretted immediately. But before she could even
grimace at the taste, Frederico whipped an arm around
her and yanked her first to her feet, then into his arms.
Her mouth went slack in surprise and the finger she'd
been about to spit out slid free. Then faster than she
could catch her breath he slammed his mouth over hers.

Her hands automatically flew up to shove him away
and as they met the cloth over his chest it was all she
could do to suppress the instinctive urge to push, and
push *hard*. She curled her fingers into the fabric to keep
herself from doing so and managed to stand docilely.
But this venture had failure written all over it because
docile was all she could pull off. She simply wasn't a
good enough actress to pretend she enjoyed this slob's
attentions.

Her brain was still rapidly looking for a way out that
didn't include her and Finn being gunned down or captured, when Frederico wrapped his hands around her

hips and lifted her onto the trunk of the car. Then he slid his meaty paws up her waist, her diaphragm, clearly aiming for her breasts.

Oh, no. That is so not gonna happen!

Luckily, before she could blow everything, Finn materialized behind the cartel thug. She watched as he raised the gun he held by its barrel and brought the pistol grip down hard against Frederico's head. The crack as it made contact sounded like thunder to her overstimulated senses.

Then Frederico's dead weight came down on her like a felled tree. It was far too late to dodge out of his way and feeling his slack heaviness picking up velocity as it tipped her upper body backward, she feared his overmuscled mass would slam her head right through the rear window.

But Finn caught the cartel enforcer by the back of his collar and belt and hauled him upright, holding him in place long enough to move between her and Frederico and shove a shoulder into the thug's gut to carry him in a firemen's lift.

"Move," he said in a low rough voice and stepped out of her way.

She moved, sliding off the trunk with alacrity to follow him.

In a few long-legged strides he was at the back of the SUV, reaching for its cargo release with his free hand. It clicked open and he took a large step back to allow the hatch to rise. He looked over at her.

For a second she could have sworn she saw fury etched on his face. But that didn't make sense. And since he merely said in a neutral voice, "See if you can find the latch to pop the hood," she decided she must have misunderstood. He bundled Frederico handily into the cargo space.

She picked up her tote, then hurried to open the driver's door on the SUV. It took her what felt like forever to locate the hood latch, but finally she released it, then quickly eased the door closed to kill the light. She turned…and literally bounced off Finn's chest as he strode toward the hood.

He caught her by the upper arms and steadied her, then set her aside. "We have to get the hell out of here," he said. "Joaquin's gonna be out any minute."

"Did you disable the car?"

"I slashed a couple tires, but I'm going to grab the distributor cap and cut the radiator hose as well."

"I thought having possession of these babies might help slow him down, too." She dangled the keys she'd found in a section of the console between the front seats.

For just a second he stared at them as if hypnotized. "Damn. If I knew the keys were in the car, we'd have taken this rig instead of the rental." But he apparently shook off the regret that sounded in his voice with a brisk roll of his shoulders and leaned into the engine compartment.

In practically the same movement he straightened back up, a car part hanging from his fist. "Let's get the hell out of here."

They dived into the car and Finn had just fired it up and put it in gear when Senora Guerrero's front door opened with a crash. Joaquin stormed out, his gun swinging around to take aim at them.

"Duck!" Finn snapped, then leaned over the steering wheel himself to provide a smaller target.

She bent below the window just as he stomped on the gas. She heard the report of a gun, but not the sound of the bullet hitting anything. A nervous laugh escaped her and she slowly sat up as Finn shot out of range between the few buildings that constituted the village center. "He missed. Oh, thank God. He *missed*, Finn!"

"What the *hell* did you think you were doing?" Darkness, not lightened appreciably by the thick blanket of stars, enclosed the countryside as they left the meager lights of the township in their rearview mirror.

She blinked...and realized her mouth was opening and closing like a trout's. She snapped it shut, only to open it again and croak in genuine bewilderment, "What?"

"With Mister Handsy—what the hell did you think you were doing?"

"Excuse me?" She hauled herself upright in her seat and swung to face him, outrage muscling aside the icy terror that the past several minutes had wrapped around the scant dregs of her courage. "You asked me to distract him, to put myself in *danger*—then believe you have the right to critique the way I handled it?" She glared at him. "What did you *think* was going to happen? That I'd pull out a deck of cards and challenge him to a game of Go Fish?"

He took his attention off the road to pin her with cold

eyes. "I didn't think you'd invite him to stargaze, then suck off your finger like it was his di—"

Rage such as she hadn't felt since she was thirteen going on fourteen exploded in her brain, red-hot and out of control. Her usual fail-safes—not engaging, taking deep breaths, hell, taking a *moment* to prevent herself from acting before thinking—went up in smoke and she launched herself at him, fists swinging.

"What the *fu*—?" He fought the car as it swerved across the dirt road.

The vehicle's wild rocking barely even registered as Mags landed blows in any undefended spot she could find. "You dare say that to me, you pimping son of a shit?" she demanded, further enraged when she became conscious of the tears welling in her eyes. With sheer determination she willed them away. *Damned* if she would let him see he'd made her cry. "That man had his filthy hands, his *mouth* on me and you *dare* accuse me of tacitly offering him a blow job?"

She didn't realize the car had rolled to a stop at the side of the road until Finn's strong arms wrapped around her, pinning hers to her side.

"Stop that," he said in a rough, authoritative voice. "We don't have time for this." But his arms tightened even more and one big hand roughly stroked her head, dislodging her head wrap. "I apologize, Magdalene. That was a crappy thing to say."

"It was an *asshole* thing to say. And my name is *Mags*." Her nose was squashed against the hard plane of his chest, her back arched at an awkward angle and, all told…? "This has gotta be the worst stinking birthday of my life." And just as she'd thought in the Santa Rosa cantina what felt like aeons rather than half a day ago, that was saying something.

He jerked against her, further torturing her nose, and she could feel him tucking in his chin to look down at her.

She wasn't about to return his regard.

"It's your *birthday*?"

Okay, maybe not technically, since it was after midnight. "Well, it was when I fell asleep," she muttered sulkily. So, close enough.

"CLOSE ENOUGH," Finn unknowingly echoed Mags's thought as guilt piled upon guilt. God, hadn't he just been a prince among men with her today? His mom would be so proud.

But they needed to focus on the here and now, and he gently moved her back to her side of the front seat.

"I really am sorry," he said. "That was uncalled for and I have no excuse except that I'm tired, stressed out and pissed off, and I took it out on you. But as willing as I'd be to give you a couple of free shots at me, we'll have to put that off. We gotta get the hell outta here and put as much distance between us and Joaquin as we can. For all we know, he and Mr. Handsy—"

"Frederico."

"He and Frederico," he amended, showing great restraint not spitting the name, "could be taking a villager's car at gunpoint as we speak."

Fear flashed across her face, but she simply nodded and leaned her head back against the headrest. So he stomped the gas pedal to the floor and sent them roaring down the highway.

He didn't try to break the silence. He fully intended, in fact, not to say a word until Mags did. He sure as hell didn't foresee that being a hardship—he was *king* when it came to keeping his own counsel.

His brothers had long ago elected him the Kavanagh Construction go-to guy when it came to dealing with difficult clients, suppliers or hired help. He could be counted on to sit quietly and simply listen to a complaint or an excuse until he had its measure. Then he'd either fix it if Kavanagh's was at fault, which on occasion turned out to be the case, or he'd set the other party straight if he disagreed with the client/vendor/employee's assessment of the problem. And if a discussion didn't supply the solution when he knew they were in the right, he was known for simply looking silently at the other person until they started squirming or blurting out all manner of things to fill the silence.

He drove without saying a word for an additional forty-five minutes.

Something about Mags, however, had a way of turning all his usual moves upside down. Apparently she didn't mind silence any more than he did. And where yesterday he could have outwaited her indefinitely, this morning he found it amazingly difficult.

"I'm playing with the idea of pulling off the road and letting Joaquin and company pass us," he eventually heard himself say out of the blue. "Hell, we could go back to Senora Guerrero's and get an actual night's sleep, then find an alternate route in the morning. Because I sure wouldn't object to being the trailer for a change instead of the trailed."

"*I* wouldn't mind going back to sleep," she murmured—apparently to the ceiling headliner, which had curled away in a few places to hang in ragged strips. God knew she'd barely looked at him directly since her blowup. "But there are risks to consider."

"Yeah." He nodded, pleased she'd noticed when she'd spent most of the ride staring down at her fingers in her lap. "It's surprisingly flat in this area and there aren't a lot of places to hide a car."

"Sure, that's one difficulty." Turning her head without lifting it from the headrest, she looked past his nose and out the side window. "Then there's the possibility that they might wait to fix the car. Because who the hell knows what runs through Joaquin's head? He might have thought of the coming-back thing and decided to stay put."

"Are you kidding me? He's too stupid to think of something that brilliant."

This time she did look at him…as if he should be committed.

He snorted. "Fine, say what you want about me." And after the way he'd dazzled her with his charm that would likely be an earful. "But trust me on this—it'd only be his unwillingness to trade down to one of the villagers' cars, *not* any masterminding skills on his part that would keep him there." He blew out a disgusted breath. "Which still leaves us in front of him."

"I have to admit, I like the idea of being behind better. It seems a lot easier to keep an eye on what's ahead of us than constantly having to look over our shoulders." She straightened suddenly. Looked at him without the distance that had veiled those blue eyes since he'd messed things up. "But if we do have to stay ahead of him," she said slowly, "we need to maintain our lead. Or, better yet, shake him entirely."

"I'm all for that. You have an idea how to accomplish it?"

She gave him a decisive nod. "It's that finding-an-alternate-route thing you brought up. We've pretty much been following the Pan-American."

"It's the best highway in South America."

"Yeah, by far. But it's not the only one." She gave him a level look. "I'd bet my professional makeup kit, though, that it's the only one Joaquin has ever considered."

He felt a slow smile spread across his face and had to fight the urge to hook a hand around the back of her neck and plant a big kiss on her in sheer appreciation. Instead, he settled on saying, "You are brilliant!"

"Yes, I am," she agreed coolly and pulled the road map out of the glove box. She opened it in her lap.

He knew damn well she couldn't see a thing. But without missing a beat—or feeling the need to look up, apparently—she said, "Does that overhead light work?"

"You didn't test all the car's features before leaving the rental agency?"

She gave him a *get-real* grunt and he shook his head. She was clearly an in-the-moment woman and not big on planning, which as a carpenter, electrician and, hell, just an all-around builder, he didn't understand at all.

It irritated him. No, who was he kidding, it bugged the hell out of him. But that was his problem and, shaking off his exasperation, he tried the switch on the light above the rearview mirror. Reasonably bright illumination came on.

"Eureka," she said, raising the map and turning it toward the light. She pored over it quietly for a few moments, then set the still-open map in her lap and turned to him.

"In what looks like fifteen or so miles after we rejoin the Pan-Am, the road to San Vito *forks* off to the east. The red line marking the roads is still fairly strong for that highway, but when we get to Cordoba and hang a right to head south again it's not nearly as bold on the map. Which means it's—" She shook her head. "Okay, I have no clue what condition we'll find it in. But I bet it'll be less than optimal. We might have to ask around about gas stations and such before we start down it." She yawned hugely.

"But that's for tomorrow," he said, reaching out and plucking the map from her hands and deftly folding it. "We're finally getting back into the type of terrain I've mostly seen today. So whataya say we find a place where we can get the hell off this road and grab some sleep?"

"Finally," she muttered. "Something we can agree on."

CHAPTER SIX

MAGS HADN'T BEEN camping since she was a kid. Well, strictly speaking she'd *made* camps with friends but had never actually gone camping with tents and sleeping bags and stuff. Mostly she'd run wild with the kids of the families her folks ministered to. And although the gritty urban streets of Tacna, where they'd lived until she was six or seven years old, were about as far from the wilderness as things got, during the years that she and her parents had lived in the village of Onoato, the lush northern Amazon had been her playground. She and the village children had spent long carefree hours exploring and playacting. And building camps.

She sneaked a peek at Finn while he set up their camp with economical proficiency. As he moved in and out of the shadows cast by a small battery-powered lantern, she watched his features change back and forth between the spare, angular beauty and hatchet-carved cheekbones of an old-time saint to a hollow-eyed, shadow-misted visage that she entertained herself by assigning more demonic labels to.

She tried to picture him as part of those old simplistic childhood games, but she couldn't quite manage it. She could, however, easily see him swinging on vines through the rain forest the way the older boys had done, and had a sneaking suspicion that if he had been part of her childhood gang, he'd have thought he was the boss of them.

She muttered, *"As if"* under her breath.

"You say something there, Goldilocks?"

She started. Then, slapping back the bump of guilt over…darned if she knew what, she said, "Nooooo?"

As if it were a *question*, for pity's sake. Holy crappacino. She was so tired she was rummy.

Finn strode up to her and, as if he'd read her thoughts, waved a hand at the small tent he'd set up. "It might be close quarters, but it's out of the elements." He gave her a wry smile, no doubt thinking the same thing she did: that it was dry and still amazingly warm given it was the middle of the night. He shrugged. "Such as they are."

Looking at the minuscule tent, she felt a moment's qualm about those close quarters. But, *lord*, she'd give a bundle to lie down. So in the spirit of getting some rest, she sloughed off her misgivings.

"I thought about setting up just the fly instead of the whole tent," Finn said. "It'd be cooler and we'd definitely have more ventilation. But I don't know what kind of critters are around here so I decided to err on the side of keeping them the hell out." The night was alive with the sound of small rustling, chirping things. The crickets had gone dead silent when she and Finn first climbed out of the car, but it hadn't taken long for them to grow accustomed to the humans in their midst and they were now back to their full nightly chorale.

"That works for me." She headed for the shelter, but then stopped halfway there. "But first I've gotta pee."

He offered her the lantern. "Take this and wait here a sec. I'll grab you some TP from my pack." He unzipped the entry flap and tossed it back. The tent's opening was larger than she expected and he bent in half but entered it easily enough.

He was back in seconds and tossed her a plastic bag with a flattened roll of toilet paper inside. "You want me to go with you?"

She was half-tempted, but if she could handle wildlife when she was a little girl, she could darn well handle it now. "No, I'm good. I'll just be a minute."

She was back not a whole lot longer than she'd predicted and found him still standing next to the tent.

"Let me take that." He reached for the battery-operated lantern. "I put your purse thing in the vestibule." He indicated the fly that stretched out beyond the boundaries of the tent, then made an after-you gesture. "Pick whichever side you're most comfortable on. I only have the one mat and sleeping bag, but it's so warm I doubt we'll need to cover up so you can sleep on whichever you think will work best. There's a door and vestibule on both sides so we won't have to crawl over each other."

"*Fancy*." She bent to peer inside and eased out a small breath of relief when she saw it looked reasonably roomy. She let herself in the way she'd seen him do. Then, turning, she saw he'd bent over to peer in at her.

"Which side appeals to you?" he asked.

"I like sleeping on the left." She was also more drawn

to the puffy sleeping bag than to the not particularly comfortable-looking thin mat.

"Left, it is," he said. "If you want to do up the zipper on the door I'll go around and let myself in on the other side."

She did so and looked around as she unhooked her bra and removed it through the sleeve of her top. This wouldn't be so bad. It wasn't nearly as cramped as she'd expected.

Which made her wonder what kind of conditions her folks had to contend with on Munoz's coca farm. They were accustomed to living rough, but what if the cartel goons had just tossed them in a closet or set them to working the fields for twelve hours a day? They were in their sixties, for pity's sake, and likely weren't as strong as they once were.

The *zzzip* of the zipper unfastening on the other side of the tent interrupted her thoughts and she turned to watch Finn climb inside. He was around the six-foot mark and his shoulders were wide. And suddenly what she'd thought was a generous hunk of space shrank.

She eased off her sandals and set them aside, then flopped down atop the sleeping bag. "Good night," she murmured and turned away from him onto her side. Her eyes burned from lack of sleep but she had an awful feeling the much-needed slumber might be elusive. Things rustled as he did whatever he did to get ready for bed and a hint of his scent wafted in her direction.

As she breathed in the bouquet of some no-nonsense guy-type soap, laundry detergent and the faint underlying aroma of man, she was surprised to find it curiously comforting. And perhaps that was why, between one breath and the next, she did exactly what she feared she'd not be able to do.

She tumbled headfirst into the deep, dark abyss of oblivion.

FINN AWOKE FROM a great dream of having a woman sprawled over him to discover that a woman was, in fact, half-sprawled over him.

For a second, he didn't know where the hell he was. Cracking an eye open, he tipped his chin to look. Magdalene was in his arms and memories of yesterday started filtering back into his brain. Unless those were part of an elaborate dream as well.

She slept on her side, partially plastered against him. Her head rested on his chest as if he were her personal pillow, her breasts nestled against a section of his rib cage and one shapely arm draped across him diagonally. Her right leg was slung across his thighs and bent at the knee, her kneecap dangerously close to brushing his morning wood.

But if she'd been drawn to him in her sleep, clearly he'd been equally magnetized. Hard to say otherwise, considering his own arm wrapped around her in return. More damning, that hand cupped the lower curve of her breast. He gazed at it blurrily through slitted eyes.

Okay, this didn't appear to be a dream. A soft guffaw escaped him. No shit, Sherlock. If he were dreaming she'd be buck-naked and crawling all over him, performing epic pornographic acts.

He shifted the hand cupping her breast and stroked

his thumb down the warm curve to her nipple. The weight in his palm jiggled slightly and her nipple hardened beneath the barely there layer of the thin T-shirt separating their bare skin.

Nope. Definitely not a dream.

Yet still he floated in a half world, caught between sleep and full consciousness as he lazily gave the nipple caught between his thumb and the side of his index finger a gentle tug. And oh, yeah. She liked that. Watching with sleepy satisfaction, he repeated the process, loving the drowsy, appreciative sounds she made in her sleep and the way she rocked her hips with restive sexuality against the side of his.

Then she suddenly went still—and he was abruptly wide-awake with the knowledge that she likely was as well.

Not to mention the realization that he'd been caught feeling her up with all the finesse of a fourteen-year-old achieving second base for the very first time. His hand on her breast went slack and he slid it surreptitiously to her lower rib cage. Then had to swallow a snort.

Because, really? *Like if you're stealthy enough she won't notice you've been getting all handsy with her tit?*

Without raising her head from his chest, she slowly tilted it back to look up at him. Her sleepy blue eyes were still heavy lidded. "Well, this is awkward," she murmured. But, yawning, she didn't look the least bit discomfited as she pushed back to sit on the rumpled sleeping bag next to his mat. "Sorry about that. Nancy always said I was a bed hog." She yawned again, long and luxuriously, stretching with feline voluptuousness.

He had to drag his gaze away and clear his throat. "Yeah, and I apologize for copping a feel. My only defense is I was mostly asleep." He hesitated, then shrugged. "Well, that and I'm a man."

She made a rude sound. "And therefore can't resist latching on to any boob within touching range?"

He winced, because put like that, it sounded even lamer than he'd thought. Still, he nodded gamely, pushed up onto his elbow and raked his hair back with the fingers of his free hand. "Something like that. I plead the guy gene." He reached for the Levi's he'd kicked off after she'd fallen asleep last night and pulled them on, lifting his hips to tug them up over his butt. Lowering the latter back onto the mat, he zipped up.

Then he rolled to his feet and extended a hand down to assist her up. He ignored the jolt that shot through his system when she slapped her palm in his.

"Look," he said as he hauled her to her feet, "what's done is done, so there's not a helluva lot I can do about it now. But I can heat up some water so we can have a cup of coffee and wash up." Hey, he had sisters. He knew the store chicks put in things like hot water and makeup and hair doodads. Plus, who didn't appreciate a cup of coffee after a night camping out?

As if to prove his point, Mags's face lit up. "That would be so great." Then she narrowed her eyes at him. "But don't think I don't know when I'm being managed."

Busted. But he merely shrugged once again. "Just using knowledge gained from my sisters. Especially Hannah. She likes camping, but the girl goes nowhere

without her makeup and the promise of water that someone else heats."

"I think I'd like her."

"I think she'd *worship* you. I thought she hauled a
lot of that stuff around, but your makeup kit leaves
hers in the dust. If she ever saw it I'm pretty sure she'd
bow before you and say 'I'm not worthy.'" He gave her
a crooked smile and retrieved his backpacking stove
from his pack, along with the set of nesting pots. After
pouring water from the water bottle into the largest container, he connected a bottle of white gas to the single
burner and ignited it with his Bic. He balanced the pan
atop the burner, made sure everything was steady, then
adjusted the heat.

"That'll take a minute or two," he said and turned
to see her fidgeting. Refraining from saying any of the
smart-ass remarks that popped to mind, he tossed her
the plastic bag containing the toilet paper.

She snatched it out of the air and trotted off for the
jungle-type woods, sending a flock of birds winging toward the trees. He counted several other types of birds
while she was gone, some colorful, others surprisingly
dull for South America. All of them twittered, chirped
or cried raucously overhead as they flew across the
clearing or hopped from branch to branch along the
forest line.

One landed not far from him and pecked up a line
of army ants that Finn was happy to see appeared to be
a one-off thing. He'd seen a Discovery Channel show
once that had shown hundreds of those ants boiling
over a carcass and picking it clean. The ten or so the

bird had just gobbled up were as many as he cared to see up close.

It occurred to him while Mags was in the woods that he needed to apologize to her about a couple of the careless things he'd said. Luckily, before he could make himself all tense over the prospect, the water came to a boil and he got out the coffee fixings. Magdalene demonstrated impeccable timing when she strolled back into camp just as he finished making them each a cup. He handed her his one and only mug, keeping the cardboard cup for himself.

She took a sip and moaned softly. "Oh, my Lord, that's good." She looked around. "Where did you dispose of the grounds?"

"This is instant, there are no grounds."

She blinked at him. "No way this is instant coffee."

"Hey, I'm from Seattle, darlin', and you gotta know what that means. We're famous for our excellent coffee, both real *and* instant."

She grinned at him over the rim of her mug, then suddenly snapped her fingers. "Hang on," she said and crossed to the tent to pull her big purse out of the vestibule. Squatting in front of it, she carefully set her coffee cup on the ground, then pawed through her bag. A moment later she made a sound of discovery.

"Something to go with the coffee. Here, catch." She tossed him an energy bar. "It's no B. T. McElrath Salty Dog bar, but at least it has a little chocolate on it." Lowering her butt to sit cross-legged on the ground, she opened her own bar, then picked up her mug again.

They ate in silence for a while. Finn killed off his

energy bar, which he'd found surprisingly tasty. It just went to show that if you were hungry enough, even girlie food tasted good. He crumpled the wrapper and tucked it in his pocket. He'd dispose of it when he got up. Right now, he planned to just sit here and enjoy a few minutes of peace while he drank the rest of his coffee.

Eventually he drained the last sip. Propping his wrists on his kneecaps, he stared at the empty cardboard cup he held in the gap between his up-drawn knees as he turned it around and around. Then he blew out a breath and looked across the short distance separating him and Magdalene.

She'd removed that fancier-than-average rubber band binding the end of her damp braid and was running her fingers through her hair to separate the strands. And, holy shit. She suddenly had crazy wavy hair that he couldn't help but stare at.

Who knew blond hair could contain so many different shades?

She seemed more at peace this morning. Yet even seemingly relaxed she projected the same sense of energy he'd noted yesterday.

And, Jesus, had it truly only been less than twenty-four hours since both their lives had been flipped sideways? With everything that had happened, it seemed a lot longer since he'd first clapped eyes on her.

On top of the emotional upheaval of having drug-cartel minions on their ass, every time he looked at Magdalene it was as if he saw a different woman. She went from one appearance to the next, and it was like hanging out with a damn chameleon. Her coloring remained the same, yet somehow she managed to project the *notion* of different women of varying ages, ideologies and sexual natures.

Take last night, when he'd watched her with Frederico the Cretin. She'd come across as someone in her early twenties, which he was pretty certain she wasn't. And even with her hair covered and minimal makeup she'd seemed more sexual than anything she'd projected up to that point. She'd been friendly and admiring, and yet at the same time somehow slightly aloof, and he'd watched it draw the asshole into her orbit as if she were a one-woman magnetar.

But thinking about the situation that had sent them on the run again placed him squarely back on the hot seat. "Hey, Mags?" he said. She looked over at him and he eased out the breath he'd inhaled. "Look, I just wanna say I'm sorry about my trash talk last night."

Her apparent relaxation dissipated and her eyes shuttered. "Yes, so you said last night," she agreed in an nonencouraging tone.

He got that he should respect her obvious unwillingness to discuss it, but he really needed to get this off his chest, so he plowed on. "I know I apologized then, but I want to say it again. You were right, it was an asshole thing to say and forget what I said about the guy gene—I can only plead a long stressful day and not enough sleep. But my mom and sisters and girl cousins and aunts and grannies would be ashamed of me. And on my own behalf I sincerely am sorry."

"Fine," she said flatly. "You're forgiven."

"That sounded a little less than sincere, but I'll take what I can get."

He thought about the way he'd blown her off when she'd told him about her folks shipping her off to boarding school when she was thirteen. The truth was, since then he'd tried to imagine what it would have been like being separated from his family when he was that age.

And discovered he simply couldn't. There had been times, especially during puberty, when he'd dreamed of vacations away from all his brothers and sisters and the assorted extended-family members who were constantly in and out of their house. But it was his brother Dev who'd had the real problem with the lack of privacy in their family; Finn had merely wanted an occasional break. The thought of being separated from his family entirely was a whole nother kettle of cod. *Her* only family was at the mercy of a drug cartel. Not that she'd exhibited so much as an inkling she wanted to talk about that. Still, it had to be painful and stressful squared for her. The drug trade wasn't exactly an industry known for its compassion.

Mags was clearly not thrilled with him bringing up last night's snafu, however, so he'd wait for another time to apologize for his insensitive crack about her being lucky to be sent away from everything she'd known. For now, he rose to his feet.

And got right down to business. "What do you say we break camp and pack up? Then we need to spread out the map and see what we can come up with as a decent alternative to the Pan-Am route."

CHAPTER SEVEN

"JUAN CARLOS!" Victor Munoz tucked the phone receiver between his ear and his hunched shoulder. Leaning back in his chair, he swung his feet atop his desk and crossed his ankles to admire the soft gleam of leather in his hand-made Italian sandals. "It is good to hear your voice, cousin. How have our guests settled in during the adjustment period since I sent them to you?"

Silence throbbed over the line for a moment. Then his cousin said, "This is the reason I called, Victor. So I need to know up front—do you want me to say merely what you want to hear? Or do you want the truth?"

That didn't sound promising. His smile disappearing, Victor steadied the phone with his thumb and two fingers, dropped his feet to the floor and sat erect. He reached for the humidor. "The truth." He didn't add "of course," because this was Juan Carlos he was talking to. And his cousin knew him well—he didn't always react well to the truth.

"The truth is, the Delucas are a pain in my ass. Maybe not the senor so much. But the senora? Ay-yi-yi! She is showing great signs of becoming the carbuncle on my butt."

Victor rolled his eyes at the ceiling but didn't lose his temper. "Believe me, I know precisely what that feels like. I thought the farm would be the best place for her, though. I figured it would be the one place she *couldn't* make trouble."

Juan Carlos snorted.

"What the fuck is she doing?"

His cousin's sigh filtered down the line. "The question is more what isn't she. She's talking to people about their working conditions or the compensation they should be getting for a hard day's work. She's talking to them about *medical* coverage. I don't even know what that is, but the fact that they don't have it is sure as hell getting everybody all hot under the collar. Worse, it's causing insubordinate mutterings."

"Sh-h-hit." Victor selected a cigar, clipped the end and fished his lighter out of his pants pocket. He took a moment to light up, then said flatly, "That woman could only benefit from a bullet in the back of her head."

"My thought exactly. If Tia Augustina didn't scare the crap out of me, I'd dump the pair of them in the jungle and let nature do its job."

"I have a line on the Delucas' daughter, who's down here to visit them. Unfortunately the story we strong-armed the neighbors into telling anyone inquiring about them sent her away, but I've got my men out looking for her. Once we find her we'll have the leverage we need to keep the parents in line."

"Let's hope to hell that happens soon," Juan Carlos said sourly. "Or I fear we'll have a revolt on our hands."

THE RENTAL CAR started making suspicious noises around hour four of their drive south. When Finn gave it gas, it leaped forward for a second, then started cutting out, accompanied by an almost cartoonish coughing and wheezing. Neither of them was laughing, however, when he finally eased the vehicle to a stop at the side of the road. Mags had been taking deep, even breaths to keep from grumbling aloud since the first sign of trouble. But why did cars always have to choose the middle of freaking nowhere to stage their breakdowns?

Because, while she could roughly pinpoint their location on the map, there wasn't a single dot to designate a town anywhere in the vicinity of where she believed them to be. She hadn't even seen a few huts huddled together recently, let alone a community sizable enough to be helpful if they needed car parts. It had been a good hour since she'd seen signs of any habitation at all.

The best they could probably hope for was to stumble across a village that wasn't large enough to be marked on the road map. "Maybe my idea to leave the Pan-American wasn't such a hot one after all," she said gloomily.

"Let me take a look at the engine before you start to panic," Finn advised, leaning down to pop the interior hood latch. The driver's door creaked when he opened it to climb from the car.

"Where do you get panic from a simple observation?" she coolly inquired of his retreating torso—the only thing she could see from this angle. "I don't frighten that easily." *And if I say it loud enough I may even come to believe it.*

But, damn him, hadn't he neatly hamstrung her? She understood her stupid pride was her problem and not his. But she also knew that if she were choking on so much panic it threatened to wring every last breath from her body, she'd likely allow it to do precisely that before she'd let him see she was drowning in it.

Her spine went rebar straight. *Oh, for God's sake, girl, buck up.* Reassuring herself his advice was sound, that panicking before they even knew what the problem was wasn't a productive use of her time, she, too, got out of the car.

The midday heat promptly wrapped itself around her like a combination straitjacket/burial shroud. And the air was nowhere near as humid as it was going to get in the rain forest, but she reminded herself this would help her adapt. The cloud of gnats hanging in the area didn't add to the comfort level, however, and she had to mouth breathe through her teeth to keep from inhaling them.

But, hey, no panicking here, Mr. I-wouldn't-lose-control-if-my-big-balls-of-steel-were-caught-in-a-flaming-vise. "Huh," she muttered under her breath, momentarily entertained by the visual. "Bet you would."

"You sure talk to yourself a lot," he said from under the hood he'd raised.

And you have the hearing of a barn owl, so I guess we're a match made in Nirvana. She bit back the urge to say it aloud and contented herself by observing, in an even tone, "Well, if a girl wants to have a decent conversation…"

She walked around to peek at the engine as if she actually had an inkling what anything under the hood was. Okay, she recognized the radiator since she'd just seen it yesterday. But that was about it. "Can you tell what the trouble is?"

"Going by the way we got a surge of power when I jumped on the gas, only to have it cough and cut out immediately after, I figure it has to be fuel-related. So I'm checking out the—"

His voice trailed away and she was debating whether it was worth asking him *what* he was checking out when he abruptly said, "An-n-nd, here's our problem."

She leaned over him. "What is it?"

He craned his head around and she suddenly found their faces so close together, they were practically kissing. She pulled back a little.

Finn's mouth tipped into a slight smile before he turned his attention back to the engine compartment. "See this?" he demanded and she looked over his shoulder to where he'd thrust one long finger, indicating... something or another. Then she saw the tube thingy he pointed out and nodded.

"This is the fuel line and it's loose."

"Oh, goody. Tighten it up."

"That might be easier said than done. My pliers are back in Seattle in my toolbox."

Her stomach flip-flopped. "Can't you use some more of that silicone tape stuff?"

"No, darlin'. It's not a split in the tubing, it's a loose connection that's allowing air in the line. But before you start to—"

She narrowed her eyes at him. "You do *not* want to say *panic* again," she instructed clearly. "Not if you know what's good for you."

His teeth flashed white. "All righty, then." He turned back to check out some more crap under the hood.

She stepped away. "I'm guessing this might take a while, so I'll go slap together some sandwiches from the groceries we bought."

"Sounds great." He straightened from the hood and headed around to the trunk. "Here, I'll set this in the front of the trunk so you can get to it," he said and she looked over to see him hauling forward the little cooler they'd bought in one of the bigger stores in San Vito.

Finn dived back into the trunk and she could hear him rummaging through it as she carried the cooler over to a downed tree that had a length of reasonably flat surface. She got out a package of tortillas, a container of pulled pork, a jar of salsa and the little container of marinated julienned veggies she'd scored in a bodega down the street from the store where they'd found the cooler. She had all the makings for lunch, but nothing to put it on.

She glanced over at Finn. "Is it okay if I look through your backpack for something to use as plates?"

"Help yourself." Making a sound of satisfaction he backed away from the trunk with an incredibly rusty pair of pliers in his hand and headed back to the front end of the car.

He'd left the trunk open and she walked over to grab his bag. She opened it up and moved aside some clothing, the fuel bottle and—whoa—a good-sized baggie full of condoms before she located a melamine plate. Knowing that he'd packed for one she figured they could share the latter, but as she was trying to put everything back the way she'd found it, she knocked the lid askew from the largest pot of his nesting pans. She had it half back on the set when she realized it was probably intended to double as a fry pan.

And that there was no reason it couldn't triple as a plate. "Score!" she whispered.

"Heard that."

She leaned around the edge of the car to look up its length at him. He stood on the same side, bent so far into the engine compartment that he was mainly a muscular profile of lower torso, long legs and that really nice butt as he did whatever it was he was doing to the fuel line. "Of course you did."

She returned to her rudimentary tree-trunk kitchen and slapped together tortilla wraps for both of them. She plated them, then remembered the mangos she'd bought yesterday and sliced one up, arranging the segments next to the wraps. Then she glanced back at Finn again. "Lunch is ready whenever you are. You want one of your beers?"

"God, yeah." His voice was fervent. "I'm just about done here."

She took their plates over to a stand of trees. After checking the branches overhead to make sure no snakes or nasty oversize insects were going to drop on her head and give her heart failure, she set the plates on the ground and went back for her drink. A moment later she sat on the ground in the shade of a tree and found a level patch of ground where she could set her can of soda. She picked up the pan-lid plate and rested it in her lap. Then, leaning back against the tree trunk, she used both hands to scoop up her tortilla. She inhaled its aroma for a moment, then took a bite.

A multitude of flavors exploded in her mouth and she moaned in ecstasy.

Across the way Finn swore in a low voice.

"I heard that," she said and grinned, tickled with the opportunity to give him a little of his own medicine. But then she considered the way he was giving up his vacation for her and the fact that he was probably par-boiling in his own sweat by now and added with more graciousness, "Come and have something to eat. I guarantee you'll feel better for it."

"Yeah, I'm a-l-l-most there. *Yes!* Here we go." He unfurled from his bent posture over the fender and stretched to his full height. Digging his fists into the small of his back, he arched over them to get the kinks out. "I'm done. I didn't even get my hands that dirty."

"Good. Grab your beer out of the cooler and come have your lunch."

He dropped down next to her a moment later and raised his beer bottle to his lips. He chugged down a quarter of it in one long swallow before coming up for air. "Damn," he muttered, looking at the bottle in his hand. "I probably should've drank some water to slake my thirst before I opened the beer."

"No, you know what?" she said. "Screw it. It's been a hellacious two days that feels more like a hellacious two weeks. So if you kill off your beer too soon, drink another. You earned it and I can drive the next leg."

He butted his shoulder against hers and his was hot, damp and solid. It was also there and gone between one moment and the next as he reached for his plate. He picked the tortilla wrap up and took a huge bite. "Omigawd," he muttered with a full mouth.

"I know," she agreed. "Freaking hits the spot, right?"

"Oh, yeah."

"Wait until you taste the *ajiaco*," she said. She had been so psyched to find the rich chicken-and-potato stew she remembered fondly from childhood. "I thought we could heat that up for dinner tonight."

"Sounds good. Where'd you get the mango?" He ate the remaining slices on his plate.

"I bought a couple outside the cantina yesterday, but with everything that went on after that I forgot all about them."

He took another big bite of his wrap, but after he'd chewed and swallowed it, he positioned himself to look over at her without having to twist his head around at an unsustainable angle. "About the car," he said slowly.

"Oh, no! You didn't get it going?"

"No, I'm sure it will hold. But I had to reassess my assessment from yesterday. I wasn't kidding when I told you it's in remarkable shape for its age. But I have a bad feeling that it's reached the stage where all kinds of little shit starts going wrong. If I had my toolbox and we were in a city where we could find replacement parts, that wouldn't be a problem. But in the middle of goddamn nowhere?"

"Problem," she said glumly.

"Yeah. 'Fraid so."

"You think we should get back on the Pan-American?"

"You're the one who's been studying the map. How

far do you estimate it is to a city of decent size, supposing such a thing even exists on this road?"

"If the legend is accurate, it looks like there's a... well, not a city, exactly. But quite possibly a good-sized town in maybe sixty, seventy miles."

"Okay, then." He gave her a brisk nod. "If it were me I'd probably risk betting on there being a place where we can turn this heap in for something newer and more reliable. But you're the one responsible for the rental. So, what do you think?"

"That you probably have a better grasp on this kind of thing than I do." She shrugged, because she really didn't have a clue what was the best thing to do. "It's all a crapshoot," she admitted. "So let's go with your idea. At least you have one—it's more than I do."

He gave her a slight smile, popped the last bite in his mouth, chewed it up and swallowed it down. Then he killed off the remainder of his beer and rolled easily to his feet. "Let me start up the car and see how she sounds. Then if your offer is still good, I will take you up on the driving thing and grab myself another brew. Because, you're right. The last however many hours feel more like a couple of weeks."

They took off a few minutes later. Slumped in the passenger seat next to her, Finn finished his second beer before they were five miles down the road. Seconds after tucking the bottle out of the way, he was asleep.

It didn't take long for the silence to grate on Mags's nerves. With no love of spending time by herself, she'd made a habit of surrounding herself with people.

But she tried to be smart about it. She'd figured out

a long time ago that it wasn't wise to fully open herself up to anyone. Relationships didn't last and she'd discovered the hard way that the instant she forgot that and tried to know someone on a deeper level, they were more likely than not to disappear on her.

If that meant she had more acquaintances than actual friends…well, that was okay. It was preferable, actually. She could talk to just about anyone, and no matter how superficial the connection, she possessed a genuine talent for making people feel like they were good friends for whatever space of time they spent together.

Yet here she was, captive in a soundless bubble, her only company dead to the world. And she'd admit it—that scratched at her last good nerve.

By the time Finn finally stirred over in his corner, she was downright antsy. Generally she excelled at finessing a conversation. Around Finn, however, that skill seemed to slip-slide away with frightening ease.

Now was no exception. She barely allowed the poor guy to stretch and blink the sleep from his eyes before she demanded, "So, why are you on vacation all by yourself?"

"Huh?" He turned his head to look at her through heavy-lidded eyes.

"Aren't hikers supposed to do the buddy-system thing? It seems dangerous to be in the wild in a foreign country all by yourself." *And why the hell would anyone* choose *to be alone anyway?*

"It's kind of a moot point, don't you think?" he said, giving her a level look out of dark eyes that had grown considerably more alert. "Since as it turns out I'm not in the wild."

"Yeah, I suppose so, but I'm curious."

"My plans with another hiker fell through."

Several beats went by as she waited for him to continue. Apparently, however, he'd said everything he planned to. Men were such a different species when it came to conversation. Would offering a few details kill them? "Why? What happened?"

He exhaled a gusty put-upon breath. But he said, "My brother Bren and I had this trip in the works for two years, then early last year he was diagnosed with cancer."

Her heart clutched. "Omigawd, Finn, I am so sorry. I hope he beat it."

"Yeah, he's now cancer-free. But his oncologist wasn't overjoyed with the idea of him taking an arduous hike in a country where neither of us speaks the language particularly well and the medical care isn't always all it should be. His doc was a pussycat, though, compared to Bren's wife, Jody. Bren fought the good fight but Jody went through a lot, too, when he was so sick, so he finally had to throw in the towel. By then it was too late to find anyone else to go." He shrugged. "I didn't particularly mind. I was looking forward to some time to myself."

Which, of course, her situation had totally screwed up. Still, she asked, "Why? Do you have a marriage or long-time relationship that's going south on you?"

His laugh was short and unamused. "No."

She waited for him to elaborate and when he didn't, she sighed. "You're not a real big communicator, are ya?"

He had the nerve to look insulted. "I'm an excellent communicator when there's something worth communicating about. This touchy-feely shit isn't."

"C'mon!" Reaching across the seat, she poked a finger in his side and merely gave him a little smile when he snapped tough-skinned fingers around her wrist and delivered her hand back to the steering wheel. "Are you pining for an unrequited love?"

"Jesus." He shook his head in disgust.

"I'll take that as a no. So, you're not married, not involved and not carrying a torch. What had you so hot for some alone time, then?"

"You aren't gonna let this go, are you?"

She shot him a cheerful smile and discovered to her surprise that something about the conversation actually made her feel that way. "Nope."

"Fine. It's my family." He must have seen her knee-jerk protest forming, because he added flatly, "I know, I know, you think a big family is more romantic than chocolates and roses on Valentine's Day. But as someone who actually lives in one, I'm here to tell you there are times when the lack of privacy is enough to drive a guy to drink. There's just no getting away from everyone. I work with my three brothers in the family construction business all day long—although, given we're all men, that's not so bad."

"Because you can scratch and spit and beat your hairy chests in male solidarity?"

His mouth quirked up. "Or at least speak the same

language. My aunts and grandmas and even one of my sisters-in-law and a few girl cousins who damn well oughta know better, on the other hand, want to see me settled. Apparently something happens to the Kavanagh females once they get married. They morph from fun chicks into nags who believe the entire world needs to march by twos, man-woman, man-woman."

"No man-man, woman-woman allowed?"

He laughed. "I honest to God think they'd be okay with that. What they can't stand is that I never bring anyone to the family events."

"Why not? Don't you date?"

"I date plenty. No—more than plenty. I date a lot."

"Omigawd," she breathed, suddenly flashing back to the memory of that I'd-do-ya-baby look he'd given her in the cantina yesterday. Her brain hit a patch of black ice and spun a fast three-sixty through a decade's worth of mental images from the myriad nightspots she'd frequented over the years. Slightly dizzied by the impressions whirling through her head faster than the sound of light, she eased her foot off the gas pedal, steered the car to a stop on the side of the road and shut it down. "Oh. My. God."

She turned to stare at Finn, a strangled laugh threatening to blow her windpipe apart. "You're one of *those* guys."

"What the hell are you talking about? Why'd you stop? What guys?"

"The ones you see cutting a different woman out of the herd every night of the week in every club in every city in the world." *Good God, Mags, hyperbole much?*

But she shook her head because she knew—she just
knew—she was right about this. "Men who are charm-
ing and fun, but most of all dedicated to getting laid
and staying single. You know who I'm talking about,
Kavanagh.

"You're one of the man whores."

CHAPTER EIGHT

A MAN...WHAT? Finn gaped at Magdalene's profile as she turned away to lounge in the driver's seat, casually draping her left wrist over the steering wheel. Did she just call him a *man whore*?

Temper sparked. Because, what the fuck? She'd known him five lousy minutes in the greater scheme of things and thought she had him all figured out? Well, excuse the hell outta him if that hacked him off some. Only one thing prevented his spark of ire from racing up a line of black powder to explode all up in her face.

He couldn't claim she was completely wrong. He had made avoiding commitments—and, yeah, sue him, getting laid as often as possible—a priority from the time he was about seventeen. Until recently it hadn't occurred to him to even question his habit of holding himself romantically aloof.

And if that wasn't enough, in his head he could hear his sister Hannah laughing her ass off, then wheezing between raucous whoops of hilarity, "Oh, God, *man whore*. She sure nailed it in one with that description, didn't she, boyo?"

Still. The spark might refuse to set off an explosion, but it didn't simply vanish in a puff of harmless smoke, either. Hannah was family; since first memory they had taken turns insulting and knocking each other off their respective high horses. *She* was allowed to dent his pride, because he knew her bottom line was she would always have his back.

Little Ms. Magdalene, on the other hand, didn't know him for shit.

Well, two could play this game. He felt as though he, too, had a decent grasp on her less desirable characteristics. He opened his mouth, ready and willing to pepper her with them like buckshot.

Only to notice that maybe she wasn't as insouciant as she appeared. When he looked closely, in fact, he could see how rigid her left leg was and how hard the foot on the end of that leg pressed against the floor on the far side of the brake pedal.

Almost as if she were bracing for him to take his best shot.

It made him remember that, unlike him, she probably hadn't had a lifetime of someone having her back. Which was not to say he felt duty bound to give her a free pass to take potshots at him. Hell, no; screw that.

He slid over and even as he stopped to leave space between their bodies, he slipped his arm the rest of the way along the top of her seat until he could tiptoe his fingers across the cap of her shoulder. He plucked up a strand of her braid-wavy hair and rubbed its ends between his finger and thumb. "Jealous, Magdalene?"

She whipped her head around, yanking the strand free. "How many times do I have to tell you my name is Mags?" she demanded. "And jealous of what?" She gave him a look that said, "One of us is deluded, Jack—and it's not me."

He picked up another thicker tendril and wrapped it around his forefinger, bringing his hand closer and closer to her face, until he could trace the whorl of her ear with his fingertip. "Of the fact," he said in a low voice, leaning near, "that I have had lots. And. Lots. Of s-s-ssex." He breathed the final word directly into her ear.

Which, okay, probably wasn't his smartest move. Not when it brought him close enough to smell the sunshine in her hair and the healthy Mags scent of the rest of her. "But, hey, don't you worry, darlin'," he said as if running off at the mouth would somehow negate his awareness. "I can always make room for one more."

He didn't need the scream of outraged she-relatives in his head to know he was out of line. But he'd say this for Mags, she lost that stiffness he'd noticed and turned to face him, cool as you please. Ignoring his hand now firmly entangled in her hair, she gave him a long, slow once-over.

"Tell you what, *darlin'*—and what's with your constant use of that word anyway? Is it just a sly way of dodging ever having to remember actual names?" She essayed a never-mind-that wave of her hand. "That's not important. My point is that I'm not really interested in being one of a faceless horde of…dozens? Hundreds?" Mild distaste flashed across her expression. "Thousands, perhaps?"

"Hey, let's not rule out millions." He watched color fluctuate under the fine-grained skin of her chest, her throat and face, and dug his fingers deeper into that warm, streaky blond hair until he could scratch his nails along her scalp. Goose bumps cropped up on her arms. "So…should I take that as a no, then?"

"Yes. You should take it as a great big resounding no. I'd have to be drunk off my ass to sleep with you."

"Yeah?" He leaned close. Lightly gripped her firm little cleft chin, pressed a here-and-gone kiss on her lips, then, setting her loose, pulled back. And in his most tempting voice murmured, "Buy you a margarita?"

She made a sound like a suppressed sneeze exploding in her throat and, knowing a muffled laugh when he heard one, he grinned, disentangled his fingers and moved back to his own side. He knew damn well their chemistry went both ways, because she'd been every bit as engaged as he when she'd kissed him in the gondola. But unable to shake his dad's edicts about the way men treated women, he merely said, "You know you're tempted."

"You keep telling yourself that." But then she laughed outright and started the car again. Pulling out onto the empty road, she shook her head, shot him a what-the-hell-am-I-supposed-to-*do*-with-you glance, then turned her attention back to her driving.

"You just keep telling yourself that, bub."

WHEN THEY ROLLED into the town of La Plata later that day, Mags was relieved to see it looked plenty large enough to house a car-rental agency. She pulled over to ask the first person they came across if there was indeed one—and if so, where they might find it. Following the man's directions, she then set off to locate it.

They couldn't have driven more than a couple of miles before they suddenly found themselves at a cross street bisecting a sizable festival in progress. The air rang with the shouts of merrymakers and music, and the long boulevard they crossed was closed to traffic and clogged with costumed revelers. Citizens dressed in their own brilliantly colored party garb filled the sidewalks, while seductive aromas of fiesta food wafted beckoning fingers, inviting one and all to come eat their fill.

The guitar, horns and mariachi-heavy music drifting through their open windows had her involuntarily dancing in her seat. She forced herself to still, but when she glanced over at Finn she discovered that he, too, was doing a seated boogie.

Meeting her gaze, he gave her a whatta-ya-gonna-do, one-sided smile and continued to rock his upper body in a subtle, sinuous rhythm. She took back what she'd thought yesterday when she'd made the snap judgment he wasn't a club kind of guy. Apparently he was.

The man rocked some serious moves, at any rate.

The music faded as they left the festival behind. Mags navigated her way to the rental agency through a maze of secondary streets until she finally spotted a sign for Paseo Las Industrias Barato Auto Rentals. And for the first time since running afoul of Joaquin in Santa Rosa, she felt as if something might actually go their way. She'd gotten her current car through a Barato agency—and while the quality of this one didn't

compare to the few cars she'd rented in the States, the
agency did honor returns from any Barato dealership
in South America.

After giving Finn the paperwork and letting him
out in front of the office, she looked for a place to
park in the minuscule lot. Judging by the vehicles she
walked past a minute later, it might have been the Santa
Rosa agency fleet that was the fluke, not the rest of
the Barato-owned agencies at all. The cars in this lot
looked far newer. That was encouraging. So was entering the tiny agency to find the clerk speaking English
and dealing quite handily with the American.

Finn looked pumped when he and the clerk joined
her a moment later. He slid a folded piece of paper and
a key on a foam ring, of all things, into his back pocket.
Reaching her, he turned her around and escorted her
right back out again.

"We have to go grab our stuff out of the trunk," he
said. "Enrique here is hot to close up for a couple of
hours to attend the festival. You and I are gonna go
check it out as well."

"Oh, but—" She glanced over her shoulder to see the
clerk locking the front door, then hustling away. She
opened her mouth to call him back, but snapped it shut
again. And nodded. What the hell. Checking out a local
festival sounded like a great break from their single-
minded drive toward the Munoz grow farm.

Finn grabbed her tote out of the trunk, handed it
to her and pulled out his backpack. He put the foam-
ringed key into the pack's outside pocket and swung it
onto his back.

"Which car is ours?" she asked, digging through her bag for her wallet and a lipstick.

"Beats the hell out of me."

She turned to him. "But what do we do with our stuff?"

"We'll have to carry the pack and your purse. The rest we'll leave here and come back for later."

"If it's still here to retrieve."

He shrugged. "Which is why we're taking the important stuff with us."

She sighed, put her wallet and lipstick back in the tote and pulled out one of her scarves. She twisted her hair up off her neck, tied it in a knot midway between her crown and the base of her skull, then wrapped the scarf around it in a style a South African makeup artist had shown her. Looping the bag's strap over her head, she settled it cross body. She looked up to see Finn watching her with a crooked smile. "What?"

"Nothing. It's just...that girlie stuff you're always doing is way outside my experience."

"Yeah? Don't your sisters or your millions of lovers do the girlie thing?"

He shrugged. "Probably. I've just never paid much attention. C'mon." He nudged her with his shoulder. "Let's you and me go do the festival."

The rental agency was on the edge of La Plata's industrial area, so they had to hike quite a way before they reached the event. Mags was hot and thirsty by the time they plunged into the heart of the party, but the music and aromas and the sheer amount of men, women and children gathered with a single shared purpose of hav-

ing fun made her forget for a while the problems that
had been piling upon her shoulders. Looking over at
Finn, she saw he had his camera out to document the
scene.

She got caught up in the crowds as she and Finn
inched their way along the sidewalk, dividing their attention between the spectacle around them and looking
over the goods for sale on rugs and flimsy tables. They
stopped to watch as a group of women in brightly patterned costumes danced past in the street, twirling and
manipulating their huge circle skirts until they swirled
around them like kites taking flight.

Mags pored over a table piled high with costume
jewelry. She particularly loved the chunky bracelets
made from what looked like old-school Lucite. Even
with the bargain-basement asking price, she was aware
of the limited amount of cash she'd brought with her
on this trip. She tried to ignore it, but it jangled at the
back of her mind and finally, regretfully, she turned
away from a particularly appealing orange-and-cream-
colored bangle.

Out of nowhere a little voice in her head demanded,
*What right do you have to enjoy yourself—and cov-
eting jewelry, for pity's sake—when your mother and
father are enduring God knows what at the hands of
Munoz's men?*

Enormous guilt threatened to consume her, but she
squared her shoulders and forced herself to think logi-
cally.

And, looked at rationally...

They weren't blowing off her parents' situation so

they could enjoy a day out of time. The car agency was closed until the festival was over and their attending it themselves was a legitimate means of de-stressing. Heaven knew their psyches had absorbed hit after heavy-duty hit ever since her original run-in with Joaquin. It felt like it'd been one craptastic challenge after another. So, she shook off her guilt as best she could and granted herself permission to take this time for what it was—a brief respite that would help refill their wells and give them the strength to fight again.

Several barely pubescent boys in elaborate costumes and headdresses the colors of the sun did a tribal dance out in the street a short distance from the jewelry tables. Beyond them two shirtless teenaged boys in white pants performed a contrastingly modern B-boy routine to a hip-hop tune blaring from an old eighties-style boom box.

Mags looked over her shoulder to share a grin with Finn over the wildly divergent cultural styles and found him gone. She looked around, but for a moment all she could see was a group of men in black bowlers and beautiful elaborately embroidered yellow ponchos with yellow and green fringe that shivered with their every move. Anxiety began to itch like a bad rash under her skin. *Oh, God, where did he go?*

She mentally kicked herself, because if he'd deliberately shaken free of her, well, it was her own damn fault, wasn't it? Why did she always have to shoot off her big mouth before she thought things through? She knew she had crummy impulse control, but couldn't she, just once, have bitten her tongue and not blurted out the first damn thing to pop into her head?

Oh, no, a voice dripping in sarcasm drawled in her head. *Not you, girl.* You *had to go call him a man whore.*

Crap. Who could blame him if he'd gotten fed up?

Then, suddenly, there he was, weaving toward her through the ever-moving throng. When he reached her a moment later, he held out a tall to-go cup filled to the brim with ice and what looked like lemonade. "Here," he said. "I thought you might be thirsty."

She walked right past his outstretched arm to wrap her own tightly around his lean middle and give him a hard, relieved hug. Because the truth was, she hadn't fully realized until this moment how much strength she gained just knowing that he was with her, shouldering a huge share of the burden.

And she really, really didn't want to find out what it would be like if she had to do this on her own.

Finn looked down at her. "He-e-y—hey, there. You okay?"

She nodded against his chest. Then, firming up her chin, which had developed an unacceptable tendency to tremble, she stepped back…and thrust up that chin. "Of course," she said coolly, reaching for the cup he'd offered and taking a huge gulp.

And God have mercy. She moaned against the cup's rim. The lemonade tasted like manna from heaven as it slid like iced silk down her throat.

"Of course," he repeated, a slight smile tugging at his lips as he checked her over. The moment she lowered the cup he reached out to rub his thumb across her bottom lip. He drew it back to study the drop of lemonade that decorated his thumb's pad, then brought it up to suck the droplet into his mouth.

The way heat streaked through Mags's veins, a person might be forgiven for thinking he'd done something a helluva lot more suggestive than licking up a drop of juice. She turned away to stare blindly at a group of young women currently parading down the street in Vegas showgirl–style outfits that were long on sequins, feathers and towering headpieces, and short on coverage. She glanced down at her own cargo shorts and double tank top and thought she could probably stand a little style herself. She had forgotten, during her years away from El Tigre, the sheer panache Latin women often brought to their fashion and makeup.

Even if it was the memories of this country that had steered her interest in makeup artistry.

"Shit," Finn suddenly muttered next to her and she looked up to see him gazing past the performers in the street.

"What is it?"

"There's a couple of thug-looking guys on the other side of the street," he murmured. Then his voice went hard and authoritative when she started to turn her head. "Don't look."

"Is it Joaquin or what's his name?"

"No, but they're definitely on the lookout for someone and they don't seem quite sure yet that we're it, so don't give them a better look at your face by facing them fully."

"Gotcha." Drinking the last of her lemonade, she

turned casually away. "Give me ten minutes and I can change both of our looks so much our own mothers wouldn't recognize us."

He looked down at her. "How do you plan to do that?"

"I'm a makeup artist and I have stuff in my bag that can transform us." And wasn't it odd that she hadn't already told him how she made a living? Even though they'd only been together one day, they'd shared so many adrenaline-fueled experiences it somehow caught her by surprise that he didn't know. She knew about *him* being in business with his brothers.

"And you can do this in ten minutes?"

She nodded. "Or less." She turned to consider the shops behind them and the tables set up along the edge of the sidewalk. "Let's go in there," she said, nodding at a shop two doors away from where they stood.

It was dim and cooler inside and she headed straight to the wall of carnival masks. "We'll make yours easy," she said and within two minutes had selected a tiger's-head mask, two arm ruffs and a beads-and-bones necklace. She carried everything to the counter to pay.

"Is there a back door?" she asked the clerk, who was more interested in checking out the action on the street than in her and Finn. Except to check the price, he'd barely even glanced at her purchase.

Without taking his gaze off another group of scantily dressed young women outside, he jerked his head at the narrow curtain that separated the front from the back of the store.

They stepped through it and she put a finger to her

lips. "Take off your shirt," she whispered. "And if you have different pants to put on that wouldn't hurt, either."

He did as she said—and for once she was too busy digging her all-gold pirate outfit from the bottom of her tote to take the time to admire the show. Throwing in the costume had been a last-minute impulse in case she needed to supplement her meager funds while she was here. She hadn't actually anticipated it would be necessary, but as she dropped her pants and wiggled into a pair of tights she thanked God for the little voice that had insisted she include it.

She slipped a full-sleeved shirt over her tank tops and buttoned it up to her throat. She added a vest atop that, tied a sash around her waist and arranged the two oversize plastic skeleton keys to dangle just right. Her sword was in her suitcase back at Senora Guerrero's boardinghouse, but she slid her plastic dagger into the sash at her side. She pulled on soft, flimsy-soled boots, then reached for her makeup kit and stepped into the small restroom that luckily provided a mirror and began sponging gold makeup on her face and neck and hands.

She turned to see Finn staring at her. "You are fast," he said in a low voice.

She nodded and unfolded her soft tricorne, reshaped it and fit it over her hair, tying the attached kerchief in an elaborate knot at the back of her head to hold it in place. She gave herself a quick once-over to make sure she hadn't missed a spot where her fair skin might show through, then jerked her chin at Finn. "C'mere."

He squeezed into the tiny room and she indicated that he should take a seat on the toilet. "You're tan enough to pass as a native so we're going to keep this simple," she breathed and dabbed yellow patches on his shoulders and upper arms, chest and abs, then squatted to paint black slashes atop them. She dropped the necklace over his head and tied the ruffs above his elbows. Strands of gold and black faux fur hung almost to his wrists. He'd changed into khaki shorts and she tied her leopard-print scarf around his waist, then handed him the mask. "Place this to give yourself the best vision possible, then turn around so I can get your back."

He did so, and moments later Mags stepped back to check out the overall effect. "Not bad," she murmured. "I'd do better with more time, but this ain't too shabby." She nodded at the mirror. "Check it out."

He rose and did as she directed. For a second it was dead quiet in the crowded little room. Then, "Dammmmn," he breathed. "You're right. I don't think my mom would recognize me. And you look amazing." He handed her the camera. "Take a shot, wouldja?"

She did, then posed with him for a selfie, before getting down to business. "Let's go see if I can make us some money." She eased out of the bathroom and headed for the door in the back.

"Wait…what?" Finn was right on her heels, moving with amazing stealth for a man of his size.

Not that he was massively large or overly bulky. She shot a glance at him as they headed for the door that opened onto the street behind the festival, admiring his wide shoulders, nicely developed arms and leanly muscled chest and abs.

He was just right.

The front door crashed open and they both froze as they heard rough-toned voices demand from the clerk if he'd seen the two of them.

"Shit," she whispered and wagged her fingers to indicate he should go back into the bathroom. She crowded in behind him and had barely managed to get the door closed past their blocking bodies when footsteps pounded past. The door to the back street opened.

And seconds later, slammed shut again.

Pressing back against Finn's front, she eased the door open and peeked out. "Coast is clear," she breathed. "We'd better go out through the front."

The clerk was still more interested in the festival than them when they appeared back in his shop and they let themselves out the door. "Let's go this way," she said as they hit the sidewalk. "I'm hoping to find a plaza."

They wove through the crowd for two more blocks and at the end of the second, Mags was rewarded, for it emptied into a plaza. "Grab me out one of your pans, would you?" she asked and walked over to a spot that was a bit clearer of people than the rest. "Just put it down at my feet, then go stand away from me," she instructed when Finn pulled the smallest pot from the nest of three.

He did as she directed with the pan, but demanded, "What the hell are you going to do?"

"My cash is low. I'm going to make some more while the opportunity is hot." And having said so, she struck a pose and froze.

Her stillness, in the midst of all the activity, imme-diately drew a crowd. People marveled at her unblinking resemblance to a statue and boys tried everything they could to make her flinch.

But she had been doing this for years and had built up an immunity to loud noises and hands clapped or fingers flicked in her face. It wasn't until a little girl maybe three years old stared up at her in awe and whispered, "Is she real, Papa?" that she gave a slow wink.

The crowd roared and tossed a rain of El-TIPs into her pan. She changed her pose and remained unmoving for an additional twenty minutes, suffused by a sense of pleasure as rich as the cash growing steadily higher at her feet. Finally, seeing Finn circle back as he'd done periodically, she barely moved her lips to ask in English, "We clear to move on?"

He gave the area a casual glance. "As far as I can tell. I haven't see the thugs again."

"Good." Giving up her pose, she stooped to pick up the container of pesos. People applauded and with a cheerful grin she rose and bowed with a flourish. Then she met Finn's gaze head-on for the first time since beginning this gig. "Then maybe we should get while the getting's good."

CHAPTER NINE

"SHIT." FINN PUT his hand on Magdalene's arm to stay her as they started around the corner that would bring them to the car-rental agency. He pulled her with him as he stepped back until the building blocked them from view again.

"What?" she whispered. *"What?"*

"They're here." He risked another quick glance around the building, but his eyes hadn't deceived him. The same steroid-fed gorillas they'd seen at the festival were standing next to the car they'd just turned in. "The cartel goons are over in the lot."

Clearly stunned, Magdalene stared up at him without so much as a blink of those big blue eyes. "How did they know this is where we'd be?"

Good question. But he thought about it as he led her back the way they'd come and, thinking out loud, he said slowly, "They probably didn't."

"What do you mean?"

"When we hit town and you asked that guy if there was a place that rented cars, he immediately named this one. It might be the only game in town, and if that's the case, it would make it the logical place to check. It's also possible Munoz got a line on the car we turned in and that's how they've been finding us. They probably came here first and found the joint closed for the festival, then tried again after we gave them the slip."

"Crap, crap, *crap*!" The sclera of her eyes were very white against the gold paint still on her face. "Now what are we going to do?"

"I actually have a plan."

"You do? What is it?"

"I'll tell you when we get where we're going." From the front pocket of his shorts he pulled out the paperwork he'd gotten earlier at the car agency. After returning two pieces to his pocket, he shook open the map.

"Tell me now." Mags reached around him for the map, but he half turned to wedge his shoulder between them and held her off as he pored over the route the clerk had highlighted.

"Dammit, Finn! Lemme see." She reached again.

Again he deflected her. "You'll see when we get there."

She narrowed her eyes at him. "Don't make me hurt you."

He made a rude noise. "Yeah, I'm real worried." He folded the map and shoved it back in his pocket. "There's nothing quite so scary as a gold pirate chick with a plastic dagger." He grinned at her indignant expression. "Good thing I'm in possession of all the real weapons."

"That's true," she agreed, then gave him a level look. "But you have to sleep sometime."

He laughed and picked up his pace. He didn't slow down again until they reached a small market along their route. "We'd better get some new provisions." He blew out a breath. "I'm gonna miss that little cooler."

"And the *ajiaco*," she said wistfully. "I was really looking forward to having that tonight. It was one of my favorite dishes when I was a kid."

They went inside and Mags asked to use the restroom, disappearing with that big-ass and evidently bottomless purse of hers behind the colorful bead curtain separating the store from the storage room. By the time she reappeared, pink-skinned from a scrubbing and wearing regular clothes, he'd selected an assortment of nonperishable groceries and a few pieces of fruit.

She looked at his selection, then grabbed a couple of chocolate bars and two big bottles of water. They took their purchases to the counter and she hauled out the scarf she'd knotted around the afternoon's take. "Here. Use this. You've been paying way more than your fair share."

He took it because he could see she'd make a fuss if he didn't. And because he'd seen what she'd hauled in during that relatively short time.

Watching her in the square this afternoon had blown him away. He never would have guessed that someone who pumped out energy in the kind of massive waves she did could stand so still. She had *been* a golden pirate statue and none of the noise or movement on that square, none of the young boys who had done their best to make her flinch or the grown-ups who had waved disbelieving hands in front of her face, had affected her immobility one bit. Hell, he'd thought only cats could go that long without blinking.

When he finished paying up, she reknotted her scarf around the hardly dented mound of El-TIPs and thanked the clerk for letting her use the bathroom. Then they packed their bags with their supplies and hit the streets again.

Not much farther on, they began to catch an occasional breeze. He steered her to the right at the end of the next street.

"We must be getting near the river," Mags said. "It feels a little cooler and I'm catching a whiff of it now and then." Turning her head, she gave him a smile that was almost girlishly sweet. "I love that smell."

"Good," he said as they reached the street running along the river and turned left. "Because we're taking a boat from here." He braced himself, waiting for all the reasons why it was a stupid idea.

"Will it get us closer to our objective?"

"Yeah. Pretty damn close, in fact."

"It's probably a good idea, then. Hopefully it won't occur to Joaquin and company that we'd take this route."

Huh. Every time he thought he had her all figured out, she caught him by surprise.

But he didn't have time to mull it over because he was beginning to note that the farther they walked toward the dock where the agency clerk had told him he'd find the boat, the rougher this section of town became. He didn't care for the way some of the men lounging and smoking outside a bar they were approaching eyed Mags.

Without missing a step, he shifted her to the street side of the wooden plank sidewalk.

"What the—"

"Keep moving and don't make eye contact with the guys up ahead. I don't like the way they're looking at you and I doubt you would, either. But trust me when I say I'm pretty sure they're the kind who'd take any eye contact from you as encouragement."

"What if they thought I was already taken? That I was all hot for you?"

He shrugged, both at the question and the way his body predictably got with the program with an immediate mental, *Oh, yeah. Come to Daddy.*

Since his body was a dumb animal that had gone without for a while and tended to show its willingness to change its luck when so much as a whiff of opportunity arose, he forgave it that. At the same time, he did what grown-ups do and ignored it. "Toss-up," he said. "It might be just the ticket—or it might set off a feeding frenzy."

"I like the first idea. Not too crazy about the second when I'm the chum." She slid her arm around his waist. "Maybe if we start off easy."

Holy crap, she felt good snugged up against his side. "Yeah," he said, sliding his arm across her nearest shoulder and hooking his elbow around her neck, his hand dangling dangerously close to the thrust of her breast. "Maybe then."

Finn knew it was playacting, but glued against Mags from shoulder to thigh as they walked in slow, sensual unison down the sidewalk, all he really cared about was her heat, her scent sinking into him. It was already sweltering, so shouldn't it have made him feel caged in? Yet it didn't. It just felt kind of...right.

They were almost to the knot of men when Mags looked up at him and laughed. "You do know, don't you, that you still have your makeup on?"

Well, hell. As soon as they'd cleared the festival he'd removed his mask and those hula-skirt-type arm things and put his T-shirt back on. But after that he'd been so focused on getting to the rental agency, then on getting *away* from it without being seen, that he'd entirely forgotten the makeup she'd put on him. Even when Mags had used the store's restroom to wash off her own and strip off her hat, swashbuckler shirt and boots, it hadn't dawned on him.

Now here he was, approaching a bunch of guys that he'd call bikers if they were in the States and, okay, had any actual Harleys outside the cantina, and he was decked out in fucking cat makeup. Great way to intimidate the South American Bad Boys. The only saving grace here was the hurkin' big knife he'd taken off Joaquin, which was tucked in his leopard-print belt.

An-n-nd...shit. Could have done without the reminder of the scarf threaded through his belt loops.

Apparently, though, Team Bikers Without Bikes thought it was cuter than the *olinguito* mammal recently discovered in the Andes, because they started whistling and making kissy sounds and generally saying things that even with his inadequate piss-poor Spanish he could tell was a version of "Here, kitty, kitty, kitty."

The tone was universal even if the words were not.

Still, he was known far and wide—at least throughout Clan Kavanagh—as Mister Mellow. These jokers would have to do a helluva lot better than make pussy jokes to truly embarrass or anger him.

It was plain to see, however, that they'd succeeded in pissing off Mags. "What the *hell*?" she growled and opened her mouth, clearly prepared to deliver a set down in her liquid rapid-fire Spanish.

He tightened the bend of his elbow around her neck and gave her a big feral grin when she looked up at him. "You know I grew up with six siblings, right?"

"Yeah, yeah—you don't appreciate them, needed some space from the whole family, but especially the women, et cetera, et cetera, et cetera. Not really the time to have this discussion again, Kavanagh."

"Yeah, it actually is, *Deluca*. Because compared to my brothers and sisters, these guys are novices. *Nothing* is more ruthless than a Kavanagh kid with a grudge and the slice-and-dice vocabulary and fertile imagination to come up with unique retribution. By the time I hit first grade I was an old hand at sucking it up and never letting anyone see that anything said to me could actually *get* to me."

"And…? Oh-h-h." She drew the word out as the answer to her own question dawned. "There's nothing a bully hates quite as much as that, is there?" She threw back her head and laughed. "Brilliant. You're rather diabolical."

"I try," he admitted modestly.

They'd drawn abreast of the clowns outside the cantina. Her laughter seemed to have shut them up, however, and the two of them sauntered past unmolested.

Or at least Finn thought they had until, reaching around him, one of the men grabbed Mags's ass in the wake of their passing.

Rage exploded in his brain and, spinning to face the assailant, he caught the groper with an uppercut to the jaw just as the guy was pulling back his hand and winking and mugging for his buds. The ass grabber went down like a felled sapling and Finn, still seeing red, pulled back his foot to kick the shit out of him, but Mags grabbed him by the arm with one hand as she fumbled in her big purse with the other. "We're kinda outnumbered here, dude," she muttered urgently under her breath. "We gotta move."

Seeing she was right, that the asshat's friends were beginning to recover from their surprise and weren't happy with him—or, by extension, Mags—he had to agree that putting some distance between them was probably an excellent idea. Clamping his fingers around her free wrist, he took off at a dead run. She'd demonstrated yesterday that she could keep up.

He swallowed a snort. Hell, who was he kidding? She could likely outstrip him if it came right down to it. The woman could *run*. So damned if he'd insult her by expecting anything less now.

They pounded down the wooden sidewalk for a full two blocks, angry nonbikers a posse of raggedly spread-out avengers in their wake. Finally, he spotted a ramshackle marina up ahead that had to be the one the clerk told him about. "This way," he said when they reached it and swerved onto the long dock.

Checking out the boats, he muttered, "No," to every

one they approached, then passed by. "No, no, *fuck* no, no, *yes*! That one!" He pulled them to a halt in front of an open, narrow craft that looked like a slightly oversize dory, with its narrower flat bottom and high sides. He could see shipped oars inside but it also had a nine-horse motor attached to the back. It wasn't exactly what he'd anticipated, but it was the only one painted royal blue with an orange keel and orange trim.

Pulling the key from his pocket, he tried to hand it to Mags. "Climb in and I'll untie it."

"*I'll* untie it," she said. "You get it started. I don't know bupkes about engines of any kind." Squatting down, she lobbed her bag onto the floor of the boat between the two middle plank seats and went to work unfastening the front line looped around the dock cleat. "And make it snappy," she added. "Those idiots will be here any minute now."

He didn't bother arguing. She was right; he should have assigned the duties that way in the first place. The motor looked fairly ancient and it was going to take some finessing from someone who actually knew something about engines. Not to mention that he was the one who'd been given instructions for locating everything they needed before he could even start the damn thing.

Climbing into the boat, he located a small lockbox beneath the bow and used the key to open it. From inside, he pulled out the starter cord and wound it around the pulley. Then he hauled out a good-sized gas can, quickly connected its fuel line to the motor and squeezed the rubber bulb in the line a couple of times to get gas into the carburetor. After pulling out the choke, he gave the wooden handle on the cord a yank. It gave a halfhearted cough, then died.

He started rewinding.

The boat rocked as Mags climbed in. "We're loose," she said, "and you might want to get a move on. Those guys aren't real speedy and a few have dropped out. The ones that are left, though, just hit the dock."

"Grab an oar and push us away," he said. "And let's hope to hell they don't have a boat of their own." He gave the bulb another pump, waited a second as Magdalene pulled one of the oars out of the oar lock, then gave the handle another yank.

He got a more promising reaction this go-round when it almost, damn near, caught. Still, no cigar. The good news, however, he decided as footsteps thundered down the dock, was that he was getting faster and more efficient at rewinding it around the pulley.

Meanwhile, Mags braced the blade end of the oar against the dock and shoved. It whipped the rear of the boat out into deeper water, but the front end, where she was kneeling, was still less than a foot from the quay, and even as he pulled the starter cord once more, he saw one of the bar boys rock to a halt in front of her and bend over the bow.

This time the motor roared and he rapidly adjusted the choke and put the boat in Reverse. They started moving away from the dock and he shot a triumphant grin over his shoulder.

Just in time to see the man lean farther and close his hand on a fistful of Mags's hair.

He roared a denial, but she didn't make a peep. Instead, she thrust her right arm out at the man who had her in his grip and shoved the tip of her index finger down on the little gray canister in her hand.

The guy screamed like a girl and let her go to claw at his eyes.

Finn took immediate advantage and turned the motor handle hard to the left, whipping the boat's front end away from the dock in a fast, tight U. He heard a splash behind him. Looking back, he saw the man's head pop up out of the water.

Straightening the boat out, he pointed them downriver. "You okay?" he asked, looking over at her as she cautiously climbed over two narrow seats and sat facing him on the one nearest his. "You mace him?"

"Pepper-sprayed." She shrugged. "Same difference."

He noticed she didn't address his first question. "And you're okay?"

"I'm fine." The look she cast around her, however, seemed less certain and when she looked back at him her delicate eyebrows furrowed. "When you said we were taking a boat, I guess I kind of expected something larger."

"Yeah, me, too." He shook his head. "Well, I didn't really give any thought to how big it would be. But I assumed it would have a small shelter on it." He studied her fair skin. "You have a nice hide. Delicate—I'd hate to see it get burned to a crisp." She was already pink from being out in the festival sun. Luckily, the sun was nearing the horizon and as he'd already learned, when it went down it did so suddenly and completely.

Which brought up another problem.

"You're such a silver-tongued devil," Mags said. "I'd feel flattered, except I bet you tell all the girls they have a good hide. But don't worry, I'm not going to burn." She leaned back to hook her bag and dragged it over the bench to the floor in front of her. Opening its top wide, she dropped her pepper spray back into it, then bent to paw through it for something else.

A second later she straightened with the thin, long-sleeved, half-zip T-shirt she'd donned in the gondola. "This is my rash guard," she explained, pulling it on. "It has built-in SPF."

"That's one less thing to worry about, then."

She gave him a funny little crooked smile. "Aw. You were worried about me?"

"Maybe a little." He held up a hand, his thumb and index finger an inch apart to demonstrate. "Right now I'm more worried about finding a spot for us to pull over for the night before the sun goes down."

"Yeah. That'd probably be a good idea. The only problem, as I see it," she added, looking around at the river and its surroundings now that they were away from town, "is that the water appears to end where all that dense foliage begins."

"Yeah," he agreed glumly. "And that doesn't leave us with anywhere to set up a tent."

"Or find a place to pee."

Given that she seemed to do *that* with much more regularity than he, he shot her a rueful smile. "Right," he said drily. "Or do that."

CHAPTER TEN

THE SUN WAS an enormous flaming orb sinking behind the river's western bank. Long rays of light spiked through the clouds that billowed with increasing denseness atop the bank's horizon, turning the mass into a spectacular wash of orange, scarlet, gold and violet. The result was stop-the-breath-in-your-throat stunning. But Mags also knew it heralded nightfall. Soon.

And that wasn't good.

"It's going to be dark in about five minutes," she said. And so far they hadn't found so much as a chink in the impenetrable foliage lining the banks.

"I know." Finn had removed his backpack shortly after they'd cleared town and he nudged it with his toe in her direction. "I have a headlamp in there. I want you to go get us the life jackets from under the bow. Put yours and the headlamp on. When it turns full dark I'll row for a while. It'll be safer than using the motor. Your job is to keep an eye peeled for anything that might get in our way and a potential place to pull over."

"And if we don't find one?"

"We hope to hell there's an anchor under the bow as well, because it's not safe to travel blind for long. The map indicated this is a tributary to a bigger river that we won't run into until we're just above the northernmost Amazon. A lot of tributaries are controlled for agriculture but I don't know if that's the case here. I'm kind of hoping so because my research before coming to South America pointed to a lot of waterways in this region having falls. And while some of them are insignificant, others definitely aren't. I'm thinking we don't want to find ourselves going over one in the dark."

"Or in daylight, either, if it comes to that."

"Oh, I don't know." He grinned at her. "That could be kind of fun." Evidently taking her unsmiling face for the lack of amusement she felt, he gave her a suspiciously unsober sober look as he added virtuously, and probably falsely, "But mostly I'm right there with ya."

She reached for the pack and pulled it onto her lap. Finn directed her to the outside pocket, where she found the headlamp and, never having seen one up close and personal, she removed it from the pack and studied it for a few silent moments. The band had a subtle black-and-charcoal geometric design, the company logo stamped in orange in regular intervals and was clearly intended to go around the wearer's head like a miner's light. The actual LED holder was a lighter gray metal that sat dead center in the band. The beam was adjustable and she tested its limits for a few seconds before slipping the band onto her head.

Unfortunately, she let go too soon, for it slipped down her forehead and over her eyebrows until the bridge of her nose stopped the lamp's protrusion. Forcefully. "Ow."

"Are you okay?" The corner of his mouth tipped up. "Want me to kiss it better?"

She made a rude noise that he correctly interpreted as a no. But she had to admit the idea of him kissing her *anywhere* was… Lord have mercy. Crazy appealing.

His dark eyes made a slow inspection of the too-loose gadget still sitting cockeyed atop her nose. "Looks like my head's bigger than yours. Which is to be expected, since I need room for my amazingly large brain."

"Or for your astoundingly fat ego." She hauled the head strap back to her forehead and slapped a hand against it to hold the thing in place as she tugged on the strap in back to tighten it up. When she got it to where it felt secure, she turned back to him and posed. "How do I look?" She turned her head first to the right, then to the left, sucking in her cheeks and pursing her lips in her best runway moue. "I hear all the fashionistas are wearing this color combo this season. Flattering, right? I think it brings out the orange in my eyes."

He laughed—then laughed even harder, as if he couldn't help himself.

As if she'd said the wittiest thing he'd ever heard.

She assured herself *that* didn't warm her right up from the inside out. It wasn't like she gave a great big rip what he thought of her.

She sneaked a glance at him, all big and competent with his wide-palmed, long-fingered hand firmly on the steering thingy. Really. She *didn't* care.

Feeling unaccustomedly flustered, she turned away to fetch the life vests and verify they did have an anchor if they needed one. Then she settled back on her seat, pulled off her scarf and sighed as snatches of a fit-ful breeze fluttered through damp strands of her hair.

The next time she looked at Finn she saw that he'd kicked off his hiking sneakers, which, he'd informed her when she'd said she thought all hikers wore boots, had a steel shank running through the insole to give it the stability of one. She studied his feet. They were ac-tually kind of nice…long and narrow with long toes and a high arch. The big toe on his left foot looked beat-up, as if something heavy had dropped on it. She thought about asking him about it, but didn't.

Little by little she found herself relaxing. It was rather calming, being on the water. The air was a hot, damp weight against her skin, yet she felt as if she could breathe, could draw a truly deep, satisfying breath for the first time since this madness had blown up in her face. It was peaceful out here.

But not quiet. The motor's hum and the water softly slapping the hull of the dory were soothing sounds. The evening itself, however, was a sometimes melo-dious, often raucous cacophony of birds trilling, cry-ing and calling out as they wheeled against the sky or journeyed back and forth across the water. Many were brilliant explosions of color against the dense greenery lining the river, others you had to concentrate to pick out among the preponderance of camouflaging cover. She watched a pair of toucans settle briefly on a tree limb hanging over the water before hopping from branch to branch to branch in what appeared to be a restless quest for the ideal perch.

Then more abruptly than the final curtain falling on

a bankrupt play, the sun dropped below the horizon and the sky went from alive with fire and light to stygian.

Finn muttered a curse and cut the engine, tipping it up until the propellers cleared the river. He locked it in the upright position and Mags felt more than saw when he turned his attention to her.

"Turn your lamp on and move up to the bow," he instructed. "You're mostly looking for a place where we can pull over for the night, but keep an eye out for deadheads or anything else that might snag the boat."

She did as directed and heard the creaking boards and slight ring of metal against metal when he shifted into her seat and unshipped the oars. Glancing over her shoulder, the beam of her headlamp caught the blade of the oar on her right as it sliced into the water. When it rose again, a thin stream rimmed its bottom edge like a slick of mercury before rolling off in silver droplets that left expanding rings in the mirror-smooth river. She turned her attention back to her assigned job as he began to pull with strong, even strokes, and the boat glided through the water with nearly the same efficiency it had under motor power.

It took her a minute to get the hang of looking within the headlamp's beam without losing focus as she slowly swiveled her head to catch everything from one side of the waterway to the other, but it quickly became second nature. Unfortunately, there wasn't much to see except the unrelentingly closely packed right-up-to-the-water's-edge plant life and less ubiquitous trees. Her eyes were burning in their sockets from too infrequent blinking and she was about to throw in the towel and

suggest they drop anchor after all, when a sudden slice
of unexpected white made her squeeze her eyes shut
and rub the hell out of the burning itch they'd become.
When she reopened them, the white was still there. Fo-
cusing on it she saw that it was, omigawd—

"Beach!" she blurted. "On the left. No, wait, my
left, your right," she amended when she remembered
they faced different directions. "And about…crap, I
have no idea how far away—my distance-judging skills
suck eggs. But it's within reach of my lamp beam." A
slightly wild laugh exploded out of her throat. "There's
an honest-to-god patch of beach, Finn!"

A big laugh rolled out of him as well and he craned
to look over his right shoulder. "You still have it in your
beam? Oh, hell, yeah, there it is! Good work, Mags!"

"I know. I totally rock, right?"

"Damn straight." Untwisting to face the stern once
more, he put his back into rowing, and the boat shot
down the river. "Tell me when to turn."

A minute or so later she gave him the word and he
pulled hard on his oar to turn the bow right, then re-
sumed rowing with both oars. Seconds after that the
gritty susurrus of hull meeting sand sounded as the
boat's bow touched, then slid almost a foot up the beach.
Mags laughed, swept the sand with her light to make
sure nothing creepy awaited them, then scrambled over
the bow and onto the shore.

Finn joined her and the two of them tugged the boat
farther up the sand until a good half of it was out of
the water. When it was safely settled, she broke into a
spontaneous little dance until he directed her to train

the headlamp on his hands. He'd retrieved the anchor
and she watched the strong bunch and flex of small
muscles and tendons as he deftly tied it onto the bow-
line and sank what he called its fluke—and she called
the pointy end—deep into the sand.

"Who the heck *knows* that kind of terminology?"
she demanded.

"Someone whose brother spent over a decade crew-
ing in races or sailing rich people's yachts from point
A to point B all over Europe."

"Which brother is that?"

"Dev. He's the—"

"—one closest to you in age and interests."

"Yeah." He gave her a hey-you-remembered! grin,
then directed her to train the light on his backpack until
he pulled out his battery-powered lantern and set it up.
In its farther-reaching light he gathered enough wood
from the beach and along the border of the foliage to
build a small beach fire and set up the tent while she
assembled something for them to eat.

They sat in the sand in front of the fire to eat their
late dinner. Even though the evening was still hot and
muggy, there was something comforting about watching the flames flicker and dance. When Mags finished
her meal she looked over at Finn. "Between running
from ass-grabbing pigs and worrying about being on
the river after dark, I didn't realize how hungry I was.
But this hit the spot. If you're done, I'll clean up."

He handed her his plate and fork, and she carried them along with her own to the river, where she
scrubbed them with sand and rinsed them in the water.

"I'll check these in the morning to see if I need to redo them in boiled water," she said as she finished up and set them inside the tent vestibule before rejoining him in front of the fire. But her bladder was anxious to relieve itself and she shifted uncomfortably on the sand. Finally she said, "I really gotta—"

"Pee," he finished for her. "I swear, girl, I've never met anyone who does that as much as you." But he pulled his backpack over and dug out the toilet paper for her. Then he dug around some more and offered her a little spade.

"What's this for?"

"Take it to the far end of the beach and dig a little hole to do your biz. Cover it back up when you're done and, boom! You've avoided having to go into the brush."

"Oh, God, thank you, thank you!" Throwing herself at him, she wrapped her arms around his neck and planted a loud, smacking kiss on his lips.

Just like the last time she'd impulsively kissed him, however, this, too, promptly jumped the tracks into something much less grateful and a lot more...lusty. Finn's hand speared into her hair to hold her in place when she started to pull back. He raised his head for a moment, looked into her eyes, then lowered it again. And his mouth was all blistering heat and I'm-in-charge aggression.

Damned if she wasn't all over that, too. She'd probably be all over him as well...if she didn't have to dig that hole so darn bad. Slowly, reluctantly, she pulled back. "I, uh, really do have to go." She held up the trowel. "Thanks for this. I wasn't wild about the idea of

going into that—" She waved a hand at the dense foliage. "Even supposing I could penetrate the dang thing."

She climbed to her feet and trotted down to the far
end of the beach, where she dug her hole and flipped
her headlamp to point as far skyward as its adjustabil-
ity allowed. Not because she didn't trust Finn not to
look. She might've only known him for a short while
in the grander scheme, but it was long enough to know
he wasn't the kind of guy to get his jollies watching her
do her biz. She simply felt less exposed knowing she
was shrouded in darkness.

She thought about that kiss. She really needed to do
something about her lousy impulse control. Because,
now what? It hadn't even lasted that long, yet it had
packed a killer punch—and she didn't believe only for
her. So, would he expect to pick up where they'd left
off? Had she made him believe she was ready and willing to share his sleeping bag as well?

Was she?

Quite possibly.

No.

C'mon, admit it…*possibly.*

No, dammit. Just—*no.*

Dang. When would she learn to take a second or two
to *think* before she threw herself headfirst into behavior
that was potentially destructive?

She could feel her cheeks flame in mortification as
she adjusted her clothing and headed back to the fire,
in no hurry to abandon the all-encompassing shadows.
Because there was no denying that once again she was
the one who had started it. And women who started

things up, then called an abrupt halt to them, tended to
be called cock teases by the men on the receiving end.
Approaching the fire, she braced herself.

Finn, however, merely looked up at her and said,
"You want a cup of coffee?"

"Yes." And if that sounded particularly heartfelt,
well, it was—on so many levels. On the taken-at-
strictly-face-value level alone, caffeine was always a
much-appreciated perk. She didn't even worry about it
keeping her up all night. Their sleep had been so spo-
radic, so hit-and-miss the previous night, that she was
pretty sure she could drink an entire pot and still sleep
like Dracula in the daylight.

Finn tossed the dregs of his own coffee into the
fire and it hissed and sent a small shower of exploding
sparks above the flames as he reached for the pot he'd
placed on a little wire grill straddling the edge of the
fire. He refilled the cup and handed it to her. "Careful. It's hot."

She took a cautious sip and moaned at the rich fla-
vor. "Oh, my God. That's heavenly."

"Yeah, a good cup of coffee is hard to beat," he
agreed. He lounged back on one elbow and smiled at
her, all easy and relaxed. "Tell me about being shipped
off to boarding school in the States when you were
thirteen."

Shock sizzled bolts of lightning through her veins,
and she froze, her hands tightening their grip on the
cup. "What?"

"I blew you off when you tried to tell me yesterday,
but I've been thinking about what you said and I'd really

like to know. Do you really believe your folks shipped you off to the States so they could concentrate on other people's kids?"

Oh, God. The last thing she wanted to do was spend her relaxing moment before the fire limping out the reasons her parents didn't love her to Finn of the large nosy-because-we-adore-you Family Kavanagh.

Well, you can always steer the conversation back to the sex that may or may not have happened if you didn't possess a pea-sized bladder.

An-n-nd, put like that— "Yeah. I do."

"Why?"

"I was born in El Tigre," she said slowly, staring into the fire. "My folks are Baptist missionaries in a primarily Catholic country, which makes living and working on a shoestring a fact of life. But it never even occurred to me that we were poor. As far as I was concerned, running fairly wild with the boys and girls of the families my folks ministered to was the best of all worlds, whether it was in poor villages in the Amazon or in the some-ways-poorer inner-city neighborhoods up north." She fell quiet for a moment, remembering, and her lips quirked up. Because those had truly been some of the best times of her life.

Rolling her shoulders, she drew up her knees and hugged them to her chest. "Then out of the blue, midway between my thirteenth and fourteenth birthdays," she said, her voice hardening, "my parents packed me up and shipped me off to boarding school—no warning, no discussion."

"No discussion at all? They didn't give you so much as a hint why?"

She laughed bitterly. "They *said* it was for my own good, that it was for my *safety*, for pity's sake."

"Maybe, darlin'," Finn said gently, "that was exactly what it was."

"Please. So, what had been perfectly safe the previous thirteen years was suddenly a minefield I was no longer intelligent enough to pick my way through?"

"You said your mom is dangerously outspoken. Maybe they were threatened by someone like Munoz."

It gave her pause, because that had never occurred to her. After reassessing her long-held beliefs in silence for several moments, however, she shook her head. She was strangely reluctant to abandon the comforting possibility that Finn's suggestion opened up. And yet—

"No," she said. "We discussed everything as a family in those days and I pretty much knew the good, the bad and the ugly of what was going on in our lives. So I think if that had been the case, they would have just said, 'We want you safe because so and so is making threatening noises.'" Turning her head until her cheek rested on her kneecap, she looked at him, noting the rough stubble that had grown on his lean jaw since shaving the night before last. "But they didn't, Finn. They didn't say a damn thing, just dragged me to the airport and put me on a plane."

"Thirteen can be an impossible, bratty age."

"Yet most parents don't throw their kids away because of it. Besides," she said flatly, "I wasn't bratty or impossible then—that came later, in boarding school. I was Magdalene then—I was a *good* girl. Not that they gave a rat's rear end. They just wanted me gone so they'd have more time to devote to everyone else's kids."

He was staring at her, arrested. "What do you mean you were Magdalene then? That's your name now, right?"

"No." Her heart pounded unaccountably, but when he gave her a puzzled look she gave him a terse nod. "Okay, yes, technically it's my legal name. But Magdalene is the sweet compliant girl I once was." She gave him a long, unsmiling look. "She's gone, Kavanagh. I've been Mags for a long time now."

CHAPTER ELEVEN

FINN WAS CONFUSED, but he had no trouble seeing Mags was dead serious. So much so that a metaphorical light-bulb went off over his head as he recalled the consistent, emphatic way she'd corrected him every time he'd called her Magdalene. Which, he had to admit, had been pretty damn often since he genuinely dug her name.

Swiveling on his butt in the sand to face her profile rather than the fire, he burrowed his bare feet into the still-warm sand near her hip. Mags's head was tilted downward, the fall of her hair hiding most of her face. "Tell me about that. When did you change to Mags? And more importantly, why?"

She glanced at him then, but looked as if she might balk, as though the last thing she wanted to talk about was this. But he merely sat quietly, leveling a steady gaze on her. He had all night.

She must have realized it, too, because looking away once more, she gave him the big sigh women were so good at and hitched the shoulder nearest to him. "As far as I'm concerned, my folks threw me away," she finally said in a tone more resigned than the sulkiness he'd half expected. "And getting hit with the parental expiration date left me in no mood to turn the other cheek. So, I reinvented myself."

"How does a thirteen-year-old reinvent herself?"

"By dumping Goody Two-shoes Magdalene. I became Mags, and she was a whole lot tougher, let me tell you, than little Miss Mealy Mouth."

He tried to envision an unsophisticated girl from the poorer areas of South America reinventing herself in the boarding school she'd been sent to a world away from everything she'd known. His brain threw up a wall against the mere idea. "How did that work for you, overall?"

She grimaced. "I admit the transition wasn't mistake-free. I was angry for a long time and got myself kicked out of three boarding schools before I decided to buckle down enough to graduate so I could get the hell on with my life." Head bent again, she looked down at the sand between her feet and added flatly, "It worked out in the end."

"Yeah?" Why did he get the impression that was less than the truth? Or at least that a lot of shit had rained down on her head before she'd gotten to that point? "What did your folks think of the transformation?" Her hair still mostly blocked his view and he reached out to scoop a hank of it behind her ear, leaning in to see her expression more clearly. "You did still see them occasionally, didn't you?" Because leaving a kid that age in boarding school year-round was a concept he could not wrap his head around.

"Sure. I went home summers." She gave him an insouciant smile. But her eyes were remote and her energy muted, as if she'd slid behind the Wizard's curtain.

"And…?"

She gave him a cool look. "And what?"

"What did they think of your transformation?"

She shrugged. "They didn't have a clue what to do with the Mags who'd replaced their little girl and their response was to get stricter and stricter." She looked directly at him, and for the first time since they'd started this conversation he caught a glimpse of the real Mags in the indignation that turned her eyes a hotter blue. "Can you believe that? They sent me a thousand miles away so they wouldn't have to bother with me, then they're *surprised* when I don't fall in with their stifling rules for the few stinking weeks I do get to come home?"

She flashed him a sudden smile filled with genuine, if self-mocking, humor. "To be fair, in the early years I went out of my way to shock them. I generally landed on their doorstep with my hair dyed black, or pink or whatever my mood was at any given moment. And for a while I wore temporary tattoo sleeves and spirit-gummed a gem to my right nostril and a safety pin to my left eyebrow." She poked the inside of her cheek with her tongue. "Fun times, those."

Her sudden self-deprecating humor grabbed at something deep inside of him. He'd give the woman this: she was far from a whiner. He hadn't heard her complain once, even with a cartel hot on their heels, and he'd go out on a limb and posit she hadn't back when she was a kid, either. "You're such a balls-to-the-walls kind of chick, I'm surprised you didn't get inked and pierced for real."

"Nah. I like to mix things up and my taste is constantly changing. Not even in my rebellious years did I wanna be stuck with holes or permanent art I might despise six months down the road. I'm much happier making temporary changes with my makeup."

"You have a real talent for transforming things," he agreed. "How did you get to be so good at that?"

"Dunno. It was just something I started experimenting with and found I had a knack for it. It was the skill that eventually helped me fit in at school." She essayed a facial shrug. "Even the snobby girls who thought I was bug-ass weird sought me out when they had a special occasion or there was a costume party."

"Is that street-mime thing you did today how you make your living?"

"Honey, please." Even in the flickering light of the fire he could see that the look she gave him was indulgent in a you-really-need-to-get-with-the-program sort of way. "Mimes are those annoying white-faced jokers who get all up in your grill and mimic your every move or do their stupid I'm-in-an-invisible-box routine. I'm a living statue. Big difference," she said, turning in his direction and giving him another of those self-deprecating smiles. "At least in my own mind. And yes, it's one way I earn the rent."

"How the hell can you stay so still?"

"Beats the heck outta me. Maybe it's an only-child thing—I've just always been able to go to a place in my head where it's quiet and still. And once I tune everything out, it's fairly easy to stay there."

"I'd have thought for someone with your energy it would be next to impossible."

She looked at him with a crooked little smile. "You think I'm energetic?"

"Hell, yeah." And if he'd speculated once or twice—or, okay, a whole lot—what it would feel like if she applied all that vigor to some down-and-dirty sex with him, well, his mama didn't raise no fool. He knew enough to keep it to himself. "I get the feeling sometimes that if it could be harnessed, you could single-handedly power a village. At the very least."

She laughed in delight. "That's maybe one of the nicest things anyone's ever said to me."

It was? He had a sudden urge to haul her in for a hug, which wasn't part of his usual bag of tricks. But, Jesus. If only one thing anyone had ever said to her counted as the nicest, shouldn't it be a compliment of mammoth proportions? It seemed wrong that instead it had been something so small.

He cleared his throat. "So, when's the last time you saw your folks?" She acted as if reinventing herself as a wild child had made her impervious to hurt, but he was guessing that was far from the case. She was here now, wasn't she, racing around determined to save her parents? He'd bet the farm she'd been coming home whenever she could since they'd sent her away.

"Twelve and a half years ago."

Finn felt his jaw literally drop. But what the fu—? "*Twelve* years ago?" He leaned into her the better to see her face and unaccountably felt red-hot fury drilling a hole in his gut. "You haven't been to visit your parents in *twelve years*?"

"And a half." That prideful little chin of hers ratcheted up, its shallow thumbprint dimple leading the way. "Not all of us have the lovey-dovey Brady Bunch family you came from."

"But *twelve*—"

She whipped around to face him, kicking up sand with the ferocity of her movement. "Oh, for pity's sake," she snapped, "I heard you perfectly well the first *and* the second time. And as much as I appreciate all the girlie melodrama you invest in the word—"

"Hey!" Girlie melodrama, his big swinging dick.

"—after completing two semesters of college, I quit both the academic life and going back home during summer breaks. It wasn't so much that I couldn't deal with Brian and Nancy's disappointment in me. It was more that the having to do so every damn time I saw them wore me to a nub."

He tried to imagine calling his folks by their first names, but had a feeling his mom would consider that a washing-his-mouth-out-with-soap offense. He met her gaze and raised his brows. "So you just gave up on them."

"Yes. Is that what you want to hear, Kavanagh? Then *yes*, as you say. I just gave up on them."

Like hell. "Yet, here you are. Back in El Tigre, putting yourself at risk to find them."

She attempted the sulky facial equivalent of a shrug.

"Well, *I'm* not the one who fell out of love with them, am I?" She drew in an audible breath and exhaled it through barely parted lips. Then as if someone had wiped the slate clean, her expression smoothed over and her voice turned brisk when she said, "Neither was I ever completely off the grid with them."

She made a little yeah-yeah-I-know-what-you're-thinking gesture. "I admit I don't call them very often because it's frequently beyond my budget and completely impractical since they spend most of their time out in the community. I have made it a point, though, to write regularly to keep in touch."

"Yeah. Okay." He relinquished the judgmental self-righteous shit—and promptly remembered previous conversations. "You said it was having your mom's letters stop after she'd talked about her differences with Munoz that made you worry they were in trouble."

"And, boy, was I right on that front," she said glumly.

"Hey." He reached over and gave her shoulder a squeeze. Noting how warm and soft her skin was, he pulled his hand back and rubbed the feel of her away in the sand next to his hip. "We're gonna find them."

"Yeah." The word might be an agreement, but her tone demonstrated zero confidence. She pushed abruptly to her feet. "Well, listen, it's been a long day. Could I talk you into heating me up some water to wash? I think I'll get ready for bed."

And without waiting for a response, she turned on her heel and strode to the tent, patently ready for this day to be done.

SUSAN ANDERSEN 155

F<small>INN WOKE UP</small> with the sun the following morning and
rolled over to see if Mags was awake as well.

And chuckled.

She lay facing him, still sleeping soundly. Her hair
tumbled across the top part of her face, covering her
eyes and one cheekbone, and her hands were pressed
together like a little girl in prayer.

Except not quite. Sometime in her sleep she'd tun-
neled them beneath her cheek, perhaps to provide
support. Whatever the original reason, their current
position pushed her mouth into what would have been
pursed kissy lips if it hadn't somehow twisted them
out of shape.

He threw back the top of his unzipped bag, scratched
his abs and gave his morning wood an absentminded
pull. He picked his cargo shorts off the tent floor and
tugged them on, lifting his hips to yank up the shorts
over his butt. After zipping up gingerly, he rolled into
a crouch and crab-walked through the tent's doorway
and vestibule.

Rising to his full height outside, he stretched, gave
his belly another scratch and headed down the beach
before hanging a left for the foliage's boundary line.
When he returned moments later, he scooped some
water out of the river and put it on to boil for the morning washups.

He had sisters, so he knew Mags was going to make
him pay for seeing what she would no doubt view as
her weakness last night. For that reason, when he heard
rustling noises indicating she was awake fifteen or so

minutes after he'd washed up and started the coffee, he braced himself. *Wait for it.*

Waa-a-aait for it.

When she emerged a few minutes later, however, the TP bag clutched in hand, she merely yawned hugely, mumbled, "Mornin'," and trotted off down the beach.

"Huh." Okay, not a full-frontal snark attack, then. Maybe she was waiting for him to let his guard down so she could hit him with the sneaky just-when-you-think-it's-safe-to-come-outta-the-water version.

Half an hour later, after they'd downed their coffee and the skimpy breakfast he'd put together, and had cleaned up the kitchen stuff, he conceded he might have it all wrong. "Okay," he muttered as he watched Mags put away her toothbrush. "Maybe it's just a Kavanagh-chick thing."

"What is?"

"Hmm?" Shit. *Good going, there, bro.* "Uh, nothing. I was just thinking out loud."

"Yeah, I got that part. What's just a Kavanagh-woman thing?" Her slender brows drew together. "I assume it's an attribute we lowly Delucas don't have."

"Trust me, darlin'," he assured her, "that's a good thing."

If the still-furrowed eyebrows were an indication, he hadn't assured her of a damn thing. He blew out a breath. "Fine. I thought you'd make me pay for the stuff you told me last night."

"What?" There was no doubting her genuine puzzlement. "That's stupid—why would you be to blame for my crappy relationship with Brian and Nancy?"

"I wouldn't. But like I said, doll, it's a Kavanagh-chick thing. Whenever my sisters demonstrated the least little thing they considered a weakness in front of me or my brothers, we always paid for witnessing it." He gave her a pointed look. "Just another fun thing you're missing out on, not having a big family, I guess."

"Oh, don't be so thick. I'm not a flipping Pollyanna. I get that being part of a large family isn't all roses all the time. What I can't believe is that you have no appreciation for it at all."

He actually had considerable appreciation for his family. Now, however, ridiculous as he knew it to be, he felt honor-bound to stick with the stance he'd originally taken. He gave her a lazy smile. "What can I say? You should have been born into my family and I should have been the only child."

She blew out a breath that contained neither vowels nor consonants, yet managed to convey *Idiot!* all the same.

He grinned, because that was quite the talent. "Let's pack up and get a move on while it's still reasonably cool."

"Yes, sir, Boss." The tone was coolly sarcastic, but she crawled back into the tent, gathered the few things she'd collected from her tote or his pack last night and stowed them back in their proper places. When that was done, she rolled up her sleeping bag. Coming out a moment later, she stacked her belongings outside the tent, then sank to sit cross-legged on the ground a few feet away and pulled a tube of SPF from her bag and began slathering it on. While he broke down the tent,

she brushed her hair and gathered it into one hand in
a ponytail, which she tied in a knot at the nape of her
neck, then applied mascara and a slick of rosy lip balm.

A few moments later, when he turned from tightening up the straps that secured the tent container to the
bottom of the backpack, he discovered she'd carried
her things down to the boat. He watched as she tucked
everything except her tote, which she never seemed to
allow to be more than a foot away from her at any given
time, neatly beneath the bow.

He carried his own load over to the boat. "I swear
you must've been born a sailor," he said and gave her
a friendly hip check as he arranged his stuff under the
bow alongside hers.

She blew a rude raspberry, but pinked up, and not for
the first time Finn thought it didn't take a hell of a lot
to please her. They shoved the boat into the river and
Mags held the line while he climbed in. Then she gave
the craft a final shove and hopped atop the bow. He unlocked the nine-horse, lowered the propellers into the
water and primed the motor. It started on the first pull.

Minutes later, they were chugging down the river.

"THIS BEATS THE EVER-LOVIN' crap out of driving," Mags
said with a big grin. It was all she could do to not laugh
like a loon.

The morning was still young enough to be fairly
cool, the sky was blue, the birds were colorful, the water
smooth as silk and, *man*, she liked this river travel.

Finn grinned back at her. "You get out on the water
much back in the States?"

"No. Except for a freebie birthday ferry ride to and from Catalina once, I've never even been on a boat."

"You're kidding me." Then he immediately twitched a muscular shoulder as if to repudiate his words, or maybe the incredulous tone of voice in which he'd delivered them. "Not that I've been out on tons of 'em myself. I have, however, been on more than a ferry."

"Yeah, I guessed as much." She nodded to the motor and his tanned, competent hand manning the tiller or whatever the pokey-outie steering stick that maneuvered the motor was called. "You obviously know what to do with that thing."

He laughed and, looking at him in the morning sun, all strong-bodied and flashing white teeth, she felt something warm and effervescent slide through her veins. Loosen all her muscles.

She looked away.

A moment later, however, she looked back again. "So, you said you work with your brothers in the family construction business. What kind of stuff do you construct?"

"We mostly do high-end remodels. We redid an old mansion a couple of years back and restored it to its former glory. That was a fun one—to take something that had been gorgeous at one time but had been updated over the years in a really piss-poor fashion and make it shine once again. Dev met his wife on that job."

She would have enjoyed following that thread, but made herself stay on track. "So you work for the rich folks?"

"We've done plenty of smaller jobs, but the Wolcott mansion kicked us up into the high-income-bracket crowd."

"I wouldn't mind being rich," she said dreamily.

"Yeah?"

"Absolutely. I've had to stretch every dollar I've ever earned." She made an erasing gesture. "Don't get me wrong, it's doable. God provides and all that."

He gave her a half smile. "Hard to throw away those teachings learned from the cradle, isn't it?"

"No foolin'. Still, I truly believe it. It would sure be fun, though, to have a bit of discretionary income every now and then." She realized it was suddenly much noisier than it had been a moment before, so she twisted around.

And saw that the placid river just ahead of them where it went into a bend was about to turn into whitewater rapids that boiled and churned like the wrath of hell.

She whipped back to look at Finn. "Oh, shit. This can't be good."

CHAPTER TWELVE

FINN LOOKED AHEAD as well. "Fuck." He should have been paying more attention, but he'd gotten caught up in their conversation and failed to notice that, little by little, the ever-present impenetrable foliage had been joined by large boulders on either side of the river. Their growing density meant a thinning of the solid under-growth behind them and the inclusion of a lot more trees than they'd seen along this stretch.

And not a single safe place to pull over to assess their options.

He raised the propeller shaft out of the water and locked the motor in place, then pulled the oars from the oar locks to use as paddles. When he had a free second, he looked over at Mags, who sat clutching her tote with white-knuckle hands.

Even as he debated putting her to work, she looked up, visibly collected herself and said, "What can I do?"

"Do you think you have the upper body strength to man one of the oars? They're made for rowing, so they're long and unwieldy."

"Pass one over, let me see."

He did as requested and she gave it her best shot. But they *were* long and unwieldy and heavy. She struggled.

Finally, she pulled it into the boat and looked at him. "I'm sorry," she said. "I can't seem to find the right hold to make it so I can paddle without doing more harm than help. And I'm afraid I'll lose the dang thing."

"Don't worry about it, we'll be okay," he assured her—and hoped like hell he wasn't blowing smoke. This wasn't the type of boat he'd have chosen for riding the rapids, although the flat bottom was a plus. The rigidity of its wood, on the other hand—

Well, that was going to be a little more problematic.

Still, they had what they had. He'd just have to take each hurdle as it came.

That made him take note of something they didn't have. Or Mags didn't, anyhow. "Where's your life vest?"

She looked down at herself. "I forgot to put it on."

"Well, grab it now before we hit the rough stuff."

No sooner had the words left his mouth than they did just that. The bow sliced through the beginning of the white water and that was all it took to suck them into a pattern of eddies and whirlpools strong enough to command his full attention. He focused on getting them through it, because along with the white water, or maybe the very factor that caused it, boulders now cropped up in the river itself. No sooner did he squeak their boat past one without scraping its side along the solid rough-rock surface, then another was there to take its place.

It was like a big game of dodge 'em and, adrenaline running high, he laughed as he shot the boat past one obstacle only to have to paddle fast and furiously on the other side in order to maneuver them around the next. Then he got tangled up in a whirlpool and was pretty damn sure he wouldn't miss the one they were fast approaching.

But Mags kept them away from it with the end of her oar and he whooped in approval.

After a period of time that could have been anywhere between seconds or a quarter of an hour, the boat flew out of the turbulence into a calm patch of water. He'd barely spared more than a quick glance at Mags, however, before he saw the small falls coming up.

After a lightning-quick assessment, he decided it wasn't much, maybe a three- or four-foot drop. Trouble was, the boat wasn't bendy the way a river raft would be and at the base of the drop the white water recommenced with a vengeance.

And Magdalene still wasn't suited up in her safety gear.

"Dammit, Mags, grab your life vest. We don't have hard hats—at the very least you gotta wear your flotation device. Then trade places with me. We have a little drop coming up and I'll have more control from the front of the boat."

She twisted to look over her shoulder at the approaching falls before leaning back on her seat to snag her vest from beneath the bow. Clutching it and her big bottomless purse to her chest, she climbed over the seat and headed toward the stern as he duplicated her movements toward the bow.

The current was fast, and as they neared the drop he only had seconds to decide whether to face it head-on or at an angle. He risked swamping the front of the boat with the first option and flipping it over with the second.

Good times. Choosing the compromise his gut insisted on, he paddled toward the drop and hoped for the best.

He maneuvered the boat to approach it at a slight angle that would put them in the smoothest part of the falls, yet still give him time to circumvent the rocks below toward which his bow was now primarily aimed.

It worked as if he actually knew what he was doing, instead of flying by the seat of his pants, but he didn't have time to pat himself on the back. The current and eddies were even stronger down here than they'd been above the short falls and he had to work like a son of a bitch to avoid each new challenge that cropped up one atop the other like in one of those police training grounds where silhouettes popped up and rookie cops had a nanosecond to decide if they were a threat or a granny with groceries.

Then the water suddenly smoothed out and there was even a beach a few yards away. He whooped and shot a grin over his shoulder at Mags.

It froze on his face when she wasn't where he expected her to be.

He looked around wildly, half expecting to see she had squeezed herself into a space on the floor between the seats.

The only thing on the decking was her life vest.

"No. No, no, no, no, *fuck* no!" He was pretty sure, in hindsight, that he knew where this might have happened and kicked himself for not having her sit in the middle, rather than the back end of the boat.

But he shook it off and dropped the motor's propellers back in the water. He yanked the cord, then turned the dory in a tight circle the minute the outboard fired up. Opening it full throttle, he headed back upriver.

He hadn't traveled that far from the demarcation line where calm met turbulent water, but the nine-horse simply wasn't fast enough to suit him. He cursed fluently as he scanned the river for a glimpse of Magdalene. *Please, God, I'll go to church again like Mom keeps telling me I oughta, if You'll just let me find her.*

An awful image appeared full-blown in his brain and he amended, *"Alive.* Please. Let me find her alive."

He honest to God couldn't imagine all of Mags's energy shut down for good and damned if he *would* believe otherwise before he was presented with indisputable proof that gave him no other choice.

But he saw nothing. Not a damn thing—she was simply nowhere in sight. He'd reached the edge of the white water and had a sinking feeling the nine-horse wouldn't be powerful enough to power through it upstream.

"Finnnnnn!"

Oh, *hell* yes! The sound of Mags's voice sent relief singing through his veins. He looked around wildly, but for several heartbeats he still couldn't spot her.

Then suddenly he did. Only her head, shoulders and arms showed above the churning water where she clung to the side of a boulder. He maneuvered the boat along the border, where the water changed from calm to wild until he was as close as he could get, then climbed over the seats to throw out the anchor on his side of the division. As soon as he was certain he'd played out enough line to hold, he hopped up onto the bow of the boat to assess the situation.

Maybe ten to twelve feet of white water separated them and there were two possible obstacles between her and the safety of the boat—only one of which he deemed a real risk. "You have any idea how deep it is?" he called.

"No. Every time I try to put my feet down, the current sweeps them out from under me." A wave hit her boulder and sent a plume of water into the air. Its rebound caught her in the face and as she coughed he could see her arms slide several inches down the rock.

"Hang on!" *Shit, shit, shit.* "You want me to try to swim to you?"

"Yes," she said fervently. But she immediately shook her head. "No. Unless you're a world-class swimmer there's no way to swim against this current. And probably not even then." She was quiet for a moment, then she said so softly he barely heard, "I'm not sure I can let go of the rock."

"I'm scared" was what she was really saying and he wanted to give her a soothing "I know, baby" in return. But he knew better than to offer sympathy to someone on the ragged edge, the way she must be, so instead he said briskly, "I know you're shook, but if you went out of the boat where I think you did, you've done the hardest part already."

His gut churned at the thought of the punishment she'd taken getting from that point to the rock she clung to now, but he made damn sure it didn't show on his face. "You can do this, too," he said matter-of-factly. "But before you do, I want you to take a look at the streams going away from your boulder and the objects in your path between there and here."

She did what he said and a moment later she said, "That one's going to be the biggest problem." She nodded at the boulder that gave him the most worry as well, and he was glad to hear her voice had lost its frightened wobble.

"I agree. See the relatively calm area between the two streams?"

She nodded.

"See if you can maneuver yourself around the rock so you can let go in that spot. You'll have a lot more control if you can stay in that one."

"Unless it has serious undercurrents that we just can't see," she muttered.

He smiled wryly, because *that* was the Mags he knew. "I won't lie to you, darlin', it very well could. But we know the other two definitely do, so I think it's your best bet. And if you can keep yourself in it, it should squeak you past the problem boulder. The white-water streams don't merge until my side of it."

As he watched, she jutted out her chin, squared her shoulders and inched one hand toward a handhold in a part of the rock that would bring her closer to her objective. It was higher than where she'd previously held on and as she got a good grip on it, she lifted her shoulders out of the water.

And...what the hell? For the first time he saw that

she had hooked the strap of her big bag around her neck and the body of the tote hung down in the water. "Lose the purse!" he roared.

She ignored him and found another handhold.

Dammit! He remembered all the money she'd raked in yesterday. A lot of it had been in paper El-TIPS, but she'd had a shitload of change-type pesos as well. She might as well have an anchor tied around her neck and he was amazed it hadn't dragged her down to the bottom of the river already. "Lose. The. Fucking. *Purse!*"

She got her feet on the boulder and pushed off.

"Son of a bitch!" He held his breath as she landed mostly in the smoother stream. But her left shoulder and thigh caught the edge of one of the turbulent watercourses, and it tried to pull her deeper into its tumultuous depths. She submerged twice and he was pretty sure he aged ten years waiting for her to pop back up to the surface each time. Eventually, however, she fought her way free until she made it entirely into the calmer stream.

Calmer was a relative word, however, and his heart banged against the wall of his chest as he watched her being whipped toward him at an incredible pace. It wasn't a straightforward plunge to the finish line— she was spun around, dragged beneath the surface and shot out of it again and again.

He held his breath as she approached the boulder, because she was too damn close for comfort. She did exactly what he'd told her she had a shot of doing, however—she cleared it by maybe an inch and a half.

Before he could cheer her victory, the calm water

disappeared on her. And what hadn't been pretty to begin with turned downright ugly as she was promptly dragged under the water—and didn't come up again.

"No!" He dived overboard and swam with strong strokes to the edge of the white water before he surfaced to assess.

She should be coming out—or have come out—right about here…provided she didn't hit her head or have that damn purse snag on something on the bottom.

If he got his hands on the thing he was going to sink it.

A sudden midbody blow knocked him under the water and—thank You, Jesus, see Ya in church!—it was Magdalene. He got his arms around her and pulled her up until both their heads cleared the water and he could see her face.

She was eerily still and her head sagged slightly to one side. "No, c'mon!" he whispered and started maneuvering them toward the boat. "Come on, baby. Don't you give up on me now."

She remained too damn still.

Then her eyes popped open and she gasped in a huge breath of air that made her promptly cough and wheeze. Her arms circled his neck in a limp hold.

Her lack of strength scared the shit out of him. "Are you okay?" he demanded, treading water to check her out. "Where do you hurt?"

"I'm fine." She rested her head on his shoulder. "God, you feel good." Her fingers softly patted the muscle they rested against. "So solid."

"You sound weak—are you injured?"

"Bumps and scrapes," she said in a low, hoarse voice. "Kinda stings, but nothing serious." Then her voice grew stronger. "But yes, I'm weak. Get a clue, Kavanagh. *I'm* not the big strong construction guy in this scenario. My arms just got more exercise than they've had in weeks and they feel like linguine. My legs aren't quite as bad, but they're not loads better, either."

"Let's get you into the boat."

"Good plan," she said fervently and let him side-stroke the two of them over to where the dory gently bobbed on its anchor.

He looked down at her when they reached the boat, tipping his chin in to see her face where she'd half tucked it into the crook of his neck. Her eyes were at half-mast. "Can you hang on to the gunwale for a second? It'll probably be easier to haul you in from the boat than try to lift you into it from the water."

"'Kay." But for several seconds, she maintained her loose grip on his neck, her head resting heavily on his shoulder. Then, blowing out a long, quiet breath that Finn felt cool on contact with the river water stippling his skin, she transferred her grip, one hand at a time, from him to the edge of the boat.

He ducked out from under her, watched for a moment to make sure she hung on, then after he firmly commanded, "Don't move," he dived beneath the dory. He came up on the other side and hauled himself into the boat, then immediately knee-walked to her side. "You still good?"

"As can be expected," she agreed with a weary nod.

That was probably as much reassurance as he was

going to get, so, bracing his knees against the boat's interior lapstrake siding, Finn sat back on his heels on the boat's deck. Then, carefully distributing his weight, he reached for Mags, sliding his hands beneath her smooth armpits. He settled the heels of his hands and his palms against the sides of her breasts, his thumbs anchored in front where the ball socket of her shoulders met her outer chest, his fingers curving around her back in a firm grip. Tightening his core for stability, he lifted her into the dory.

The instant he set her loose, she collapsed to sit on the floor between the back and middle seats. Leaning her back against the side of the middle one, she pulled her knees to her chest and wrapped her arms around her shins, her body bending around that damn anchor of a purse. She bowed her head and pressed her forehead against her kneecaps.

Finn watched her back lift and fall with her every breath. Her hair was a sleek cap that clung to her skull before separating into dozens of soaked strands that stuck to her face and fanned across her shoulders, her breasts, her back.

Water dribbled down her torso. Some of the river water ran pink when it crossed her various scrapes, several of which oozed tiny droplets of blood. He started the motor. "Let's go over to that beach and take a look at you."

She merely nodded without lifting her head and he turned the boat and headed for land. Moments later, its bottom scraped shore and Finn stepped over both Mags and the seat she leaned against. He got out and turned to drag the dory's bow farther up the sand. After burying the anchor up the beach, he went back to collect his pack and assist her onto solid ground.

"Will you be okay for a second if I go set up the tent?" He didn't know if she'd need to lie down or not, but sand wasn't the best place for someone with open scrapes.

She nodded and he grabbed the backpack from the boat and in minutes had the tent set up and a towel-covered sleeping bag for her to lie on.

When he turned back to her it was to see her sitting cross-legged on the hot sand, her big bag cradled in her lap. She was pale, her clothing soaked, her pretty skin marked up from the rocks she'd encountered in her wild tumble through the rapids, and sudden fury exploded in his gut.

He tried to repudiate his feelings as he dug his first-aid kit out of his backpack. Hey, he couldn't be mad at her for failing to don her life vest when he'd told her—twice!—to do so, because God knew she'd already paid a steep enough price for it. So he laid the blame on her bag. That fucking monster of a bag that only by the grace of God hadn't dragged her down to a watery grave.

He leaned down, plucked it out of her lap and flung it as far as he could into the river.

"What the hell!" She leaped to her feet. "Go get that!"

"No! The damn thing nearly killed you!"

"You *shit*! Go get it!"

He crossed his arms over his chest.

She ran to the water's edge, waded to her thighs, then dived in, her gaze locked on where the bag was half-submerged but still floating as it moved lazily away from her in the light current. Then she set off swimming.

Finn swore and went after her. She was clearly exhausted and he caught up with her in about three strokes. When he tried to pull her to him, however, she snarled, "Get your hands off me!" and kicked out with her feet, catching him high on the thigh, way too close to his junk for comfort.

Swearing under his breath, he scooped a hand under her stomach, slapped the other on her butt and sent her sailing through the water toward shore.

"Go back," he said. "I'll get it."

"I don't trust you," she said flatly, treading water and glaring at him through spiky, water-spangled eyelashes.

He was surprised how much it hurt to hear her say that, but he supposed he'd earned it.

Hell, he'd tried to deep-six the queen's share of her belongings, including, most likely, her passport. Clearly, he hadn't been using his head. "You have my word," he said quietly. "I'll get it." And he took off with strong strokes toward the big tote.

When he swam back with it a short while later, he found her still standing, calf-deep, in the shallows. He handed her the purse and watched as she hugged it to her stomach without looking at him.

"I'm sorry," he said to her stiff back as she turned it on him and waded ashore, then followed as she strode up to the rough grass that bordered the sand at the top of the beach.

She squatted and began pulling items out of her soaked purse one by one and settling them carefully atop the grass to dry.

He touched her shoulder, but she shrugged off his fingers and he blew out a frustrated breath. "Look, I really am sorry. I thought for sure that was going to be the weight that sank you, but I realize now that I was reacting to the whole having-you-missing thing and the much-too-close call you had by turning all my fear into anger and transferring it on to your stupid bag." There. That sounded new age sensitive and enlightened, right?

Even if he had a sneaking suspicion he spoke nothing short of the truth.

She continued the silent treatment as she set the rest of her things out to dry. But out of the blue as she tried to pat her big makeup case dry with her hands, she muttered, "Not all of us have a secure job in the heart of a family business—or have a family at all, for that matter."

He dropped to his knees behind her, his hands reaching for her before he forced himself to drop them to his sides. "I know."

"Do you?" she demanded wearily, turning to face him. "I don't think you have the first idea." She gestured at the bag now limply bleeding dye into the sand. "Every cent I own was in that—I cleaned out my bank account to come down here. I did leave my main makeup kit in my apartment, but I brought enough of the good stuff along that it could make a difference in getting a good job if something comes up, because I can't afford to replace it."

Okay, he was going to get slaughtered for asking, but... "Why do you need all of that?" He looked at her washed-clean face. "You don't even wear that much makeup."

"It's my livelihood!"

"Oh, sure, I guess you told me that. For your street performance stuff."

"Well, that, too, of course. But my real skill is as an actual almost-up-and-coming makeup artist."

Knowing better than to smile at the almost-up-and-coming part, he said, "Yeah? Like in the movies or something?"

"Almost." She shrugged. "I got my first big break when a huge sci-fi production I worked all *year* to get on actually hired me. Then I had to tell them I couldn't take it when Mom and Dad went missing."

He thought this might be the first time he'd heard her call her parents *Mom and Dad*, but he bit his tongue and didn't remark on that, either.

See? He was teachable. "I'm sorry. That must have been rough."

"You have no idea. I could have given up the street performing."

"You don't like it?" That surprised him. "You're so good at it."

"It's fun to do, occasionally." She shrugged. "But I never know what I might rake in and that makes my income killer undependable."

Her hair was starting to dry in crazy strands and he

reached out to brush them out of her eyes. "I'm sorry," he said and almost winced. He'd said it so much in the past several minutes, it had likely lost its impact.

Yet he truly was. She was right—he'd always had the safety net of Kavanagh Construction. He worked hard at his job, but he also took his financial security for granted. Absentmindedly, he finger-combed her hair into a fat ponytail that he gathered in one fist. "Seriously," he said, gazing down into her blue eyes. "I am honest-to-God sorry. I was a douche to throw your purse in the river."

Her eyes brimmed with sudden tears. "I was so scared, Finn," she whispered. "So, so scared. You're not the only one who thought I might drown. A couple of times there when I was bouncing off the bottom of the riverbed, I was pretty sure I'd used up all my luck."

"But you didn't," he said in a low, firm voice, knee-walking closer until they were nearly body-to-body. "You made it—you're a survivor." He bent his head and pressed a kiss on her forehead. Raised his head and looked down at her, then kissed both of her eyelids. "You're safe now." He slid his mouth down her cheek and kissed her lips.

And they both froze, staring at one another. Then Mags swore softly.

And, pushing him over onto his back, she dived atop him.

CHAPTER THIRTEEN

HEART BEATING LIKE the wings of a trapped bird, Mags straddled Finn, her knees and shins hitting the sand on either side of his thighs, her hands bracketing his shoulders. The feel of hot granules invading her various scrapes and cuts, however, had her promptly sucking in a sharp breath through her teeth.

Finn jackknifed upright, one big hand clamped spread-fingered against the small of her back to keep her pressed against him as he sat up. "Straighten your legs," he said in a gravelly voice.

She gingerly adjusted them before loosely crossing her ankles behind his back. When she settled on his lap, the rigidity of how happy he was to see her met the crotch seam of her cargo shorts.

Right back atcha, big guy, she thought and, tipping her head, caught his earlobe between her teeth and gave it a little suck.

He shivered, but pulled her gently back on his thighs until her tingly bits lost contact with the source of all that pleasure.

"Hey," she said, looking down at him. She attempted to squirm back into position, but his hands on her hips easily kept her away from the goodies. "What are you doing?"

"We need to take a short intermission to clean up your scrapes."

"Oh, *hell*, no," she protested. "They can wait." Her nipples, harder than diamonds, throbbed right along with the heartbeat between her legs. She'd always believed the lion's share of her past sexual encounters had been pretty darn good—well, once she'd smartened up and became selective. But she couldn't recall feeling quite so out-of-control *needy* as she did at this moment.

One thing she did know with complete certainty: she had no time for doctoring. Reaching back, she gripped his legs just above the knees. Her move made him relax his grasp and, sliding back into place, she used the leverage she'd gained from bracing herself to rock her hips, desultorily stropping herself against the hard length of his sex.

He hissed in a breath, lifted his hips to press into her slow up-and-down slide, then secured her hips in his hands again and held her still. "No," he said with obvious regret, "they can't wait. You grew up here, you know how the tropics can take a simple cut and turn it into a festering mess in no time flat if it's left unattended."

She did know that, but at the moment she simply didn't care. She was itchy and restless and just… "I need to feel *alive*," she said, moving as best she could against his erection. "C'mon, Finn. You can play medic later. Right now I need you to fuck me."

Whoa, Nellie—seriously? Hearing that emerge from

her mouth in its carnal context yanked her out of the moment. She freely admitted she was a bit of a split personality when it came to cursing. *Mags* could swear with the best of them, but in truth, prissy Miss Magdalene held the reins more often than not as far as language went. As Finn said, early training was hard to shake.

But, dammit, fucking was exactly what she wanted right now.

No. Who was she kidding? *Wanted* was too pallid a word for the way she felt.

She needed it more than she needed her next breath. There had been too many horrific moments in those pounding rapids when she'd truly believed she was going down and staying down for the count. So right now she needed to celebrate the fact that while she'd been terrified out of her mind, it hadn't freaking *ended* her. And, face it, sex was probably the most fundamental life-affirming act of all.

"First aid, first," Finn said sternly. "Then I'll make you feel so alive you'll beg for mercy."

"Pffft." She put all the skepticism at her command into the sound. Then said, "I'll make you a deal. I'll let you tend me if you take off a piece of clothing for every scrape or cut you fix up."

"I'll take off a piece for every *third* bit of doctoring *if* you behave—no teasing—while I get the job done."

She shifted restlessly. "Oh, God, Finn, I don't know if I can sit still that long." Straightening in his lap, she spread her hands over her breasts, pressing them toward the wall of her chest and massaging them. Her head dropped back. "I'm just…so…dang…*hot.*"

"Sweet mother Mary," he muttered in a rough half whisper and rose to his feet as if he didn't have a hundred-and-thirty-pound woman atop him.

She emitted an embarrassingly girlish squeak and wrapped her arms and legs around him like a squirrel monkey around a canopy tree vine.

He strode over to the tent and set her down carefully outside the vestibule. "Brush off the sand and then get inside. I'm going to heat some water real quick. My first-aid kit is on the sleeping bag. Grab out the triple antibiotic and a handful of bandages, and I'll be right back."

Squeezing her thighs together to assuage the heavy pulse thumping between her legs, she pulled off her tank top, shook it out, then used it to carefully brush her arms and legs as free of sand as she could get them. Some of her abrasions had suffered more skin loss than others and the sand in those would need to be rinsed out. But for now she shook out her top again and arranged the garment over the top of the tent to dry. Then she stripped off her nylon cargo shorts and spread them atop the tent as well, although they were already close to dry.

Finally, clad only in a damp mocha-colored lace bra and matching panties, she brushed her hands together to rid them of the sand still stubbornly clinging to them and bent to enter the tent.

Had she been able to stand upright she would have paced within its confines. Denied the option, she sank to sit cross-legged on the floor next to the bag to avoid leaving faint butt prints on the latter from her not totally dry undies.

At first she was so twitchy she could barely breathe and restlessly she butterflied her knees up and down as she pulled out the first-aid supplies. But little by little, with nothing to fuel this mad out-of-control urgency for wild monkey sex, the sensation started to fade.

She pulled her legs in close to her chest and wrapped her arms around them, lowering her forehead to press against her kneecaps. *Dear God.* What had she been thinking? She'd always liked sex, but she could say with complete honesty that she'd never burned from the inside out to jump all over a guy the way she just had with Finn. She believed in keeping things easy breezy, not getting all intense and involved.

Nothing good ever came of involvement. It was fun for a while, but in the end inevitably led to disillusionment.

She blew out a breath. Thank God Finn had insisted on treating her scrapes. Of course now she had to break it to him that he wasn't getting lucky after all.

Or maybe not, she thought a moment later when the outer flap was pulled back and he bent to enter, a pan of gently steaming water carefully balanced in his big hands, a water bottle tucked under one arm and his ultra-absorbent backpacker's towel thrown over a muscular shoulder. Because to her surprise, all the crazed sexuality she'd thought firmly extinguished roared back to life as if someone had tossed gasoline on a banked fire. Her grasp around her shins went slack, then dropped away and her legs slid back to their original cross-legged position.

Finn had clearly been watching his footing and trying to keep his bent back from brushing the ceiling of the low tent. But once he was all the way in he raised his gaze to glance at her.

And stopped dead. "Holy shit," he breathed in a raspy voice. "*Look* at you."

He did just that, his gaze zeroing in on her breasts, stiff nipples poking against the mocha lace of her demi cups, then at the plump lips of her sex already growing damp behind the until-then unnoticed abrasion of her panties. When he finished looking his fill, he leisurely mapped the expanse of the bare skin that curved and hollowed between the two scraps of fabric.

Then he blew out a quiet breath and, assuming a neutral expression, squatted next to her hip and set the pan on the floor of the tent. "Here," he said, reaching to roll up the flap on the mesh window to let in more light. "Let's take a look at the damage."

He checked her over with methodical thoroughness, having her reach her bent-elbowed arms toward the ceiling so he could see the undersides in one instance, and then roll up onto first one hip, then the other so he could inspect the backs of her thighs in another. And all the while he gently probed her various scrapes, bumps and bruises.

Finally, he sat back on his heels. "You look like you were on the losing end of the war, darlin'."

"Hey, I'm alive and ambulatory. That says 'won it' to me."

"Valid point." He twisted around, snagged the wash-cloth she hadn't realized was in the pan of water and wrung it out. Then, exerting obvious care, he began cleansing her wounds.

She sat quietly as he finished blotting dry the wounds he'd washed, then applied the triple antibiotic cream. This wasn't half as uncomfortable as she'd anticipated.

Then he capped the tube of salve and sat back. Giving her a level look, he said, "Now for the hard part."

She must have shot him a look every bit as uneasy as his words made her feel, for he shrugged and brushed a hand over her hair, making her realize how much sand clung to the damp strands.

"I left the ones that took off the most skin for last," he said. "It's going to take more effort—and unfortunately discomfort for you—to remove the grit from those than the smaller scrapes did."

Hadn't she suspected precisely that when she'd knocked off as much sand as possible before entering the tent? All the same, for a brief moment she'd gotten her hopes up and she blew out a wordless breath that managed to convey the "oh, shit" she was feeling.

"I know," he agreed as though she'd actually verbalized the sentiment out loud and held up the water bottle. "Let's step outside. If I use this to stream water on the worst areas it might clean them without having to scrub. And that's our primary aim in the let's-keep-Mags-comfortable sweepstakes. It's gonna be messy, though."

Mags shrugged and rose to her feet to follow him from the tent. She had a moment of self-consciousness as she straightened to her full height in the brilliant sun-

shine. Yet except for Finn there wasn't a soul in sight—
and he'd already seen her in her underwear. So when
he led her over to a piece of driftwood, she sat where
he indicated and leaned over, bracing her arms against
her knees to open the landscape of her back for his perusal, since he'd indicated that where her tank top had
separated from her shorts and her right shoulder had
sustained the worst of the damage.

But instead of immediately starting in, he said, "You
know that I've slept with a lot of women. But I want you
to know that I've always worn a condom and I have a
clean bill of health."

"Me, too," she said. "I can't claim to have always
practiced safe sex. I was all about the stupid risks when
I was a kid, but someone must have been looking out for
me because I dodged both pregnancy and all the com-
municable diseases, which was more than I deserved."
Looking at him over her shoulder, she said, "Can we
get this over with? I don't deal well with suspense."

"You bet," he agreed gently.

Determined not to whimper like a baby, she drew a
deep breath, but still had to grit her teeth when the first
stream from the water bottle set the wounds to throbbing. It helped to hear Finn swearing beneath his breath
on her behalf as he cleaned the deeper abrasions. All
the same, some of the things he had to do hurt like the
dickens and she suddenly felt way too emotional. She
found herself battling a serious urge to cry.

And Mags Deluca didn't do the crying thing in front
of people.

Well, okay, she had almost done so a couple of times

with him, but, c'mon, that was just now when she'd admitted how afraid she'd been she was going to drown and on the first night when things had been brand-new crazy. Fear tears were understandable and that first night she'd come close only after episode upon episode had piled up. Anyway, in the end she hadn't full-out cried either time.

All the more reason to steel herself against breaking down now, though. Those two almost slipups could be forgiven. A third, genuine one? No, no. It just plain wasn't gonna happen.

Suddenly she remembered her earlier bargain and grabbed on to it, welcoming the starch it infused in her backbone. The instant he finished putting antibiotic salve on the second scrape she said, "Lose some clothing."

For a second he went still behind her. Then she heard rustling and his hand and lower arm came into sight, dangling his T-shirt in front of her, before opening tough-skinned fingers to let it drift to the ground.

Her mouth went dry over his corded, hair-feathered forearm—an *arm*, for God's sake—and she made a rude noise in an attempt to pretend it hadn't gotten her all hot and bothered. "That's it?" she said coolly. "I've seen your naked chest before. I was hoping for something a little more revealing this time."

"We wouldn't want you getting too excited too soon."

"Please. I've let you slide but we both know with all the doctoring you've already done, by rights you should be buck-naked right now."

"Trust me, Magdalene—"

"Mags!"

"Mags," he said easily. "Trust me when I say a sun-burned dick won't do either of us any good."

A snort of laughter escaped her. Damn him. He had a habit of working his way past her guard. Still… "What was that you said? You make a valid point?"

"Damn straight, baby. Just thinking about it's got me hunched over."

She grinned down at the sand.

The smile was wiped from her face when he set back to work, but eventually he circled around to finish up a place on her left shin and arm. Moments after that, he pushed back and sat on the sand in front of her log. "An-n-d, we're done. You holding up okay?"

She took a second to take stock, then nodded. "The ones on my shoulder and back are a little throbby, but it's probably nothing an Aleve won't cure." Her adrena-line high had long since crashed, however, and she was abruptly exhausted.

It must have shown, because he helped her to her feet. "Let's get you one," he said and led her to the tent.

She stopped outside the vestibule and bent to run her fingers through her hair to knock the sand loose before letting herself into the tent, Finn following on her heels.

"Have a seat on the sleeping bag," he said and squat-ted in front of the backpack.

She did as directed while he rummaged for some-thing to take the edge off her various aches and pains. It was hotter than the devil's handmaiden in here, with only the vaguest of breezes drifting through the mesh window and door screen. Yawning, she rolled to lay on her stomach since that was the most comfortable position. Or more accurately, the only one she was willing to try, even though he'd put gauze pads over the worst of the abrasions. Folding her arms, she used them as a pillow to cushion her cheek for the second or two it should take Finn to find a pain reliever.

Then they'd get down to business.

A GRUNT OF SATISFACTION sounded in Finn's throat as his hand closed around the bottle he'd been searching for and he turned with a grin to present it to Mags. But his smile froze in a poor imitation of the real deal before dropping away entirely. "Well, shit."

She was sound asleep.

Thunder rumbled in the distance and the occasional flash of dry lightning brightened an already not particularly dim interior. He unfastened the sleeping mat from the bottom of his backpack and crab-walked over to roll it out next to the sleeping bag where Mags was sprawled. He gazed at the long groove of her spine and the round curve of her ass for a moment, then shrugged.

What the hell. Sex was clearly off the table—at least for now—and being out on the water in an open boat anytime lightning was part of the equation, even if, as he suspected, it was a fair distance away, wasn't the brightest idea. Sleep had sure as shit been hit-and-miss the past few nights, so he might as well catch some shut-eye himself.

He flopped down on the mat and stretched out.

But his eyes remained open. He stared up at the tent's ceiling until he'd damn near memorized every seam.

It, in return, didn't divulge clue one. Finally, he rolled onto his side and propped his head in his palm to stare at Mags.

The woman sure as hell grabbed his attention by the balls, and it felt like more than your average proximity-based *me man, you woman, things are gettin' hairy, baby, so let's get down and dirty while we're still alive* kinda way. He remembered being drawn to her from the beginning and wondering why, since she hadn't struck him as all "that."

"My mistake," he murmured, reaching out to gently move her hair aside to see her face. "You're definitely all that."

She mumbled in her sleep and rolled to face him. Her lips pursed and she made a few soft smacking sounds, then wrinkled her nose. Her hand came up to knuckle its tip. A second later her fingers went slack and slid back down onto the bag as she settled more deeply into sleep.

He smiled, because she looked so girlishly innocent like this. Awake, she had a kind of knowing look about her, as if she'd been there, done that and had the T-shirt to document it. Studying her, he realized that while she likely had been around the block a time or two since reinventing herself as Mags, part of the impression she projected might stem from the shape of her eyebrows. The right one arched higher than the left, as if she were perpetually amused at life and raised a sardonic eyebrow at its vagaries.

Her skin, on full display in that skimpy bra-and-panties getup, was so creamy he just wanted to lick her all over—particularly where her breasts rose out of the demi cups and pressed together to form that deep, lush cleav—

"Jesus." He rolled onto his back once again and glared up at the ceiling. What the hell was the matter with him? Viewing her sexually was one thing, but he was feeling downright *moony*, for God's sake, like he was, what? A fourteen-year-old? That wasn't his style at all—and he was going to stop all this middle school bullshit, starting now.

Lightning lit up the tent again and much sooner on its heels than its earlier counterparts, thunder boomed. *You've got yourself some downtime, dammit,* he thought grimly. *Take advantage and grab an hour or two of sleep while the grabbing's good. If Magdalene can do it, so can you.*

It took a helluva lot longer than it should have, however, before slumber finally claimed him.

CHAPTER FOURTEEN

MAGS WOKE UP hot and groggy. Raising her head, she blinked at the red wall of the tent—and realized she didn't have the first idea if it was early morning, high noon or headed toward sundown. She'd slept so heavily she couldn't recall a thing that had happened before she'd dropped off and, yawning, she rolled onto her back.

Her various doctored abrasions immediately made themselves felt, clearing her mind in a red-hot hurry. "O-kay," she murmured as everything came back in a rush and she slowly sat up, head hung low as she took several deep, slow breaths to lessen the discomfort. "Could use that anti-inflammatory right about now."

She remembered now that Finn had been looking for some in his pack. And…oh, crap. She must have fallen asleep on him. She turned her head toward the door, wondering if he was out by the river.

She almost looked right past him sleeping on the mat next to her. On the other side of him, on the tent floor, sat the water bottle with a blue oval pill on its cap.

"Oh, bless you." She sat up and reached over him for the pain reliever. She threw it in her mouth, washed it down with a swig of water and realized—big surprise here—she needed to find a potty bush.

Taking care not to wake Finn, she climbed over him and let herself out of the tent. Blinking in the bright light, she saw it still appeared to be the same day—and by the direct overhead position of the sun, likely somewhere around noon.

She was back within moments and reclaimed her spot. For about five seconds, she considered trying to go back to sleep, but she was awake now and knew that wasn't going to happen. So, crossing her ankles and hugging her thighs to her breasts, she rested her chin in the notch between her kneecaps and took advantage of this rare opportunity to check out Finn at her leisure.

Had she given the matter any thought, she would've expected that once the adrenaline-fueled craving for him burned away, she'd be a teensy bit mortified by the way she'd talked to and climbed all over him. Mulling it over now, however...

Eh. Not so much.

She always tried to see things as they actually were and not simply the way she wished them to be, and more often than not she was successful at it. So, squarely facing the reality of her earlier behavior, she admitted it was hardly a shock. She'd been drawn to Finn from the moment she'd set eyes on him in that hilltop cantina.

There was certainly nothing wrong with that and she refused to be embarrassed about it. Who cared if they wanted to screw their brains out? They were two consenting adults, neither of whom had other relationships they'd be betraying. So, if they found passion and a measure of comfort in each other's bodies on this wild run across El Tigre…well, good for them.

They'd already faced more adversity and perilous situations in the past few days than she, at least, had experienced during her entire lifetime. And considering the emotional landscape she'd inhabited in her teens, not to mention her attitude those first few years after being banished from home and the stupid, risky things she'd done, that was saying something. She'd willfully allowed herself to be in too many situations that a reasoning individual would have given a wide, wide berth. Not that she could honestly claim she'd ever been in real physical danger before this trip back to El Tigre. But that was due more to sheer blind luck than intelligent planning on her part. God knew that, more times than not, she'd sailed too close to putting herself in harm's way.

But she'd been a heedless kid then. Now she was an adult, a fully grown woman who didn't hesitate to check Finn out. Hard to see the downside in that venture.

He was long and lean, yet in no way skinny. His wide shoulders were the kind that had some bone with the muscle, rather than that muscle-upon-muscle, no-neck bodybuilder look. Not that she hadn't known some fine-looking guys who'd spent a goodly amount of time in a gym. But she had a feeling Finn's body had been honed from the hard, physical construction work he did rather than pumping iron in front of a mirror.

Her lips curved up. Because a mighty fine build it was.

His skin wasn't what she thought of as Irish coloring,

but rather had a slight olive cast—the kind that tanned quickly and easily. She wondered if it retained at least a hint of its color in the dead of winter.

A light dusting of dark body hair fanned across his chest and the happy trail arrowing down from it widened just above and below his belly button before disappearing beneath the low-slung, unfastened waistband of his once-beige but now bleached almost-white cargo shorts. His thighs were muscular, his shins lengthy and calves round. Like the feet she'd noted earlier, his hands were as long and lean as the rest of him, and she'd felt their strength, witnessed their proficiency.

She found herself wanting to explore every inch of him.

So...why not? Smiling softly to herself, she rolled onto her stomach to do just that.

FINN AWOKE FROM a sex dream he couldn't remember but was pretty damn sure had been really good to find Mags kissing his body.

At first he thought he was still dreaming. But when he raised his head to stare groggily down himself, he discovered Magdalene sprawled on her stomach, half-atop him, her fingertips splayed through his chest hair as she licked a light outline of the ridges that etched his abs below his diaphragm. She'd loosely braided her hair and he watched as her full, pink lips and pinker tongue moved across his abdomen.

"Hey," he croaked—and cleared his throat.

Raising her head, she lifted her upper body slightly to meet his gaze. The movement rubbed her cleavage's pale skin against the darker skin of his lower abs and the lace of her bra lightly scratched the skin it touched with her slightest shift of position.

"Hey, yourself," she said softly. "Sorry I fell asleep on you."

He shrugged. "You clearly needed the rest—and I gotta admit I did, too." He ran a fingertip down the groove of her spine as far as he could reach. "How are you feeling?"

"Better. I found the anti-inflamatory you left out for me. It's taken the edge off the worst of the discomfort." She gave him a lopsided smile. "I'm just grateful it wasn't worse—I know it could have been a lot more so." Lowering her head again, she pressed another kiss into a lower muscle in his six-pack.

Watching her look at up him as she did so made his dick, already half-hard from his dream, stand up and salute.

"But I don't want to talk about that right now," she whispered against his navel.

Worked for him. But he wanted to kiss her, and reaching down, he slid his hands beneath her armpits to lift her up until her mouth was where he could get at it.

She squealed at the surprise of being shifted, then laughed at herself and wiggled around until she evidently found her optimal comfort spot atop him. Following the directive of the hand he'd wrapped around her nape, she lowered her head until their mouths aligned.

He loved how soft and full her lips were and much as he'd like nothing more than to just eat her alive, he remembered in the nick of time that she wasn't in tip-top shape. So he took his time and kissed her softly, tenderly, instead. He sipped at her lips, changing the angle frequently but keeping his tongue to himself.

Until the moment she made an impatient noise deep in her throat and grasped his head to hold it still as she opened her mouth over his.

Then all bets were off and with a guttural sound he sank his fingers in her hair, framed her cheekbones with his thumbs and held her head still in order to plunder the spicy-sweet interior of her mouth. The way their tongues dueled for dominance, however, he was as much the plunderee as plunderer. Mags sure as hell gave as good as she got—and all the while making soft, urgent sounds that drove him to longer and more elaborate ways of plying his tongue just to hear yet more of her little do-me noises.

He rolled her onto her back on the sleeping bag, but at her involuntarily inhaled breath, he shifted them back onto his mat with her on top once more. Lifting her head to break their kiss, he gasped, "I'm sorry, Magda— Mags. I forgot for a second. I'll be more careful."

She tightened her grip on him and all ten of her fingernails pricked his skin. "I don't want more careful. I want down-and-dirty, total out-of-control, runaway, wild and woolly sex."

Aw, Jesus, girl, you're killin' me, here. But he met her hot-eyed look coolly. "And I'll give you that—just as soon as some of your skin grows back."

She uttered a derisive snort, but he continued to hold her gaze. "Lack of pain doesn't have to mean boring, darlin'." But that set his brain to speculating and he narrowed his eyes at her. "Unless…you into that?"

She guffawed. "Oh, hells to the no."

He shot her a cocky smile. "Then I promise to make you scream."

"I'm holding you to that. And if you don't, I'm calling a do-over—and we will be doing it my way."

"Deal." Cupping the back of her head, he tugged her closer. "Now shut up and kiss me."

She did, and within moments her enthusiasm had severely undermined his much-lauded control. Their breathing grew choppy and, dying to get his hands on more of her, Finn slid one free to cup her breast. Her nipple drilled into his palm like a tungsten carbide bit and, shifting his hand, he slid his thumb to squeeze it against the side of his index finger. Then gave it a tug.

She moaned and he grinned against her mouth, which made her lift her head, separating their lips. "What?"

"Sensitive nipples. I wonder if I can make you come just by playing with them."

"Pfffft." With an as-if look, Mags sat up on him. But when she tucked her bent knees next to his hips he saw her wince and he brought his hands down to wrap around her hips and raise her as he, too, sat up. "Sit in my lap and straighten your legs the way you did earlier."

As soon as she complied, he lifted her until her breasts were on a level with his eyes. But instead of checking them out up close, he looked into her eyes.

And licked his lips. "Lose the bra."

"Ooh." She wiggled on him even as she reached for

the clasp behind her, an action that all but thrust her tits in his face. "I just love me a forceful man."

Without lowering his gaze, he moved to catch a nipple between his teeth, loving how heavy-lidded her eyes grew, how her cheeks flushed. Lightly grinding the lace against the stiff point, he raised his eyebrows, then gave the sweet bead a hard suck and turned it loose. "Handy, that," he growled. "I like being forceful."

THE SENSITIVE SHEATH deep between Mags's legs clenched hard and her brain blanked out for a second. Then... *Omigawd*, she thought. *Oh. My. Ga-a-awd.*

Okay, so she'd never actually been with a genuinely forceful guy before—or at least not the kind who watched her when he did things to her, who said things that weren't really dirty or anything, but made her crazy aroused.

But if the way Finn made her feel was any indication, this was going to be *good.* She licked her lips and unhooked her bra, shimmying it down her arms and tossing it aside.

Still, protested her inner I-do-things-my-way self.

She'd started this rodeo; did she really want him wresting control out of her hands? Hooking her arms around his neck, she chafed her now bare breasts against his chest. And leaned forward to lightly grasp the lobe of his ear between her teeth. "How 'bout you lose those shorts," she said in a low voice. It wasn't a question.

"Feeling a little forceful yourself, are you?" He pulled his head back just far enough to slide his earlobe free, then lowered his chin to catch her bottom lip between his own strong teeth. "Who do you think's more likely to win that contest?"

His tongue touched her lip with the *th* and *L* sounds and closed around it pronouncing *more*, making her shiver. But looking him straight in the eye, she said, "Me, of course."

He laughed, freeing her lip. "Not even close, baby." He flopped backward and reached between them for the zipper of his fly. Given the usual bird racket and the noise of the river outside, she shouldn't have been able to hear the soft sound of its teeth disengaging. Yet somehow it seemed preternaturally loud in the tent's quieter interior. She startled slightly when he said, "Lift up so I can shuck these babies as commanded."

She got her feet under her and raised her butt. The backs of his hands brushed her as he crunched up to push his shorts down. He bicycled them to his ankles and kicked them free. She lowered her hips again—and found herself sitting on his bare penis.

"Holy crap!" She stared down at its darkish head and the two or so inches of hard, veiny shaft showing in front of the mocha lace of her panties' crotch and slid backward to see more. "You didn't say you weren't wearing any undies!"

"Men don't wear *undies*," he said in disgust. "That's for little kids and you chicks. Men go commando."

She wiggled even farther back onto his thighs and his dick sprang free. Reflexively she reached out to grab it, but then ignored it for a second to bounce her free fist off her chest and give a guy grunt. "Big man eat nails and crack open nuts on head." She had to admit, however, that the girth she'd wrapped her hand around felt very manlike and she stroked him through her fist.

Finn hissed in a breath and arched his hips to push into her grip.

She grinned down at him. "Who's your mama, now, hotshot?"

His eyelashes tangled in the outer corners when he narrowed them at her. "You did not just say that."

She merely gave him a brash smile and waggled her eyebrows at him.

"I am so gonna own you." Gripping her hips, he lifted her an inch or two until her breasts were level with his mouth, then he latched on to her left nipple.

"Oh!" Lust was an electrified arrow shooting straight to the jangling nerve center between her legs. Her head dropped back and her hand slid away from his erection as she grabbed for his shoulders, anchoring herself with her nails. She watched him through slitted eyes as he worked his tongue against her nipple's underside, pressing it against the roof of his mouth. His cheeks hollowed with each slow, strong suck.

She didn't realize she'd been supporting her own weight until one of his hands left her hip to move inward. Hooking the leg elastic of her undies aside, he burrowed his thumb between the drenched lips of her sex and glided up its slick furrow. A needy sound escaped her as the rough pad of his thumb bumped over her straining clitoris.

He stilled for a nanosecond, then looking up at her, drew harder yet on her breast and made a second pass at her clit.

"Finn!" Oh, God, she was so, so close. "I need you in me. Now."

He released her nipple with a pop, lowered her to sit on his upper thighs and cast a frustrated glance at his backpack. "Shit. The condoms are clear over there."

He started to set her aside but she locked her ankles behind his back to prevent it. The movement pulled her forward to press right up against his hard-on and they both moaned.

"No," she said with faux calmness, pleased to be the first to recover—if one could call all this thumping desire pulsating through her every nerve ending a recovery. She reached beside her to flip back the top edge of the sleeping bag.

Beneath it were a handful of Bareskins in their black foil-wrapped glory. XL, no less—although, please, like all rubbers wouldn't stretch to accommodate a fricking bowling ball? "I grabbed a few from your gallon baggie." Her lips twisted in a half smile. "You certainly are an optimistic guy."

His eyes were so dark and hot, they all but smoked. "We'll see about that, won't we?"

Her damn Finn-aware channel clenched once again and she grabbed up a condom and tore its foil package open with her teeth. She'd been unconsciously rocking herself against his erection and scooted back now to give herself room to suit him up. "C'mon, c'mon," she whispered as she fumbled the job, and Finn's hand closed over hers.

"I'll do it," he said. "Much more of you touching me and things might be over before they begin."

"Don't want that." She kicked off her panties.

"Nope. Really don't. There." He'd had his eye on the job at hand, so to speak, but looked up to shoot her a grin. "C'mere, you."

She didn't wait for a second invitation, but rather scooted forward and, bracing her hands on his wide shoulders, raised herself above the thrust of his sex.

His big hands grasped her butt to steady her and she delved between them to align his hard-on with her opening. Holding him in place, she slowly lowered herself. As the head of his penis penetrated her, she sighed out, "Ohhhhh."

"Oh, *hell*, yeah." His voice was low and raspy and his hands moved to her hips as though to press her all the way down. But he didn't, even though her legs, in their lap-sitting—or in this case, lap-hovering—position, were beginning to tremble. "God, you feel good. You're so tight."

She clenched around him.

Finn groaned, then met her gaze head-on. "So talk does it for ya, huh?"

She tipped her nose up but lowered her hips another inch as she lied without a qualm. "I have no idea what you're talking about."

"Mags Deluca has pretty tits and a tight pus—"

Clench, clench. She slapped a hand over his mouth. But, dammmmmn. "Okay, maybe I like it a little."

He removed the hand and kissed her knuckles. "I'd say more than a little." His smile was knowing. "But, sure, let's go with that."

Oh. It was so time to grab hold of the reins and see

if she couldn't wipe some of that cockiness off his face. She relinquished the control she'd been maintaining over her thigh muscles and, dropping smoothly, impaled herself fully. But when she darn near came at the feel of him, so hard and deep inside of her, she had to question the intelligence of the move.

God, he felt good, though. And that was *before* he began to move.

The way they were situated, with her on his lap facing him, their range of motion was limited. But sitting loosely cross-legged beneath her, Finn did the butterfly wing thing with his knees, letting them rise one moment to slide her up his hard-on, then pressing them toward the mat the next, sinking her back down on him.

It caused that crazy itch inside her to build and build, yet something in the position wasn't working. Well, it was *working*—in the respect that it felt amazing. But it wasn't enough to push her over. "I can't…" He had a grip on her butt and she made an involuntary shrugging-off motion. "Let go for a second."

His hands slid away. "Not doing it for you?"

"It feels so good—but it's just not quite right." She licked her lips. "I can't—" She planted her feet next to his hips. "You want to straighten your legs?" They must be going numb by now.

"I do." He did so with alacrity, and having more room to move and the leverage of her feet under her, Mags raised her hips, then slapped them back down. And— "Oh, God—there!"

"Yeah?" He grinned at her.

"Oh, yeah." She raised and lowered them again,

raised and lowered. "Oh, definitely, yes. *Um!*" Her eyes slid closed as the sensation suddenly hitting just the right spot sent a preorgasm zing through her. "Oh, God, Finn, I'm going to—I'm so close. So, so, so, so—"

He slid his thumb over her clit and, on the apex of her next rise, licked her nipple into his mouth and gave it a hard suck. Sharp, undulating contractions detonated around the steely sex seated hard up inside her, pulling at it and trying to coax a climax out of him in return. "Oh, God, Finn," she panted. "Oh. My. Gaw-w-wd."

He shifted slightly and her breath caught in her throat as the small movement started an entire new cavalcade of contractions.

"Christ," Finn muttered, staring up at her flushed cheeks, at her white teeth sank into her reddened lower lip and her slumberous blue eyes as she stared blindly at him while she clamped like a velvet vise all around him. His testicles drew up, making him lose track of everything but his own drive for release. He fell back on his elbows and thrust his hips upward to shove deep inside of her.

The move lifted her off her knees and she slapped her hands to his chest to keep from being bucked off. He barely noticed as he held his position high and hard inside her. Then, groaning low in his throat, he exploded in pulsation after hot, mind-bending pulsation, with the feel of tight, slippery tissues still clasping and unclasping up and down his dick. "Ah, *God*, Magdalene!"

For once she didn't correct him. The clutching around his cock ultimately slowed, then faded away and she sat atop him, blinking heavy-lidded eyes as she stared down without speaking. And a tiny smile curved her lips.

"I hate to break it to you," she finally said. "But you didn't make me scream."

Then she collapsed atop him hard enough to drive the breath from his lungs.

CHAPTER FIFTEEN

IT TOOK MAGS a while to catch her breath. She sprawled bonelessly atop Finn while his callused fingers moved lightly up and down her back, tracing her vertebrae, outlining her shoulder blades and gently circling within the shallow dimples above the rise of her butt. His fingertips against those particularly smooth-skinned spots felt scratchy and very male. She didn't know quite what to say, because this felt…different from any sex she'd ever had.

It wasn't, of course. She might feel a bit more emotionally fulfilled than she had with other men, but in the end nothing had truly changed. She certainly couldn't afford to let Finn get too close. It was simply too mother-lovin' difficult when things fell apart as, face it, they invariably did.

And truly, it was hardly surprising she'd experienced more emotions with him. Since the day they'd both arrived in El Tigre, they'd been thrown together in one outrageous circumstance after another. Yet the bottom line remained the same: Finn was a love-'em-and-leave-'em kind of guy and the last thing they needed was for her to go all hearts-and-flowers schoolgirlie on him.

Especially when what she actually felt was undoubtedly more gratitude than anything else.

Because she *was* grateful. For what had been one of the best orgasms of her life, no question. But more than that, for the way he'd taken on the troubles of a woman he'd never even laid eyes on before a few days ago. He'd thrown himself between her and the dangerous situation she'd found herself in without blinking an eye or counting the cost to himself.

So, making sure to plaster on the same free-and-easy smile she'd used to great effect with other men, she raised her head and let her hands slide from his shoulders to the mat on either side of his neck so she could lever herself upright. The move pressed her pelvis to his and arched her back into a cobra pose. It also squeezed him right out of her. Instinctually, she clenched deep inside in an attempt to keep him inside. But it was too late.

She ramped up her ain't-we-got-fun smile.

"Dammit, Mags," he snapped, "don't do that!"

"Don't do what?" Okay, so playing dumb was never particularly attractive. Still, sometimes when she felt cornered, faking ignorance was the only way to go.

"Don't give me that big life-of-the-party smile when your eyes are saying 'Get me the hell out of here.'"

"Oh, what bull. They aren't saying anything of the kind." *Were they?*

"The hell they're not. And I'm not just blowing smoke out my ass, here. I've met women like you before."

"*Have* you?" Probably way too much frost coated

her tone, but please—women like her? "And what, pray tell, are woman like me like?"

He looked her dead in the eye. "As I said, at first glance you give off this vibe of being, hands down, the coolest, most fun woman in the room. But the reality is, you're one big ball of emotional dodge 'em."

"Wow. Thank you, Dr. Phil," she said even as an inner voice murmured, *Okay, pretty much.* But if so, he said that as if it were a bad thing, rather than intelligently well thought out and self-protective. Feeling rattled and defensive, she lifted herself off of him to sit on the sleeping bag. Suddenly uncomfortable with her nudity, she reached for her underwear. As she pulled on her panties, she gave him an insolent up-and-down before adding flatly, "I'm surprised you could bring yourself to have sex with me, me being so screwed up and all." She slid her arms into the straps of her bra and reached behind her to fasten it.

He rolled to face her, propping his head in his hand. Clearly he wasn't the least bit self-conscious about being naked and he met her gaze levelly. "Maybe I hoped I'd be the exception to your don't-let-'em-too-close rule."

"Please," she scoffed. "This from the man ho who's had a bazillion lovers?"

Genuine amusement lit his dark eyes. "Trying to put me on the defensive, darlin'? I give you points for the good ol' college try, but it's not gonna work. My man-ho days may well be behind me. I came on this trip in large part because I've been wondering lately if maybe it's time to change my ways—to think about settling down. But to do that I knew I needed to be away from my

family so I could honestly say no matter what I end up
deciding that it wasn't due to any pressure from them."

"Sure, blame it on the caring family."

His dark eyebrows slammed together and for the first
time he looked annoyed. "I'm not blaming jack, I'm giving you the facts. And the facts are, I know what I read
in your eyes and that was 'Get me the hell out of here.'"

"Well, guess what, Kavanagh? You can't read eyes
for shit, because they were saying 'That was *really*
nice.'" With maybe a pinch of *And now that it's over,
get me the hell out of here.*

"Nice? Seriously?" He sat up, his expression downright offended. "You thought it was *nice*? Then let's
try this again, Deluca, because I can sure as hell do
better than fucking nice. I admit this round was short
on foreplay."

She'd thought it was just right, but panic at the idea
of making lo—having sex again and being left feeling even *more* emotional made her heart drum out a
rhythm like Thumper's twitterpated hind foot. Somehow, however, she managed to arrange her expression
into something she hoped at least appeared cool and
collected. "Oh, let's, do. Because being told I'm emotionally stunted really puts me in the mood."

He swore under his breath, raked his fingers through
his hair, then efficiently disposed of the condom, found
his shorts and pulled them on. It was sweltering in the
tent and he wiped his forearm across his forehead, then
brought his wrist down to look at his watch. And said
coolly, "You want to break camp then and get a few
more hours farther downriver?"

His sudden shift in conversation might have been jarring if that panic thing hadn't started up all over again. Even as she struggled to get her racing heart under control, however, she gave him a terse nod. "Yes. I think it's probably a good idea to get going while I still have the nerve to get back in the boat."

He cursed again and moved in on her, his hand reaching out to brush back a hank of hair that had escaped her braid. "I didn't even think about that. You gonna be okay?"

"I hope so." Almost immediately she sucked in a deep breath and gave a decisive nod. "No. I *will* be fine. You can be sure, though, that I'll put my life jacket on the minute I step into the boat."

He gave her head a knuckle rub and she blinked in surprise. She was having a tough time keeping up here, what with him trying to argue her to a standstill one moment, then getting all chummy playful with her the next.

"You know what, Magdalene?" he said. "You're a damn good sport. And I have a feeling you're a helluva lot tougher than you think you are, too." Then he became briskly efficient. "Why don't you take our packs down to the boat while I roll up the mat and bag and break down the tent."

Fifteen minutes later, they shoved off the beach. For the first half hour, Mags sat stiffly vigilant, but little by little, as the water remained calm and nothing more exciting happened than spotting an occasional group of little squirrel monkeys swinging through the increasingly dense trees lining either side of the river, her tense posture relaxed. She lifted her tote onto her lap and hauled out the items that hadn't fully dried during her earlier attempt, spreading them across the empty seat between her and Finn.

I have a feeling you're a helluva lot tougher than you think. His words kept running through her mind even as she tried her best to ignore them.

She *wished* she were tougher than she thought. Physically, she'd been known to display an occasional moment of bravery. Or foolhardiness. It all depended on who you talked to. As far as emotional toughness went, however, Finn had pretty much hit the nail on the head. When she ventured out to clubs and bars, she was the life of the party and it made her all warm and fuzzy when people thought she was fun and wanted to hang out with her.

But while she was a master at fooling herself on occasion, trying to do so in the long run simply wasn't sustainable. She knew she had mama and daddy and what a shrink would undoubtedly call abandonment issues. She also knew it was past time she let them go. Unfortunately the latter was easier said than done. And when the only two real friends she'd made during her boarding-school days disappeared from her life, she'd taken it as a sign. God knew it was less painful to simply avoid deep, genuine connections in the first place. Because, show people your real self and odds were they were gonna walk away.

Okay, Heather had died in a car accident, so Mags could hardly cry abandonment over that one. That sure hadn't made it hurt any less, though. As for Sarina—

The three of them, she, Sarina and Heather, had

been the Three Musketeers—or Teeretts, as Heather
had dubbed them—since practically the first day at
Mags's final boarding school, the one in which she'd
decided to apply herself instead of willfully screwing up
and getting herself kicked out yet again. She and Sarina
had clung together after Heather's death, but when Mags
dropped out of college, Sarina had just blown her off.

It had been like a kick in the stomach, but apparently
she'd no longer fit in her former friend's plans. Sarina
had always been ambitious, constantly seeking people
to meet, social ladders to climb. And that apparently
meant friends with connections, or at the very least,
college degrees.

An-n-nd—*this is getting me nowhere.*

She'd been doing her best to ignore Finn by keeping
an eagle eye on the water. Her spirits lifted when she
saw hundreds of brilliantly colored butterflies gathered
on a tiny sandbank.

Soon after that, however, the water lost its clearness
and grew cloudier until eventually it became downright
muddy-looking. Here and there tiny villages comprised
of a handful of open-sided huts cropped up. Straddling
the shore and the edge of the river, they were built atop
slender poles and looked as if they'd been constructed
from mud and straw.

Really? her inner critic demanded. *This is what it's
come to? Deciding what a handful of rickety huts I'll
never see again are made of?*

She sighed. Considering how often she'd sneaked
peeks at Finn even as she'd tried to keep her atten-

tion directed elsewhere, there was no getting around the facts. Her best in the ignoring department sucked.

He'd shaved the night before last, but the stubble on his hard jaw had grown almost thick enough to qualify as the beginning of a beard, or the precursor to one, any-how. His mouth, framed by all that dark scruff, looked sexy, dammit. It was thoroughly sensual…and she could honestly say that wasn't a word normally found in her vocabulary. She looked back out at the water before he could catch her gawking.

A few minutes later, however, she glanced at him again down the length of the boat. Only this time, in an attempt to avoid looking at his face, she studied his hands.

That turned out to be even worse than thinking about his mouth, because like a needle stuck on an old-fashioned, scratched-up vinyl record and endlessly playing the same few words over and over again, mem-ories and remembered sensations of those hands on her kept repeating themselves in her mind.

She clutched her head. "Errrrgh!"

Pulling his watchful attention away from the river, Finn pinned her in that direct, dark-eyed gaze of his. "Taking up growling, darlin'?"

She grimaced. "I hope not—at least it's a new-to-me skill. I guess I was thinking out loud."

"Quite despondently, too. What's bothering you?"

She shrugged. But his willingness to demand an-swers or start discussions on subjects she'd avoid like an Ebola outbreak made her revisit him saying that maybe he hoped to be the exception to her penchant for avoidance. He had put what *he'd* like right out there as if it didn't take courage, even though he'd basically said he'd like her to let him in. And the ease with which he'd owned up to it made her ashamed of her own cowardice.

So maybe she owed him a truth in return. She took some deep breaths, then raised her head to look straight at him for more than the fleeting seconds she'd been directing his way since she'd settled down enough to look at anything other than her white-knuckle grip on her seat. She licked her suddenly dry lips.

And confessed, "I didn't require more foreplay." She waved a hand. "Earlier, you know?" she clarified, in case he didn't have a clue what she was babbling about—even though it hadn't been that long ago. "Your foreplay was the exact right amount."

JESUS, SHE WAS killing him here. Finn had been doing his damnedest not to look at Mags too often since leaving the beach. Not only did he think she needed the space, but every time he got her in his sights, he also promptly pictured her all naked and hot in his arms, which in turn made him relive the expression on her face and the little sounds she'd made when she'd come for him. And God knew he didn't need that.

Even with her in his direct line of sight, he'd done a damn fine job of keeping his eyes off her by concentrating on the river—which, after this morning's mess, was probably a better use of his focus anyway. Plus, after having had the river virtually to themselves, boat traffic was beginning to appear. Way more than he would've guessed.

Despite the increased need for vigilance, however, he hadn't been able to prevent his mind from going around and around what he might have done to make the sex better than *nice* for Mags. It was hard to deny he'd been long on slam-bam-thank-you-ma'am and short on foreplay. Having her tell him that she'd been satisfied with the little he'd managed took a huge load off his mind, and his smile was spontaneous. Happy. "Yeah?"

"Definitely. I was so hot to reach the finish line that any more would have been overkill."

"Then why the hell did you call it nice?"

"Because it was! And I said *really* nice." She scrubbed her hands over her face before dropping them back in her lap. Then she fixed those big baby blues on him. "Look, I'm not used to critiquing sexual performance. No one's ever asked me to do that before." She gave him a stricken look. "Oh, God. Maybe because my own stunk and I was just too oblivious to realize."

"Trust me, you're far from lousy," he assured her, then added slyly, "It was really nice."

She flashed him the sweet beam of delight he thought of as her "Magdalene" smile.

"Oh, good. That's a relief," she said and he realized *nice* honestly was praise in her mind. She peered at him through thick, pale eyelashes that had been washed almost clean of their usual mascara in her tearing tumble through the rapids. "I'm sorry if I messed up the post-game quarterbacking. I know now that it's all wrong to call it nice. Even if I don't quite understand why."

Then she blinked and hurt flashed across her face. "Oh." Her open Magdalene expression shut down and she looked at him with the cool gaze that had Mags's ask-me-if-I-give-a-damn cynicism written all over it. "I guess that wasn't a compliment, was it?"

"I was teasing you, darlin'." Which he'd take a wild stab here and surmise no one had bothered to do much of in her life. "If you'd been any better you'd have had to bury my cold, played-out corpse back on that beach."

And just like that, her open smile exploded back on the scene, all wide and genuine and clearly pleased. "Sweet."

He shook his head, a half smile tugging at his mouth. "Not from the corpse's perspective."

Her delighted laugh was loud, raucous.

The afternoon definitely started looking up after that. They talked about the increasing boat traffic and Mags pointed out some of the more stunning birds—which, given the wide variety of vibrant plumage within the species, was saying something. The sun had begun its downward arc toward the horizon and he was trying to remember what they still had left in the way of food when they motored around a bend in the river and he saw a small town up ahead. "Whoa. Lookit that, Mags! Civilization."

"What?" She whipped around in her seat to stare at the small town that grew closer by the minute. After she'd looked her fill, she swiveled back to give him another big smile. "Food! And a shower. And maybe even a real bed to sleep in." She sighed. "I dream about thick, comfy mattresses and here we are with a sporting chance at actually sleeping on one. I still have half my take from yesterday's fiesta gig."

"A real bed sounds like Nirvana to me, too." Give him an evening with her in one of those babies and he'd lay odds he could do some of his best work ever.

But, clearing his throat, he shoved the image springing full-blown in his mind into a deep dark closet. "And a nice cold beer."

Her smile grew bigger yet. "Make mine a margarita. Alongside a big bowl of chips and salsa."

As if on cue, his stomach growled and Mags laughed.

Hearing the sounds of a cantina as they pulled up to the rickety pier that thrust out into the river, they exchanged grins as he maneuvered their boat between one similar to theirs and a long orange dugout canoe with a blue open shelter on one end. Mags climbed out and squatted to secure their boat to a couple of crude bent-nail cleats.

He hauled out their belongings as she finished up and extended a hand to pull her to her feet. "You want to find a place to wash up first or to eat?"

"Ooh, God. Both sound equally wonderful. You choose."

"I vote for a cleanup, then—if we're quick. 'Cause I'm pretty sure that beer's got my name on it at the cantina."

"Deal."

From what he could see, the town's business section was comprised of this long block of single and two-storied buildings painted in colors that looked as if they'd once been vibrantly hued but had faded over the years to grubby pastels. They headed for the only hotel, passing by a second cantina on their way.

Finn found himself salivating at the scents that floated out of it and Mags moaned low in her throat.

"I want to eat there," she said.

The sign on the hotel they walked toward read merely Hotel, so it was probably a safe bet it was the only one in town. When they entered its tiny lobby they found the small counter that served as check-in desk unoccupied. But it had an old-fashioned bell atop it and Finn slapped it a few times.

A man came out through the door behind the counter, tugging a napkin out of his collar. He greeted them in Spanish and Finn let Mags step forward. What followed was a rapid exchange in which he understood maybe one word in ten. The upshot, however, was that Mags ultimately began rooting through her big purse, no doubt for yesterday's leftover earnings.

He put a hand on her arm. "I've got this," he murmured and pulled out his wallet. "How much?"

She told him and he paid the clerk. The man passed him two keys with different room numbers.

He promptly pushed one back and said, *"Uno habitación. Uno."* But stomach sinking, he turned to look at Mags.

She shrugged. "I requested two rooms."

CHAPTER SIXTEEN

"UNREQUEST IT." The flat demand in Finn's voice and hard look in his eyes made Mags's heart thunder in her chest.

But damn his eyes if she'd let it show. "No." Sticking out her chin, she returned hard look for hard look. "I need breathing room." Okay, and maybe she was running away rather than having to face how this afternoon's sex had affected her. But if that were the case, so be it. She really did need some space that wasn't filled to the rafters with Finn's testosterone.

"Then ask for a room with two beds and we'll hang a blanket between them," he said in a way that let her know she'd have a fight on her hands if she didn't follow his demands pronto. "Did you even look at the numbers on these keys?" He held them out for her to see that one was on this floor while the other was upstairs. "If Joaquin or his hired muscle show up here, you have some plan in place for contacting me?"

Feeling naive and stupid, she shook her head in silent admission that she did not. Then she sighed...and acknowledged what was truly on her mind. "I get the feeling you're expecting more sex."

His dark eyes did the impossible and darkened yet

more. "I won't lie, darlin', I've been thinking about just that." He slicked his hands over his hair from his temples to his nape, where they locked at the base of his skull, one palm stacked atop the back of his other. His bent arms squeezed the sides of his face, his elbows pointed her way as he locked her in the bull's-eye of an intense gaze. "But I'm a big boy," he said unequivocally. "I take no for an answer."

She blew out another sigh. "Maybe I'm worried about my own poor impulse control."

"Oh, baby—" his grin was wide, white and wicked "—you don't wanna be telling me that. Because unless you have a gun to both defend yourself and bring me running, we *are* sharing a room." An odd expression crossed his face as he took her arm and walked her away from the desk clerk. "I forgot all about Joaquin's gun in the bottom of my pack. I'll give it to you if you really want to be alone and can get two rooms on the same floor."

Revulsion surged quick and hot and her hands jerked up, palms out, fingers spread in an age-old, if involuntary, don't-even-go-there reaction. "I've never touched a gun in my life and I don't plan to begin tonight. I believe I already mentioned, the last time you offered it to me, it's a better bet I'd shoot myself or have it taken away and used against me than be a threat to anyone else."

"Then one room it is." He jerked his head at the clerk, who gazed longingly toward the door behind which his dinner was no doubt growing cold. "Tell him."

"Finn—"

"Those are your options. The gun. Or me."

She swore under her breath. "Fine." She walked over to redo their arrangements.

"And keep the one on the main floor in case we have to bail like we did at Senora Guerrero's," Finn called softly from behind her.

She rejoined him a few moments later, shoving the refunded money at Finn as she reached him. "The only room with two beds available is upstairs," she said, handing him the key.

"Dammit, I said—"

Something in her expression must have given him pause, because he cut himself off midrant or demand or whatever it had been about to be. But just in case he was merely marshaling his arguments, she used his own words against him. "That's your only option," she said evenly. "Deal with it."

He grunted but let it go, and they headed up the stairs to the second floor, walking in silence until they reached their room. He unlocked the door and opened it, then stepped back with a gesture that invited her to enter first. They'd barely cleared the door when he stabbed a forefinger toward the small attached bath.

"Be quick, will ya? I don't know about you, but I could eat a live cow with my bare hands."

"Your mouth would probably work better," she said, "but you got it." Tote slung over her shoulder, she walked straight into the bathroom and closed the door behind her.

The shower was small, its water the color of weak tea and its pressure feeble. Yet it felt like a little piece of heaven right here on earth. She would have loved to

linger, but she, too, was hungry and she had no desire
to fight with Finn all night and ruin what promised to
be a mammoth treat. She'd gotten her way with the two
beds and he hadn't beaten to death her failure to notice
the different floors the rooms occupied when he'd seen
the original keys.

She quickly soaped up and rinsed off, washed and
conditioned her hair, then cranked off the water. After
squeezing as much of it from her hair as she could manage with her hands, she stepped out of the shower stall.

When it came to a clean change of clothing, she
didn't like anything her tote had to offer. The river
drenching they'd received certainly hadn't done them
any favors. She used the towel to absorb more of the
water streaming from her hair, then wrapped the now-
damp towel around her and stuck her head out the bathroom door.

The first thing she noticed was a blanket hanging
between their two beds that he'd managed to jury-rig
just as he'd said he would. At the moment part of it was
flipped over the line, giving her a direct view of Finn
lounging on one of the narrow beds reading what appeared to be a pamphlet of some kind.

But still.

"You wanna change places with me?" she asked.
The damn man had kicked off his shoes and stripped
off his shirt and she looked away when she found herself tracking the curves and dips of his musculature.
Seeing a piece of peeling paint on the doorjamb, she
tore it off. "I'll get dressed in here while you shower."

"Sounds like a plan." The bed creaked slightly as he

pushed off the elbow he'd propped himself up on and she nonchalantly stepped into the room.

That's when she realized which bed he'd left for her and she whipped around to flash him a spontaneous, genuine smile as he passed her. She didn't even care that she caught him seriously scoping out where her towel hit the tops of her thighs. "You gave me the bed closest the bathroom."

"Well, yeah." His mouth tipped up on one side. "That's a no-brainer."

She laughed. "Get your shower. I really need to eat. When was the last time we did that?"

"Too long ago, if neither of us can remember." He disappeared into the bathroom and she went to find something to wear.

Digging through Finn's backpack where she'd put some of her clothing when he'd made her lose her suitcase, she came across a red sleeveless top. It was girlie and its cotton scroll lace made it feel kinda dressy even though it, like most of her shirts, was a tank top. Unlike her usual body-hugging style, however, this one skimmed her curves and had a pretty scooped neck and a shirttail hem.

Dropping her towel, she pulled on clean panties, then rapidly slathered on lotion and donned a pair of white capris. She'd only brought one other bra and it didn't make her feel as pretty as the one she'd been wearing. But that one was grubby and no way was she putting it back on her clean-for-the-first-time-in-what-felt-like-forever body. With a little sigh, she donned the more utilitarian one, then slid the red tank top over her head and twitched it into place.

Her hair was still damp, but she combed it out, then dug through her tote for her makeup case. Standing in front of the flyspecked mirror above the room's only dresser, she used navy and metallic gold shadows, black liner and navy mascara to design smoky eyes that made her irises bluer, her whites whiter. Then she studied her bare lips, carrying on a silent debate for several seconds. She didn't ordinarily wear red lipstick, but if this wasn't the time for a celebratory color, when she was clean and all awash with the prospect of a cold drink and a hot meal, she didn't know when would be. She dabbed on MAC Good Kisser lipstick with a light hand, however, because her coloring was too all-over pale to support a deep slash of red. She blotted a good portion of that away, dabbed on more and blotted again. Then again, until, finally satisfied, she stood back and smiled.

Until she looked down at her feet. Dang. She sure wished she had a pretty pair of strappy, dressy sandals to complete her look.

"Yeah, well," she sighed. *If wishes were horses.* She'd just have to make do with her Tevas.

Making do was something she had down cold, so she pushed the minor dissatisfaction aside. It didn't pay to get all stressed over things you had no earthly chance of changing.

The bathroom door opened and she looked up as Finn strode into the room. All the moisture left her mouth.

Ho-ly crapuccino. The man really was sex on a stick—or maybe it was simply that she now had knowledge of what he could do with that body, those hands, those lips.

His normally rich brown hair was inky with the water still clinging to it, and that newly shaven jaw gleamed like old satin under gaslight. Not that she knew from personal experience what the latter looked like, but she'd read enough historical romance to be fairly certain she was at least in the ballpark. And that towel, wrapped around his hips and tucked low—

Well.

The thing was shabby and on the thin side, and it acted like neon arrows pointing out all the good stuff that wasn't covered. The long, muscular legs. The corded belly and that strong chest with its virile dusting of hair. Those wide shoulders. Not to mention his strong arms.

God, those arms. She'd had a couple of dreams about them holding her through the night. She'd bet it would feel like security squared to sleep wrapped in Finn Kavanagh's arms.

But that was a slippery slope she was staying the hell away from. She could hardly tell the guy she wasn't interested in having sex with him again, then expect him to merely hold her so she could sleep without feeling the need to do so with one eye open.

As if physical proximity ever improved anything anyway. It was that exact illusion of depending on someone else for her security that she'd worked so hard to eradicate. Besides, even if they survived this, when it was over she'd go back to her little apartment in LA, where she hoped to get her makeup-artist career back on the track she'd almost gotten it on. And Finn would go home to his big, supportive family.

She snorted. Not that he had the good sense to appreciate how lucky he was to have them.

"Ladylike," Finn murmured. But he gave her an appreciative smile. "You look very pretty. Red's a good color on you."

"Thanks. Throw on some clothes and let's go get something to eat."

"I'm with you there, doll." And he dropped his towel.

"FOR GOD'S SAKE, KAVANAGH!"

Finn watched as Magdalene whirled to give him her back. And smiled to himself as he shook his head. She was a dichotomy: so bold and freewheeling and pulsing with sexuality one moment, then damn near bashful and prudish the next.

Even as he watched, she reached toward the line he'd strung between their beds to hang the divider he'd promised her. She grabbed the bottom corner of the blanket that he'd flipped back up over the line to keep things airier and mostly open until she absolutely needed her privacy.

Which was now, clearly. Or so her twitching the blanket free and letting it drop between them told him.

He blew out a gusty breath and turned to look at the clothing he'd laid out while Mags was in the shower. The wardrobe he'd brought on this trip, if you could even call it that, ran mostly to shorts and T-shirts. Given how nice Mags looked, however, and the obvious attention she'd paid to putting herself together, he went back to the pack and pulled out the pair of khakis he'd thrown in at the last minute and the silky golden-brown Perry Ellis T-shirt his sister Hannah had given him "just in case you find a senorita you want to impress."

Not that he was out to impress anyone. Still… *Thank you, Hannah.*

He got dressed, tried to hand press the worst of the wrinkles out of his pants, then gave it up as a lost cause and dragged a comb through his hair. After putting on his shoes, he called it good. Feeling great, he sang a section of an old favorite song where a man urged a woman to "wear a dress, babe," while he wore a tie. And added how they'd laugh at that old bloodshot moon, in that burgundy sky. Then, drumming his fingers on the little nightstand next to his bed, he made his voice go falsetto for the bluesy piano-and-drums instrumental that normally followed the lyrics.

He heard Mags's muffled laugh from the other side of the blanket.

"How 'bout it, Mags? You ready to put a new coat of paint on this lonesome old town?"

"I am." She came around the corner of the divider. "I'd probably appreciate your musical abilities more, though, if I weren't starved half to death."

"I hear ya, darlin'. Let's go get us a drink and something to eat." He hovered his hand just above the small of her back as she preceded him out the door. "Did I tell you that you look really pretty?"

"You did." She flashed him a smile over her shoulder before turning her attention to navigating the stairs. "I have to admit, though, a girl just can't hear enough of those sweet nothin's."

They crossed a lobby that once again was empty, then stepped out the front entry to find that night had fallen. A silvery sliver of the rising moon barely crested the flat horizon to the east.

"I'm still not used to the way the time here is divided into equal hours of day and night," he said as they walked toward the cantina they'd decided on earlier. "That, give or take a few minutes, it never varies—you still get twelve hours of daylight and twelve hours of dark. In Seattle in the summertime it doesn't get truly dark until ten o'clock at night, but in the dead of winter it's full dark by four in the afternoon."

"I know what you mean." she agreed. "We don't have the kind of long twilights in LA that you get up north, but when I was first sent to the States I was amazed at the way the seasons affected the number of daylight hours. Up until then I'd spent my entire life down here where, as you said, the light and night hours are divided into twelve hours each no matter what time of the year it is. I'd just assumed that was true everywhere."

Rich aromas, laughter, and the clink and clatter of cutlery and crockery reached them before they arrived at the cantina, making Mags turn a delighted smile in his direction. "Omigawd. Will you let me know if I start to drool?"

"I will if you will. God, I'm hungry."

They entered a room that was crowded but not, thank God, entirely full and wove their way between tables to an empty narrow booth against the far wall. There were two handwritten menus atop its table and they both snatched one up the instant they slid in, even though Finn could only figure out a few of the dishes offered when he looked at his. He looked across the table at Magdalene. "What's *sancocho*?"

"It's a soup that, depending on the cook, is either stewlike or more brothy. Both varieties usually have lots of corn on the cob that's sliced into narrow rounds."

He made a face. "Today's been stressful enough— I'm not in the mood for soup with stuff I have to fish out to eat with my fingers." He looked down at the menu again. "So, how about this *asado*?"

"That's basically barbecue—it refers to both the technique and the social event. In this case it looks like beef alongside other meats, which are likely to be either pork, chicken or alpaca."

"Meat," he said reverently and closed his menu. "That's what I want."

She laughed and tossed her own menu atop his in the middle of the table. "Works for me. Protein sounds divine right about now."

The waitress showed up a minute later and Mags ordered for them, starting with a beer for him and a margarita for her. The waitress chatted at her in rapid-fire Spanish, then reached out to touch Mags's hair.

"Bella, bella," she murmured before whirling away in a swirl of brightly colored skirt.

Finn watched her departing back as she dodged through the room, then turned his attention on Mags's flushed cheeks. "I'm guessing she hasn't seen many blondes."

"Apparently not. Oh, please don't let this be the day Joaquin or his goons show up, because clearly I stand out." She blinked. "Oh, God, Finn. I forgot all about the goon squad for a while. It's all wrong that I'm enjoying myself like this when my parents are probably lucky if they get rice and beans, isn't it?"

"Oh, *hell* to the no." A fierce wrinkle gathered Finn's brows above his nose. "What does one thing have to do with the other? You're knocking yourself out and putting yourself in a lot of danger to get to them. You don't think you deserve to grab your moments of enjoyment where you can?"

"I—" She shook her head. "I actually thought something very like that when we were at the festival in La Plata—that being able to occasionally relax helped me feel stronger for the challenges to come." She straightened in her seat. "So, okay. I'll try to stop feeling guilty during these rare happy moments." A small, self-deprecatory smile tugged up one corner of her pretty lips. "I can't promise it'll stick with any kind of consistency, but I will try." Then she full-out grinned at him. "I ordered you a fancy potato to go with your red meat."

He eyed her suspiciously. "Define fancy."

"You'll just have to wait and see."

"O-o-kay," he said slowly, drawing out the word. "What's the worst they can do to a potato?"

She wiggled her eyebrows at him.

"Shit."

She laughed again. "No, you'll like it. Tru-u-ust me."

"Do I look like I was born yesterday? Everyone knows never to trust someone who says trust me."

She merely smiled innocently.

He found himself enjoying her enjoying herself. He'd never seen her this relaxed, never mind feeling light-hearted enough to tease.

Then their drinks arrived and he discovered that a margarita on an empty stomach made Magdalene down-right chatty.

She told him a little about how she'd envisioned some of the creatures in the space-epic gig she'd had to give up. She was amazingly descriptive and made them come alive in his mind's eye.

"I'm sure they had detailed drawings of what they actually wanted," she admitted. "But it's fun to envision what my creations would have looked like." She leaned into the table, planting her elbow on its scarred top and her chin in her palm. "But enough about me. Tell me about your family. I know you have a brother named Dev and sisters named Kate and Hannah."

That she remembered reinforced in his mind how family happy she was. He swallowed a smile. "The girls and I are the only ones still single in the family. My married sibs are Maureen and my brothers Bren and David. And Dev, of course."

"And grandmothers and aunts and girl cousins?"

He nodded. "Both my grandmas are still alive and one of my grandpas. Then there are two uncles, four aunts—and their spouses—and too damn many first cousins and *their* kids to name."

She looked at him with big wistful eyes. "You are so lucky."

"I know."

She gawked. "You do?"

"Sure." He shrugged. "I feel crowded sometimes and definitely maneuvered—if you met my aunt Eileen, you'd understand what I'm talking about. She makes our generation want to run as fast as possible in the opposite direction."

"Oh, I'm sure—"

"No, you're not, because you've never met her. At the same time, I love my family and I appreciate how lucky I am to be part of a loving, functional tribe. It doesn't make them perfect, though, Magdalene. Family relationships are messy."

"Tell me about it." But she gave him a little self-deprecating smile. "Mine is certainly messed up. And I know I romanticize the whole idea of family." She shrugged and took another sip of her drink. "It's just... I was part of that once upon a time and I loved it. I've always wished I could re-create it." Her shoulder twitched. "Though I guess for now I should just focus on saving the family I've got."

"And cut yourself some slack while you're doing it." He studied her for a moment, then felt a sardonic smile tug at his lips. "That re-creating thing must be hard to do when you pull in people with one hand, then hold them at arm's length with the other."

She looked away to watch their waitress come toward them with two loaded plates. Just before she got there, Mags looked at him across the table, her face serious. "Yeah. Then there's that."

CHAPTER SEVENTEEN

"ABOUT DAMN TIME you checked in!" Joaquin snapped into his cell phone, having snatched it up the moment he recognized the caller's number. "Where have you been?"

"Sorry, Boss," said one of his enforcers, and for a brief instant Joaquin was placated. He loved it when they called him *boss*. It made him feel almost as all-powerful as *his* boss, Victor. Then he realized he hadn't heard what his man was saying and tuned back in.

"—sight of the Deluca woman in La Plata, but she disappeared on us again. The chick is fuckin' *smoke*. So we tracked down the town's only car-rental agency."

There was a pause and Joaquin snapped his fingers impatiently. This was the trouble with working with American mercenaries—all their idioms aside, which made Joaquin wonder half the time what the hell they were talking about, *yanquis* as a whole loved stretching out the drama of every damn situation. "And? Spit it out, Palmer!"

"And we discovered she and the man she's traveling with turned in their car. But—get this—they didn't rent a replacement car."

Another silence settled over the line and he felt his

blood pressure climbing into the red zone. "If you drag
this out one more time, I will make you pay."

"Sorry, Boss," Palmer said again. "This whole business has been a case of one strange-ass thing after the
other goin' wrong. Me and Vasquez learned that Deluca
and her guy rented a boat, so we rented one, too—only
ours has a faster motor. We figured they'd have to pull
over for the night, which would allow us to catch up
with them wherever they parked their butts and bring
'em back to you. We had no real way of knowin' how
far behind we were, but figured it couldn't be more than
a couple-a hours at most. But here's the bizarre part."
His exhale rode the radio waves. "Vasquez and me, we
were jumped down on the docks by a gang of pissed-
off…hell, I'm not even sure what they were. But these
guys were just standing around, talking quietly to each
other and not payin' us any mind at all as we walked
by, then—bam! They fuckin' ambush us from behind."

"You're armed to the teeth—and you let a group of
amateurs *ambush* you?" *Dios mío.* What were they paying these morons for?

"How the hell was we supposeta know they'd go
ape shit on us? I mean that's fucking suicidal, right?
Because we *were* armed to the teeth and in that neighborhood we were lettin' it show. They kept their eyes
lowered and talked strictly to each other—until we
passed them. Then suddenly there's like a dozen of the
crazy fuckers knockin' us on our face, holding us down
and stripping us of our weapons. Once we were trussed
up like a couple-a Thanksgiving turkeys, they kicked
the shit outta us. It was during the beat down we learned

they were still all jacked up on rage because Deluca and her man had somehow gotten the best of them maybe a half hour before."

"You were only a half an hour behind them?" *¡Dios!* The gods were just shitting on them left and right.

"That's what it sounded like from what the goombahs kept ranting about. Then, to add insult to injury, the fuckers tossed us in a storeroom and didn't let us out until about a half hour ago. Vasquez is still in bad shape. They broke one-a his ribs and it punctured a lung. I think his breathing problems were the only reason they cut us loose at all—they were afraid they'd have a murder rap hanging over their heads if they didn't. I took him to the hospital and the doctors inflated the lung and say he's gonna be okay. But he's out of commission for now and I need to know what you want me to do."

"Where are you now and what's the name of the river?" As soon as Palmer told him, Joaquin ordered, "Wait while I pull up a map on my computer." He looked up the river and followed it toward the Amazon from La Plata. "Okay. It looks like the only town anywhere near your location is Rio de Villanueva. Are you familiar with river travel?"

"Hell, yeah. I grew up on the Mississippi."

So maybe this would actually work out—something he'd been seeing damn little of these days while Victor breathed more and more heavily down his neck. "All right, then. I'm counting on you to bring them to me. Same rules apply—the woman doesn't get hurt. And Palmer?"

"Yeah, Boss?"

He stroked his thumb over the finely honed blade of the knife he'd gotten to replace the one stolen from him by the *americano*. "You do not want to let me down."

ON THEIR WALK back to the hotel, Mags thought about Finn's singing earlier in their room. "So, what *is* the name of this lonesome ol' town?" She lurched a little over nothing that she could see. It made her laugh.

"You a little lit, Deluca?"

She smiled at him companionably. "I may be the tiniest bit tipsy, although all that wonderful barbecue soaked up quite a bit of the tequila from my margarita."

"Tiniest bit tipsy looks good on you." He stopped and looked around. "And where are we is a good question. I haven't seen any kind of a sign. If this was small-town America I'd look for the water tower. But I'm not see-ing one of those. Senor!" he called to a man smoking outside a bodega near the corner. *"Que es tu nombre—"* He turned to her. "How do you say town?"

"Pueblo."

"Pueblo," he raised his voice to say to the man. He gave her a crooked smile. "I know that's not quite right, but it's the best I've got. Hopefully—"

"Rio de Villanueva," the man called back.

A big grin that did something to Mags's insides split Finn's face. *"Gracias!"* he yelled, then turned to her and crowed, "An-n-nd...he shoots, he scores!"

And just like that something cracked open in her heart. God, she liked this guy. She'd been assuring herself he was an idiot, partly, she admitted, as self-preservation. She was attracted to him in a way so mammoth, it was ridiculous—and she wasn't afraid to admit it scared the bejesus out of her. In her defense, she'd thought the label applied if for no other reason than how unappreciative he'd seemed of his family. Since it was something she'd give a bundle to have for herself, anyone who had a loving family and didn't recognize the value of the gift he'd been given *was* an idiot.

Except it turned out he appreciated them just fine. He was merely fed up with the way they stuck their noses in his private business. And while she personally believed being surrounded by people who cared enough to show an interest in the things you did was pretty damn close to heaven on earth, she supposed she could also understand his desire to carve out some space for himself.

When they arrived back at their no-name hotel, Finn looked around the minuscule lobby and said drily, "Deserted as usual, I see." They climbed the staircase in silence, but she couldn't stop herself from sneaking looks at him when she was reasonably certain his attention was focused elsewhere.

Because…oh, God.

It didn't make sense and she couldn't say what made her do so, but she found she'd changed her mind about sleeping with him again.

Of course it would be better not to act on it, she sternly, if silently, lectured herself and ticked off the various reasons why on her fingers.

She'd consumed booze on an empty stomach—even if she no longer felt particularly impaired.

They had to live too closely to each other as it was. Too intimately.

Then there was the fact that the few times she'd allowed herself to get even the tiniest bit involved with someone, it had always ended badly.

With all those cautions front and center in her head, she headed straight for her bed behind the still-dropped bedspread. She shimmied out of her outer clothing, peeled off her bra and panties and donned the boy shorts and tank she'd adopted as sleepwear. Hearing Finn rustling around on the other side of the curtain, she gathered her washcloth and facial cleanser, along with her toothbrush and toothpaste, and took them into the bathroom, using her bare foot to close the door. The soft click it made behind her was the sound of privacy, something that had been scarce since arriving in South America.

It was a rare luxury not only to have an indoor toilet, and hot and cold running water, but to also have it en suite rather than in a room down the hall they had to share with the other occupants on their floor. Running lukewarm water in the sink, she held her cloth under the stream, wrung the excess water from it, then applied the damp cloth to her face, pressing it against her closed eyelids.

And sighed with pleasure. Perhaps even moaned a little. She grimaced, however, when she lowered the cloth and saw it generously smeared with her eye makeup. She had an excellent bottle of remover and her favorite ultrasoft cotton pads in her tote for the express purpose of taking this stuff off before she washed, but had she remembered? Oh, no. She squirted her skin cleanser on the cloth now, however, and managed to scrub it almost

238   RUNNING WILD

clean of the makeup before returning her attention to washing her face.

She thought she was pretty relaxed when she returned to her bed and put away all the toiletries except the washcloth, which she'd left hung over the edge of the sink to dry. She lowered herself onto the mattress and sighed with the pure pleasure of having something this soft and giving beneath her.

But after the first few moments spent reveling in the unaccustomed luxury of sprawling upon a real bed, she started thinking once more about having sex with Finn. And unfortunately once the thought entered her mind that was all she wrote, for she couldn't seem to expel it. She sat up, punched her pillow into shape, then lay back down, this time on her right side, which left her looking at the wall rather than the lightweight spread separating their beds.

A few minutes later, she flopped onto her back again and lifted up enough to flip the pillow to its cooler side and stuff it back under her head. Her feet started tapping air.

She tried slow, deep breathing.

Mentally listed all the movies she would adore to do makeup on.

Tried to calculate how much longer it would take them to get to Munoz's grow farm.

Nothing helped and she jerked upright and swung around until she was sitting cross-legged, staring at the colorless-in-the-dark spread. And demanded, "You still want to have sex with me?"

There was dead silence on the other side of the blanket and she waited one moment. Two. Then blew out a disgruntled breath. "Crap," she groused. "You're asleep. Doesn't that just figure? I'm lying here all horny and you're sleeping like a baby."

"I am not effin' sleeping," his low voice snapped, sounding thoroughly bad tempered.

"But you're cranky." Catching herself reaching a hand toward the blanket, she let it drop to her lap. "Sex would probably improve your mood."

"I'm not sleeping with you while you're drunk, only to have you turn around and be pissed at me in the morning for taking advantage."

"Please." She made a rude noise. "I said I was slightly tipsy, not drunk. Shoot, I'm probably not even that now. Want to watch me walk a straight line? Tip my head back, close my eyes and touch alternate fingertips to my nose?"

"No. I want you to go to sleep and ask me again in the morning."

"But I'm horny *now*."

"And a few hours ago you were never sleeping with me again."

She shrugged even though he couldn't see her. "So I changed my mind. Woman's prerogative." She wistfully patted the mattress next to her hip. "I'd sure like to do it in a bed." She smoothed the sheet with long sweeps of her hand and didn't even notice that its thread count was a fair distance from silky smooth. "It's a very nice bed."

He groaned and whispered a short, succinct swearword. She heard a rustling on his side of the blanket and smiled at the thought of what he could do for her.

What she could do to him. They should probably have a discussion about the rules for a sexual relationship, but at the moment she was simply happy knowing he was about to make her feel. So. Good.

Instead of coming around the edge of the hanging curtain, however, she heard him walking in the direction of the door and shot to her feet. "Hey!" She jerked aside the blanket.

Just in time to hear him say, "I'm going out," as the door closed between them.

She threw herself on her back on the bed. Clenched fistfuls of her hair and tugged. "Well, crap," she said to the ceiling. "Just…crap."

"SHIT. SHIT, SHIT, SHIT!" Eyebrows clenched over his nose, hands fisted in the pockets of his khakis, Finn strode down the sidewalk, barely registering a couple around his parents' age skittering out of his way. "What the hell's the matter with you, boyo? You shoulda jumped all over that offer."

He laughed sourly. *Yeah, right.* Da had drummed certain codes into Finn and his brothers' heads when it came to dealing with what he'd loved to call the fairer sex. And one of the biggies was that you never, but never, took advantage of a woman who'd had too much to drink. Not even if that possibility was only bastard stepchild to a "might have."

"Consider how you'd feel if she were your sister," their dad had invariably added, which got him scornful as-if sneers.

Because, really? Like Finn or any of his brothers

would ever be drawn to a woman who reminded them of any of their sisters. Still, they appreciated the guiding principle behind the old man's directive. Each and every one of them would beat the bloody hell out of anyone who took advantage of a Kavanagh woman, be she sister, aunt or cousin.

He'd only known Magdalene a handful of days but Jesus, she'd gotten under his skin. Usually, he was perfectly happy with a single night with a woman. It was essentially his preferred duration for most dates. Aside from Julie McMurty in high school, it'd been rare for him to keep company with the same woman for two or three consecutive nights.

So why had it bugged him so much to be told she wouldn't sleep with him again?

He hadn't been looking for this thing with Mags and when he'd stepped in when Joaquin was hassling her, he'd assumed it was a one-time adventure his family would ply him with single malt to tell and retell for years to come. He hadn't known it was the start of a mission to rescue Magdalene's family from a drug lord. Yet, he didn't regret a damn thing about it.

And that was the truly scary part: he couldn't envision *not* doing this with her. She drove him nuts sometimes, but something about her just grabbed his attention by the short hairs and refused to let loose. She was the most interesting woman he'd met in a long time.

Maybe ever.

Little by little, his sexual frustration lost its grip and he started to pay attention to his surroundings. He'd stalked to the end of the small business district in a haze and, given that men with guns were trying to run them to ground, that wasn't the smartest thing he'd done today. So from now on, he was on full alert.

Not that there was much to see until he noticed another short street behind the one hugging the riverfront. Following it, he entertained himself trying to read the various signs on the storefronts and small businesses. Then he came to a building that needed no interpretation. Holy shit. He went inside and strode up to the lone clerk behind the counter. He tried out his high school Spanish on the man.

And, okay, he already knew it was pitiful, but apparently he hadn't realized how pitiful, because the reply he got was far too rapid for his comprehension. *"Uno momento,"* he said lamely, and about-faced to race out the door.

He ran all the way back to the hotel and burst into the room and straight past the blanket that divided his bed from Magdalene's. "Sorry," he said when she bolted upright. "But get dressed, I need your interpretive skills."

"What for?" she asked even as she rose from the bed and reached for the stack of neatly folded clothing she'd set on the floor next to it. She began pulling things on over her little boy-shorts panties and tank top.

"This burg's got a train station," he said and grinned. "And if it goes anywhere near where we need to be, you won't have to get in the boat again."

"That would be most excellent," she agreed, "considering we can't predict how much more rough water we'll run into." She stood on one foot to put on her sandal, then switched to the other. After tweaking the strap into place over her heel, she dropped her foot and gave his chest a light slap as she brushed past him. "So what are you waiting for?" she demanded. "Let's go!"

"Hang on a sec. I need to dig out the map so we have some frame of reference." It took only a little longer than that before he'd done so and they headed out.

It took no time at all to walk to the end of the riverfront and as Finn escorted Mags around its corner to the avenue behind, she gave him a delighted smile. "I had no idea another street was back here!"

"I know, right?" They arrived in front of the station. "Let's see if we can get where we need to go from here."

It turned out they could get close and a short while later they had tickets for the next morning's eight-thirty train. Finn dragged out his wallet and handed it to Mags to pay for them. "Ask him if we can use the phone to call the rental place in La Plata to see how to get their boat back to them. The card's in there, too."

"Oh, good thought. I forgot all about that." She twirled back to the man and launched into a discussion with him in her liquid, fast-paced Spanish. A few minutes later she turned back to Finn.

"This is better than we could have hoped for. They work with this company all the time and had an inquiry just today for a boat to get four people back up that way, but they didn't have anything available. He said he'll call them back, and if you bring him the key and your paperwork in the morning, he'll write us up a receipt for proof of delivery."

He laughed, snatched up Mags and swung her in a circle. "At last—something going our way!" He planted a swift kiss on her lips, then set her back on her feet before he was tempted to linger. Smiling at the man behind the counter, he said, *"Gracias!"* Then, wrapping his hand around the back of Mags's neck, he escorted her out of the station.

"Let's go see if that bodega is still open," he suggested. "There's no telling how long the train ride will be, but I'm pretty sure it won't have a dining car. I wouldn't mind picking up some provisions."

"Good plan. I don't like it when the food gets dangerously low."

They were in luck and reached the little mom-and-pop just as the proprietors were about to close up. Mags charmed them into staying open a few moments longer with the promise of being quick.

And they honored her word, the two of them snatching up whatever looked useful or tasty. Their items were rung up thirty seconds shy of five minutes later. They both said *"gracias"* several times and were escorted to the door by the smiling owners.

Back in the room, he squatted in front of his pack to make room for their purchases and carefully zipped their tickets inside the exterior pocket. Giving it a final pat, he rose to his feet and turned to find Magdalene standing fairly close behind him.

Naked as the day she was born.

CHAPTER EIGHTEEN

"You owe me a screaming orgasm," Magdalene said. "And before you bring up the tipsy thing again, tell me, could someone too drunk to know what she wants do this?" Standing on her right foot, she held her arms out to her side as she brought up her left foot until her entire yardstick-straight leg was perpendicular to her body. She pointed her toes at him, then flexed her foot back toward her shin while pushing out her heel.

He'd barely gotten used to that—never mind the whole package of Magdalene in all that exposed baby-smooth skin with its dangerous curves and intriguing dips—when she swept her still elevated leg around to the side and back to center, affording him flashes of her satiny pink parts.

Cheeks flushed, eyes bright, she looked him in the eye. And demanded, "You in?"

He caved like a cheap paper plate. "I'm in." And he tackled her, taking her down onto his bed.

She squeaked, but gave him a cool-eyed look as he pushed up on his palms to loom over her. "Good," she said. "I'm up for doing this until we go our separate ways if you are. But if so, we need to establish a few ground rules."

The idea of ground rules generated an unfamiliar resistance. It didn't make sense since he was generally all about laying his cards on the table. Still… "There are no rules in sex."

"Please. There are rules in everything."

"Like places I can't touch you?" he demanded. "Things you won't let me do?" His gaze was slow and thorough as it traveled over her from the top of her head to where his fully clothed body met the blond triangle where they'd fit together if he were as naked as she. He winced slightly at the abrasions she'd gathered on her trip through the rapids this morning, but didn't lose track of his goal. Meeting her eyes once again, he licked his lips. "Because I can make you like them all."

"Ooh." She performed a sensuous little supine wiggle, which did interesting things to her beautiful beige-nippled breasts. "I like the sound of that. But I'm talking more about what happens when the sexin' is done."

Some of the heat dimmed in her eyes and for the first time she avoided his gaze. "I'm not good at relationships. So that's not what this will be."

Best of all worlds, he assured himself. Just sex, with none of the clinging and being overburdened with all her personal shit.

And yet… "Define *not good*."

"I just…don't do them. I've tried occasionally, but either I mess things up or I actually do things right, but people disappear from my life, anyhow. Either way, I learned a long time ago it's easier just not to have expectations." She ran her fingers through her hair, pushing it off her face. "Look," she said, pinning him in place with the weightiness of her attention, "I know I have issues I'm long overdue addressing. But who can afford therapy?"

"Someone with insurance?"

"Yeah, okay, those people. But unless I get hired on another movie like the one I had to turn down, that's not even a glimmer on my horizon." She essayed a facial shrug. "I've told you what I do for a living. It's hardly in the neighborhood of a nine-to-five gig loaded with Bennies." She looked at him through a pale forest of lashes. "And frankly, Kavanagh? You don't sound like a steady-relationship kind of guy, yourself."

"I haven't been so far, although I've told you that may change. But whether it does or it doesn't, I have a condition of my own."

The look she leveled on him was chock-full of suspicion. "And what might that be?"

"We agree to be honest with each other. If something doesn't work we say so and why."

"Isn't that what we're doing already? Neither of us has been particularly shy about voicing our opinions."

"True. But there's just something about sex and ch—" Recognizing trouble when he heard it tripping off his own tongue, he shut the hell up.

Unfortunately, too late. "Tell me you were *not* about to say sex and chicks," she said.

"Okay, I wasn't going to say—"

She gave him a shot to the shoulder. "You so were!"

He grasped her wrists and pressed them down on the mattress next to her head. "You might not want to get too handsy with me, darlin'. When you're this close, touching me and wearing nothing but that pretty, pretty skin, my dick's all about the naked wrestling."

"And yet in your mind it's women who can't stay rational when sex is on the menu."

"I know," he said deep in his throat and bent his head to kiss the side of her neck. God, she tasted sweet. "What was I thinking?" He pressed another open-mouthed kiss a bit lower, smiling a little when her breath hitched and she shifted restlessly beneath him. "Do you really want to spend our one night in an honest-to-God bed arguing about this?"

"No." She licked her lips. "I want you to get naked, too."

"I can do that." He shoved back and rose to his feet at the end of the bed. Looking at her bare sprawl atop the bed made him feel almost as if he might start to beg. Jesus, he could almost hear the words pouring from his mouth—*please, baby, please, baby, please.*

He stiffened. Finn Kavanagh didn't beg any woman. Ripping his shirt off over his head, he tossed it aside the moment it cleared his face. Then he focused his attention back on her.

She lay with her hands where he'd placed them, next to her face, her fingers loosely curled toward her palms. Her thighs, however, were pressed together as if to hide that gorgeous little blond pelt between them, which he now knew, even if he couldn't currently see all of it, had been waxed from the midway point of her labial lips down. "Spread your legs."

"What?" she said blankly. But he noticed that her nipples shot on point.

His cock followed suit. "You heard me. I'll strip for you but I want to see that sweet pu—" The word dried on his tongue as she did what she was told and spread them. "Jesus," he whispered hoarsely. "That's gotta be one of the wonders of the world. America oughta have a national monument dedicated to it."

"Yeah, maybe they could add it to Mount Rushmore," she agreed drily. "They have all those busts of American presidents. All that's missing is Deluca's vajiggy."

He laughed, shoved his pants down his legs and kicked free. "Bet you'd have a helluva lot more climbers scaling you than Roosevelt's nose."

He wasn't sure if she heard him; she'd pushed up onto her elbows and seemed pretty preoccupied with staring at his dick, which had sprung out in happy relief when he'd released it from the constriction of his khakis. She licked her lips.

He licked his own. "Wanna kiss it?" He knew he should stop talking trash to her, but he couldn't help himself, he got such a charge out of teasing her. Mostly she was a shock-proof, take-no-prisoners kind of woman. But she had these little pockets of innocence, times when he could tell he *had* shocked her, and he loved finding—and exploiting—them.

Apparently this wasn't one of those times, however, for she merely said, "Yes," and rolled up onto all fours to cat prowl across the bed toward him.

And oh, sweet mother Mary, watching her coming at him just fried his brain.

She halted inches away and without hesitation leaned

right in to press a prim little close-lipped kiss on the head of his dick.

Finn's breath exploded from his lungs, which seemed to tickle her, for she shot him a faint knowing smile. Then without taking her eyes from his face, she lapped the flat of her tongue up the length of his cock and bumped over the flange of the head to the slit in its crown. She took her time tickling that with the tip of her tongue.

Watching it happen, *feeling* it and seeing her open her mouth wider to suck him inside, he bent to grab her shoulders. Hardest thing he'd ever done, but he couldn't believe what a hair trigger she gave his dick every time she came near it.

The maneuver pushed his hips away from her even as he hauled her up onto her knees. Ordinarily he wasn't one to turn down a blow job, but nothing about sex with Magdalene was goddamn ordinary. He wasn't thrilled about it, but he didn't have the first idea how he'd go about reversing the phenomenon. Where she was concerned, years of experience seemed to go up in smoke.

But, dammit, he *was* more experienced than she was—he'd put money on it. And if he couldn't take command of this situation, right here, right now, he might as well turn in his man card.

There wasn't a woman on earth had the power to make him do that. "You under the illusion you're in charge here?"

"Who said anything about being in charge? You asked if I wanted to kiss it, I said yes and I kissed it."

She grinned at him. "French-kissed it, in fact. If you didn't want me to, why ask?"

Yeah, Kavanagh, why ask? Hell if he planned to tell her he'd thought it was a way to keep the upper hand. So he ignored the question. "I like you on your hands and knees. But turn around."

He loved the way sexual direction seemed to turn her on. She was by no stretch of the imagination a compliant woman. Yet without protest, she whipped around and presented him with the curve of her long, pale back and that pretty heart-shaped ass—which she wiggled at him as she looked at him over her shoulder.

He gave one smooth cheek a spank with the flat of his hand as he climbed onto the bed to kneel behind her. "You are a saucy wench, I'll give you that."

"You have no idea. Give me five minutes where I was a minute ago and I'll show you just how saucy I can be."

That made his already hard cock impossibly harder, and he bent over her back. Reaching around her side with one hand, he palmed a breast even as he opened his mouth over the muscle where her right shoulder met her neck, gripping it lightly between his teeth.

She froze beneath him. Then she shuddered.

Whispered, "Oh, God, Finn!"

And pressed her butt back against his hard-on. Her nipple turned diamond hard and he caught it between his thumb and index finger to give it closer attention.

She began to pant.

Jesus. She had to be the most responsive women he'd ever been with. Reluctant to abandon her plush tit, but needing one hand planted on the bed for stability, he smoothed the one he'd been teasing her with down her diaphragm, her abdomen. He dipped his forefinger briefly into the shallow cup of her navel before stroking it down the soft hair crowning her mound and into the wet, slick slit between her legs.

Simultaneously, they inhaled sharp, deep breaths and he raised his head from her neck. Mags reached between them, groping for his cock.

"Wait," he said as her fingers closed around him and began tugging his dick toward her opening. "I want to look at you while I fuck you. I want to see you when you come."

She set him loose and flipped over onto her back, scooting up toward the boardless head of the bed. He dived face-first across the corner of the bed to hook the shoulder straps of his pack and haul it onto the mattress. It was already unzipped and he dug through it for his bag of condoms.

It only took him seconds, yet it was enough time to realize that what he wanted with Magdalene wasn't simple fucking. He wasn't a complete cretin—he liked women. He didn't think of them as just fucks.

Okay, he occasionally did.

But he'd never slept with a woman he didn't genuinely enjoy talking to as well. But Mags…

She was in a class of her own. And he wanted to make lo— No. He couldn't say he ever did that. But he wanted to take his time with her.

Show her a little tenderness, which he'd done damn little of last time.

He grabbed out a handful on condoms and lifted his upper body back on the bed.

Mags was lying on her side, her head propped in her hand, watching him. "Think you've got enough protection, there, cowboy?" She cut her eyes toward the wrappers in his fist and raised her brows.

"For starters."

One corner of her mouth tilted up. "I have to say, I admire your confidence."

"Yeah?" He scooted up to face her, mimicking her posture. "You're not exactly a slouch in that department, yourself."

She flashed him that pleased, sweet smile that grabbed him by the balls and showed no inclination to let loose every damn time he saw it.

"That's true, I'm not," she agreed. But if she were trying to hide from him the way his saying so had tickled her, it wasn't working.

"Ah, man." He reached to wrap a hand around her nape. "You do things to me, Magdalene. Crazy, wicked things that mess with my head." And scooting closer, he moved in to kiss her.

He'd been around the track more than a time or two—hell, more than Secretariat, Seattle Slew and War Admiral combined—so kissing should have been the least of what they planned to do to each other. Yet it didn't feel like a "least." It felt so damn fresh every time he kissed her amazing lips, every time he got within licking distance of her flavors. And he wanted more of them.

He wanted them *all*. Including the ones he may have

licked off his fingers, but had yet to taste from the source. So after what could have been fifteen seconds or the same number of minutes, he slid his mouth from hers to kiss his way down her throat. As his lips moved lower, he eased her over onto her back and propped himself over her, lowering his chest to rub against her breasts in a long, luxurious undulation.

Her breath hitched in her throat for one second, two. Then she moaned low in her throat. He loved how responsive her nipples were and slowly he worked his way down to them. Cupping the full bottom curve of her right breast, he pressed it up to bring the hard bead of her nipple to his lowering mouth. Even as he wrapped his lips around it, he reached to toy with its mate.

And that was all it took to make Mags's hips perform a languid little horizontal bump and grind against the bed's top sheet.

Finn smiled against her breast, letting the nipple slide free. Releasing the other nipple he'd finessed, he scooted lower.

"Oh," she murmured in disappointed tones as she arched her back and shifted restively. "*No.* Don't stop."

"I'll give you something that'll make you feel even better," he promised. And slid down her body.

He loved the feel of her skin. It was so smooth and so soft, and he mapped it beneath his fingertips as he kissed his way down her diaphragm, her rib cage, her abdomen. Nothing, however, compared to the sleek wet furrow between her legs when he lowered himself to exhale upon it and his fingers finally arrowed in on their target.

"Oh," she breathed. "Oh, yeah, that is even better. Omigawd, right there!" she commanded as his forefinger quit circling her clitoris and bumped over the little ball bearing straining out of its hood.

But he was already sliding his finger down the slippery path bordered by plump outer lips and frilly inner ones until he reached her opening. Gently inserting a fingertip, he circled, dipping a bit deeper here, rubbing the ring protecting her entrance there. She started making breathy little noises and he had to resist the urge to either rock his cock against the sheets beneath them to get a little satisfaction for himself, or seat himself inside her to the root with one strong thrust.

Her hips rose and he slicked his finger back up her slit and thumbed her lips open. Then, looking up to meet her heavy-lidded gaze as she pushed up on her elbows to stare down at him, he lapped her the same way she had his dick, from her opening to her clit.

Another breathy "oh" exploded out of her throat and her elbows melted out from under her. She thrust her hips up as though trying to follow his tongue as it slipped down again to tickle the gates to her—what the hell had she called it, her vajiggy? Blocking everything else from his mind, he pressed her splayed thighs flat against the sheets. When he was sure she'd stay the way he'd left her—wide-open to him—he concentrated on driving her over the edge with his mouth and his fingers.

He could feel her getting closer...closer. But he continued to tease her, to bring her close only to back off. Finally, circling her clit with his lips, he tickled it with the tip of his tongue, then softly sucked. And hands gripping his hair, she exploded with a high-pitched little moan he took to be her version of a scream.

He stayed with her until the last clench and release faded and the hips she'd thrust ceilingward settled back on the bed. Then he pushed back and grabbed one of the rubbers he'd dumped on the mattress. Within seconds he was suited up and he dropped over her, catching himself on the palms planted by her shoulders. He thumbed down his erection, then aligned the head of his dick with her canal and slowly sank into the hot vise that was Magdalene's sex. It wrapped around him like a Chinese finger puzzle, enclosing him, *enveloping* him, clutching at his cock when he retracted his hips, massaging it with lubricious strength when he thrust deep again.

"God," he panted and lowered his head to kiss her for long seconds, minutes, years. When he finally raised his head, he gazed down at her. Her cheeks and lips were flushed with the blood that had risen to the surface of her skin and her eyes were heavy lidded and hot, the blue bluer than her day-to-day color. *Please, baby, please, baby, please.* "You are so fucking *hot* and you feel so good. I could rock inside you for years. Decades."

"Centuries," she said, tightening around him. Her head tipped back on her pillow, turning restlessly from one side to the other. The position thrust her breasts up at him. "You make me feel so-o-o good, Finn. You're so hard and you touch me in places...oh!" He'd shoved her knees up and caught her thighs in the crook of his

elbows as he fell forward, tilting her pelvis to give him a straight shot to her G-spot. He wanted desperately to hammer inside her like a runaway pile driver, but gritted his teeth as he held himself to a slow in-an-out. But his testicles were drawing up and he didn't know how much longer he could hold out. *Please, baby, please, baby, please.*

Dipping his head he captured her nipple and sucked it into his mouth.

"Oh, gawd," she panted. "Oh, my...harder?" she said hopefully. "Please, Finn, a little harder."

He thought she meant the pressure on her nipple, but her hands slapped down on his ass and tugged him to her.

"That's it, baby," he muttered and pulled almost all the way out before slamming back in. Pulled back and slammed in.

And bless her, Mags's breath started that "Oh, God, I wanna come, I wanna come, I wanna come" rhythm that signified she was close. He adjusted her hips a fraction of an inch until he felt his cock slide against a knotty roughness again. Thrusting hard, he held, oscillating his hips to stay in contact with the spot.

And she almost—*almost*—screamed his name as she clenched and released around him, her breath shuddery and fast, and her fingernails raking across his hard cheeks, almost but luckily not quite scraping furrows in them.

It set off his own climax and he ejaculated hard and long inside the channel that still clasped him so securely.

When the last shudder of satisfaction faded, he disengaged his inner arms from behind her knees and carefully straightened out her legs. Then he slid in a heap atop her. He was wiped out, but raised himself long enough to look down at her. "You tell me this was a one-time thing again and I won't be responsible for my actions."

She blinked up at him, then gave him a sleepy smile. "Got it. Luckily for me, I guess, I had no plans to tell you that."

"All righty, then," he said and made himself comfortable atop her until she was ready to do this again.

CHAPTER NINETEEN

SINCE THEY HAD no way of knowing how many people would be on the train, Mags and Finn arrived at the station early the following morning. Neither of them had thought to ask the stationmaster last night. Vacating their room was fine with her. She had been filled with gratitude, in fact, for the bustle of gathering their belongings because she honestly hadn't known quite how to handle waking up in Finn's arms.

She'd like to lay that entirely on him. It would let her keep the sense of comfort and security that being all wrapped up in him, skin to skin, had given her—which, Lord love her, had been even better than she'd imagined it would be—with none of the accountability. But she'd awakened to find one of her arms flung diagonally across his chest and her hand curled around his strong neck. Plus she'd been draped half on top of him, her right leg tangled intimately between his from calf to crotch.

Not that there was anything wrong with that. Still, she wasn't a stay-the-night kind of woman, so this was new territory for her. And she didn't actually sleep around much these days. Discounting her showerhead, it had probably been two or three years since she'd gotten any sat-is-fact-shun. God knew she'd participated in her share of indiscriminate sex as a teen. She'd surrendered her virginity way too young and had slept with far too many boys who, once they'd gotten theirs, hadn't even pretended to give a flying flick about her.

And who could blame them? It wasn't as if she'd made them work for it. If you didn't respect yourself, you could hardly kick when nobody else did, either.

She cast a glance at Finn as they walked down the outdoor platform to the first of the three cars attached to an engine that looked as though it'd rolled off the factory floor during Grover Cleveland's administration. He climbed the metal two-step connecting the platform to the car, twisting to look inside.

Only to promptly step off again. "Full."

"Holy crap." She met his gaze. "It's a good thing we decided to get here early."

He nodded his agreement. "Let's hope not everyone else decided the same thing and got here even earlier."

They lucked out toward the back of the second car. It was definitely filling up, but there was still an available wooden high-backed bench on the right. Mags put her tote on the floor under the window while Finn swung his backpack onto the rickety overhead rack.

If trains came with rafters, their car would have been packed to them by the time the engine rumbled to life. More people crowded the benches than the benches were designed to hold, chickens in crates were stacked up in the aisle-three seats and a goat bleated behind them. Finn stood his ground when a family of five tried to crowd onto their bench built for four and already occupied by the two of them, sitting solidly between her and their attempt to shove him over. Glaring at him in disgust, they crowded onto someone else's bench and she and Finn ended up with a beefy twentysomething man and a boy of about six.

It came as no surprise that the car wasn't air-conditioned, but the good news was the windows opened. Mags enjoyed the almost cool breeze on her face as they chugged out of the station. The only thing she enjoyed maybe even more were the myriad conversations she eavesdropped on. The more entertaining ones, she translated for Finn.

And she felt...happy.

Several hours later, the bloom was off her pleasure. Her butt felt numb, she was hungry and her bladder was near to bursting, but she'd been in the bathroom once already and the longer she could put off revisiting that particular horror show, the happier she would be. She managed not to squirm in her seat, but her stomach felt no compunction about emitting a low growl in protest over its emptiness.

Their train wasn't exactly a bastion of quiet, but Finn, who had pulled the bill of his baseball cap low over his eyes and slid onto his tailbone to doze, once again demonstrated his bat-like hearing when he turned his head against the back of the seat and said, "Y'hungry, darlin'?"

"Starved."

"Sorry. I really slept like the dead for a while there." Yawning, he pulled himself upright on the hard bench and stretched with enough vigor to make cracking/

popping sounds in his joints. "I'll get the backpack down." He looked at her. "You need to use the can?"

"Oh, God, I really do. But, Finn, that room is a disgusting *pit*."

"What's worse, though, doing your biz real quick in crappy—you'll pardon the pun—conditions, or trying to hold your bladder, only to have it scream at you forever?"

"Well, when you put it like that," she said grumpily, which made him laugh and reach over to scrub the crown of her head with his knuckles as if she were a twelve-year-old kid. He added insult to injury by pretending not to notice when she sulkily jerked her head out of reach.

"C'mon," he said, rising to his feet. "I'll clear the way for us, then get some stuff out for lunch while you use the pit."

She had to admit she felt much cheerier when she got back, and even better still once they'd eaten a portion of the provisions they'd bought at the bodega the night before. As Finn returned the pack to the overhead rack, she noticed the young boy straining to see out of her window from his position two seats away. Leaning forward, she invited him to sit by the window for a while.

He eagerly accepted. His name, she learned, was Maximilliano and for quite some time he knelt with his arms braced on the narrow sill and his head out the window like a puppy on a joyride.

But he didn't believe in enjoying the view in silence. Instead, he kept turning to her with a smile that showcased a big new front tooth alongside an empty gap to point out some species of wildlife—or anything else of interest he spotted, be it the colors of a patch of flowers, a particularly brilliant bird or a sinuous emerald boa with a white dorsal line that he spotted as it looped back and forth on itself while settling on one of the tree branches.

She hadn't spent much time around kids and even as she enjoyed his enthusiasm, she found his nonstop chatter kind of exhausting.

Apparently, it was even more tiring for him, for he began to yawn. At one point, he actually laid his head down, resting his right cheek atop his arms on the sill. His eyes slid closed and stayed that way for a couple seconds before he forced them open again. Mags had the feeling he'd fight sleep to the bitter end and, remembering the chocolate bar she'd bought last night, something she'd totally forgotten until this moment, she pulled her tote up onto her lap and dug through her stuff until she located it.

Maximilliano watched with big eyes as she ripped open the paper and split the bar into three pieces. She offered the largest one to him with the suggestion that he sit down to eat it, then gave the second to Finn and kept the last piece for herself. She enjoyed watching the boy's absorbed delight as he slowly savored the treat. She hadn't realized how much she'd come to take for granted after years spent living in America.

When the candy bar was gone, Maximilliano circled his tongue around his lips, paying special attention to the corners, then carefully licked each finger until he'd removed every vestige of melted chocolate.

Leaning around Finn, the boy's father instructed Maximilliano to thank the senor and senora for sharing their window seat and their candy and to come sit with him now. Mags didn't bother to correct her marital status; she simply returned a gentle *"De nada"* when the child followed his instructions.

When she looked over a few moments later, Maximilliano was slumped against his father's side, sound asleep. She turned away with a smile to look out the window once more.

She couldn't say how much time had passed when she suddenly sat forward in her seat.

Finn, who had been dozing next to her again—how on earth did he *do* that on this uncomfortable bench?— jerked and turned to look at her, fully alert. "What is it?"

Unexpected tears rose to her eyes, but she did her best to blink them back. "Home," she said, turning to him with a tremulous smile. "At least…it's starting to look like the area where I spent the most time back when I still lived here."

"Yeah?" His face alight with interest, he leaned around her to peer out the window, his shoulder and side a warm, hard brand against hers. Almost as quickly he shook his head and straightened back up to give her a puzzled look. "I don't get it. It looks exactly like it did the last time I looked at the scenery."

She whipped around to stare out the window again herself and saw that he was correct. It took a moment to straighten things out in her own mind, but she finally turned back and said, "We're entering the top of the Amazon basin and the lines of demarcation weren't drawn with a ruler. So we'll go in and out of it for a while. But that shouldn't last long—pretty soon, now, we'll be fully in the rain forest."

"Are you nervous?"

"I probably should be, considering I've spent far more years away than I ever spent living here—and you and I will likely have to make our way on foot, perhaps from as soon as we reach our station." She laughed, however, and thought wryly that if her expression were anywhere in the neighborhood of matching the way she felt at this moment, she must be lit up like a Texas stadium on game night.

And she admitted easily, "But I'm not—not even a little. I'm excited. God, just so completely excited. I loved it here as a kid and to finally *be* here...well, I'm more thrilled than I can say." The light shining through the windows suddenly dimmed and she whipped around.

"There!" she said, reaching back to grasp his hand without taking her attention off the view. She ended up latching on to his wrist instead, but she simply worked her hand down his until she could thread their fingers together. And gave them a squeeze. "*That's* what I'm talking about, Finn—that's Amazonia. The canopy sucks up most of the light, which is why it's greenish down here on the floor and, as you can see, dim and murkyish.

"What I don't know," she admitted, reluctantly prying her attention away from the addictive rain forest and swiveling around to face him again, "is whether goons will be waiting for us at the station. Joaquin didn't strike me as the smartest guy in town, but we've been steadily heading in the direction of Munoz's drug farm, so he has to have at least considered we'll try to break Nancy and Brian out of it. And if he's bright enough to figure that out he must realize the station we're heading toward is one of Amazonia's likely entry points." Lowering her chin, she rubbed the furrow she felt gathering between her brows as all the potential problems started edging out her momentary euphoria.

"*One of* being the important part to remember," Finn said matter-of-factly. "It's *one of* the possibilities, Mags. It's by no means the only one."

Moving just her eyes, she looked up at him. "I wish I'd tried harder to find some hair dye. Problem is, everyone in this country already has dark hair and apparently even women going gray don't use it because the few boxes I saw were blond and red. The latter of which," she added, "I should have gotten. Guys can be very literal at times. If they were instructed to look for a blonde, they might have overlooked a redhead."

"Quit beating yourself up," he said in that nononsense voice of his that smoothed out the budding hysteria sending out threatening feelers. "We both know how good you are at disguise by makeup—so get cookin' on that."

She straightened her shoulders. "You're right. And we both need to change into long pants, long-sleeved T-shirts and closed-toe shoes. Which—ugh—means a longer time in the loo, but there's no help for it. A bazillion more insects inhabit the Amazon than we've run into so far." She loosened her hold on his hand and dragged her tote up onto her lap. "I've got bug spray in here somewhere—we'll put some on when we reach our destination.

"Crap." She blinked at him as consternation pleated her brows. "That's *if* we even reach it while the sun's still up. I didn't think to ask the stationmaster how long this trip would take."

"No sense borrowing trouble at this point," Finn said in that easy way he had of dealing with the negative possibilities they bumped up against, as if nothing—*nothing*—was insurmountable. "Let's just assume, if we get in late, that they'll have a hotel or hostel or whatever to accommodate travelers. And if they don't—" He shrugged. "Hey, we've always got the tent. We'll figure out a way to make things work."

She threw her arms around his neck and hugged him, rubbing her smooth cheek against his harder one. Bristles were already displacing the close shave he'd given it. Pulling back, she smacked a kiss on his lips, then pressed her face forehead-to-forehead, nose-to-nose, with his. That brought him so close his face was a blur, but she didn't care. "Have I told you how grateful I am that you threw in your lot with me? I honestly don't know how I would have handled all this on my own."

"You kidding me?" Leaning back a little, he grinned down at her. "You would have figured it out just fine. You're smart, you're resourceful and you're brilliant with makeup. Face it, you've gotten us away from the goons more often through the use of your makeup kit and costumes than because of anything I've done."

"I don't think that's necessarily true, but thanks for saying so, anyhow."

"It damn well is, but you're welcome." He cupped her face in his hands and pulled back enough so they could see each other without going cross-eyed in the attempt. He kissed her gently, then dropped his hands to his lap. "Now get busy. Paint yourself up to look like a senorita."

It was growing late when Joaquin's cell phone rang its person-specific ring. "This had better be good news, Palmer," he said the instant he thumbed it on. But hope scratched for entrance in his brain. Because maybe finally—finally!—he could call Munoz to tell him he had the Deluca woman.

"I'm sorry, Boss," Palmer said. "I broke my leg on the trip down the river."

"You told me you knew rivers!"

"I know the *Mississippi* River, but that ain't got no motherfucking rapids—something nobody bothered to warn me this one had before I started down it! I'm lucky I got out alive. As it is, I swallowed half the river. The boat broke up on the rocks and it was only because another boat came along that I got off with just the broken leg—it coulda easily been my neck."

Works for me, Joaquin thought viciously, but didn't say so out loud. The mercenary had at least been actively trying to capture the Deluca woman. And to be fair—something Joaquin was having a difficult time doing at the moment—he'd been injured in the commission of that attempt.

So Joaquin would have to…what did the Americans call it? Suck it up? Yes. He took several deep breaths to get this rage in his blood under control, then sucked it up and inquired, "Where are you?"

"Those people who fished me out of the river and pumped the water outta my lungs brought me to Rio de Villanueva, where a doc set my leg. It's the same town we figured Deluca and her muscle were headed. So, as soon as my pain pill kicks in I'll see if anyone remembers them. She's a damn blonde—you can't tell me she didn't stick out in this dark-haired burgh like a lap dancer in church. Soon's I getcha some information, you can at least send someone else after her."

"That would be good. Call me back the minute you know something."

They disconnected and Joaquin paced his office. This was *not* good. *¡Dios mío!* Not good at all. That bitch Deluca kept giving his men the slip and he'd had to come up with creative ways to avoid telling Munoz.

The drug czar was losing patience, however—that became increasingly clear with every telephone conversation they'd had. And no one needed to tell Joaquin twice that an impatient Munoz could be very, very detrimental to his health.

He'd said it before, but at this point it simply couldn't be said enough. His future wasn't looking bright.

And maybe, just maybe, it was time he started considering an exit strategy.

CHAPTER TWENTY

THE SUN'S TRAJECTORY was in a flaming free fall toward the horizon when Finn and Mags's train chugged into their station. Finn was ambivalent about finally reaching it. The past half hour hadn't been a whole lotta fun, since he and Mags had spent it debating whether or not they should leave the train separately.

He suppressed a snort. Hell, why pretty it up? They'd spent it arguing, a word a helluva lot more accurate than *debating*.

Because Finn was nowhere near as pumped at the idea of splitting up as Magdalene seemed to be. He got that as diversionary tactics went, this was a good one. The men sent to hunt them would be on the lookout for a blonde woman accompanied by a man. Joaquin had to know by now that she was damn good at, the very least, covering up her hair. But damn few people mistook *him* for anything other than the American he was—even though his coloring reflected that of the general population of El Tigre, he stood out. It didn't mean he liked the idea of not being right there if she ran into trouble.

Because, no two ways about it, he didn't like it. Not one damn bit.

He felt a little less stressed about it, however, when

he saw her fall in step with Maximilliano and his dad just as they reached the exit vestibule between this car and the last one. She'd wanted Finn to stay a good ten feet away from her, but the best he could do was slouch along behind her with maybe three feet between them. Four, max. Still, he was relieved she'd latched on to the kid's father. Because the guy was big. Not merely tall, but built with massive shoulders, thighs the size of tree trunks and muscular arms that looked like they had a nice long reach. Finn wouldn't hesitate to bet on most people thinking twice before messing with him.

Even goons with guns, who had likely been instructed not to use them in well-populated situations.

Plus, as she chatted with Maximilliano's father—to whom she was no doubt spinning some amusing tale to explain her sudden impulse to cover up her blond hair and darken her skin with cosmetics—the child tugged Mags's hand for attention on her other side.

They looked like a family.

When he reached the door, he kept one eye on their progress while also casting swift glances around to see who, if anyone, might look interested in them—or him, for that matter. There were several single men hanging around, but two he discounted right off the bat. A couple of others were harder to peg. They were much tougher-looking than the first guys he'd written off, but it was impossible to tell if they were searching for Mags and him, or were simply tough-looking guys waiting for a family member to exit the train.

Someone behind him made an impatient noise and, eschewing the steps, he jumped down onto the platform.

He couldn't say why, exactly, but he felt more conspicuous by himself than he ever had with Mags.

Ahead of him a young man struggled to carry a stack of chicken crates. Since everyone had to exit through the station, Finn strode up to him and offered to lend a hand. At least, he hoped he'd asked if he could help with that—and hadn't insulted the guy's ancestry.

The boy—for that's what Finn saw he was now that he was up close—looked at him suspiciously for a moment. Then he looked at the crates stacked almost as high as his less-than-brawny shoulders and nodded.

"Gracias," he said, then added something in rapid Spanish that Finn thought was a lament about the kid's worthless brother not showing up after he'd promised to help. Or maybe that was his own experience projecting, having had brothers who'd shirked their own share of duties in their younger days.

Still, he'd recognized *el hermano* as brother, so he didn't think he was completely off base.

They split the pile between them, the hens in his crates smelled surprisingly pleasant, sort of a combination of sun and corn. By the time they got organized and were on the move toward the station house, they were a good ten feet behind Magdalene after all. He had to crane around the side of his crates to keep her in sight, but that also had the advantage of making him nothing more than legs carrying chickens to anyone who might be looking for the *americano* accompanying Mags Deluca.

The men waiting on the platform remained outside when first Magdalene and her party, then he and the kid tromped into the station. They crossed toward the exit on the other side of the narrow waiting room.

Happily, neither did anyone suspicious-looking lurk out front when they exited into the warm golden wash that was the last of the evening light.

He'd barely taken three steps from the entrance door when a boy who looked even younger than the kid he accompanied rushed up. If his tone and Finn's less-than-fluent comprehension of the language were anything to go by, he was apologizing profusely for his tardiness.

The boy he'd been helping set down his crates and smacked his brother on the back of the head with the flat of his hand. But he turned to heap lavish thanks upon Finn, who relinquished his share of the crated chickens to the other boy. Grinning, Finn took his leave, lengthening his stride to catch up with Mags. He arrived just as she was saying goodbyes of her own.

She turned to him as soon as their former seatmates walked away. "Tomas said there is a hotel in town *and* he gave me the name of a cheap restaurant with good food." She flashed him a big smile. "Life is good."

"For today, at least."

She shrugged. "Seems to me living minute to minute is about all we can do."

That wasn't necessarily a bad policy, given their situation, he decided a short while later as they opened the door to their hotel room and hauled their belongings inside.

In order for Mags to remain in disguise, they decided to grab dinner first and shower when they got back. They spent the next hour slowly unwinding with drinks and steaming plates of beautifully prepared food. After their meal, he stood on the walkway while Magdalene talked to some locals about the best route through the Amazon to the general area of Munoz's grow farm. An old guy drew them a map on the back of a paper bag and she thanked him profusely before carefully folding it into her tote. Then they headed off to buy more provisions.

Back in the hotel, Mags started shedding her clothing the minute they shut their room door behind them. Leaving a trail of discarded duds in her wake, she made a beeline for the bathroom to run a shower. He gave her five minutes of privacy, then let himself into the room.

Steam billowed over the shower rod and he watched as the cotton shower curtain to the little stall adhered to her shoulder and elbow at one point, then to her very nice butt when she bent to—hell, he didn't know what—shave her legs, maybe? Wash her feet?

He didn't really care why, his only thought was to get in there with her.

He kicked off his pants—the only thing he hadn't already stripped off in the other room—and slid a condom on his already raging dick, then ripped back the curtain in a whoosh of fabric, clattering rings and additional clouds of steam.

With a squeak, Magdalene whirled to face him, her posture defensive, combative. That brief I'll-fight-you-to-the-death attitude quickly turned to recognition, however, when he climbed in with her. Leaping on him, she twined her legs around his waist and her arms about his neck. Lifting herself up to meet his mouth, she kissed him hotly. The water had run cold by the time they climbed out again.

But they were both relaxed and smiling.

He patted her dry with the thin towel, noticing for the first time that her skin was washed clean of all the makeup she'd applied earlier. Then he swiped the now damp towel over himself while she did the girlie thing and slathered lotion all over that baby-fine skin. When she was done, he swooped her up in his arms and carried her back to the bed, where he settled them both, him on his back and Mags curled against him with her head on his chest, her ear pressed against his heart and her arm looped loosely around his neck.

He looked down at her, soft and sleepy in his arms. "Talk to me."

Yawning, she raised her eyes to look up at him. "Hmmm?"

"Tell me something about yourself that you haven't told many people."

"CRAP." MAGS ROLLED away from Finn. Feeling naked where she hadn't twenty seconds ago, she looked around for something to put on.

Finn turned onto his side and braced his head in his palm. "What the hell, Mags?"

"Why do people always want to talk about all that touchy-feely stuff?" She honestly didn't get it. It only led to raised hopes and she knew from hard-earned experience that hope was a bitch just waiting to kick your teeth down your throat.

His face lost its amusement. "Why are you always so emotionally standoffish?"

"Oh, will you give the emotional dodge-'em accusations a rest? I connect with people all the time!" And if her sociability was a way to fill a lonely void that had chiseled a permanent home deep inside of her? Well, she felt no need to air her dirty laundry for everyone in the known universe to paw through.

She blinked. Okay, Finn wasn't "everyone." Still, he was poking a raw nerve.

"Yeah, we've established you're the goddamn life of the party. It doesn't make you emotionally available."

True. And every now and then she hit the wall and just couldn't bring herself to be "on" yet one more time. But if she went to a venue where people hung out laughing and talking, it was almost enough to sit quietly and eavesdrop on the conversations of folks who were unafraid to conduct relationships.

She didn't fool herself—she *knew* that made her pathetic, which was not a feeling she tolerated well. But she sure as hell had no desire to drag her loser tendencies out to be analyzed like one of those idiots from daytime TV who seemed actually *proud* about spilling their guts and thus demonstrating how ridiculous they were to people who, up until then, might have only suspected as much.

Dammit. Now her back was really up, but she tried her utmost to rein in her temper before she ended up spewing it wholesale all over Finn.

Only to instead do what people who felt cornered had been doing since the earth's crust cooled: she turned it around on him. "Seriously? The man ho is questioning *my* ability to commit? Hello, pot. Black much?"

He shrugged. "I work hard and I play hard and I've always liked a frequent changeup in my playmates. I know I can be a little emotionally distant myself, but that's kind of my point. Like recognizes like, baby. I, at least, am attempting to put that attitude behind me."

"Well, bully for you."

"He-e-yy," he said softly and pushed upright, swinging around to sit facing her, supremely unself-conscious in his nudity. "How did this go from you coming around me so hard and sweet it damn near blew the top of my head off to all this anger?"

Fair question. "I'm sorry," she said stiffly. "I'm not good at the deep stuff. But you already knew that, since that's what this whole conversation is about. So you want me to tell you something not many people know? I'm...lonely, okay? Pretty much all the time."

Oh, God. That made her sound too pitiful for words and damned if Mags Deluca would be pitied. Chin up, she said, "But here's something juicier that *nobody* knows. Remember when I told you how I was all about the risk when I was a kid? I slept with half the lacrosse team at the Camden Boys Academy before I turned fifteen and—"

"Wait, what? Back up a minute, Speedy Riggs. You slept with half a lacrosse team?"

She shrugged. "It seemed like a good idea at the time."

He stared at her. "Like a gang bang? All of them at once."

"Ewww." She didn't need a mirror to know her expression was a study in horrified disgust. "*No*. One at a time's not stupid enough for you? I thought it was a big *fuck you* at my parents. But I finally realized the only one I was hurting was myself, because it left me feeling, God, so icky. So I quit sleeping with boys I felt no honest attraction to, which didn't happen until I was quite a bit older."

And, oh, God, just shoot me now. He sat there looking so stunned and she pushed onto her hands and knees with no thought in her head as to where she'd go—she simply wanted to remove herself from this humiliating situation.

But before she could scramble for the door, he hooked a muscular arm around her waist and tumbled her onto his lap. Settling her as easily as he might a forty-pound child, he then wrapped a long hand halfway around her head and pressed her face against his bare chest.

"Aw, darlin', I'm sorry," he said, his voice above her head not only as dark and smooth as a bolt of black velvet, but a subterranean rumble beneath her ear as well. "I've been surrounded by people all my life, so I had help when I screwed up. But you had no support system for your mistakes. I can only imagine how rough that must have been."

She shrugged, wanting him to believe she was too tough to be overset by her screwups. But to her horror tears threatened to breech the dam with a flood of biblical proportions.

Dammit, she'd learned young to defend herself against just about anything. But this sympathy thing—

That was a killer.

Through sheer force of will, she got herself under control and surreptitiously blotted her tears against the swell of his pec, counting on the fan of hair growing sleek and black atop it to absorb the wetness leaking over her lower lids. For a second, when he stilled, she feared he'd felt them and would now feel *sorry* for her, a concept so abhorrent her skin literally itched with mortification.

But he merely shifted slightly, causing her cheek to slide closer to the muffled thump of his heart beating strongly beneath the hard, safe haven of his chest. And for a few comforting moments he held her close with no apparent need to say anything at all.

Then he slapped her on the ass and rolled her over onto her side so that she faced away from him. Spooning his long body behind hers, he wrapped his arm around her waist, jerked her back snugly against him and said gruffly, "Get some sleep. I have a feeling tomorrow is going to be a long day."

CHAPTER TWENTY-ONE

"HOLY SHIT." Finn strode behind Mags on a trail that was all but nonexistent. "It's hotter 'n hell in here."

"It's the humidity," she said, glancing over her shoulder, and by the sweat dewing her face and throat, he realized she was no more immune to the enervating heat than he was. She'd seemed so in her element since they'd entered the rain forest late this morning that he'd assumed it was just him struggling with the moisture-weighted heat.

There had been humidity all along, but nothing like this. *This* was so palpable he could literally feel it entering his lungs like a viscous gas with every breath he drew.

For the first time since they'd started running from Joaquin, he felt out of his comfort zone—and it wasn't just the weather. It was being in a place that made him distrust the effectiveness of his long-taken-for-granted skills. "Temperatures tend to stay at around eighty degrees at the equator," she added, "but the humidity from all the rain in the Amazon jacks the heat index up closer to ninety. I haven't been here for an age but I still remember how frigid it'd get at night, even though the actual temps are probably only around fifty degrees." She shot him a wry smile. "I know, no one would call that cozy, but it generally doesn't feel like the dead of winter, either. As with the heat, the constant damp messes with the line between actual temperatures and what it *feels* like they are."

Clearly done with that topic, she sketched an infinity in the air with the hiking pole he'd given her. "I know I've raved about your awesome pole before—"

He shot her a cocky grin and she gave him a *Seriously—are you for real*? look in return and said, "What are you, fourteen?" Then, as if she were that age herself, color flooded her cheeks. And it had jack all to do with the heat radiating off the rain-forest floor.

He had to hand it to her, though—she forged on as if she were taking high tea with the queen. "As I was saying, your *hiking* pole was awesome before, but it's particularly handy down here on the forest floor."

"No shit," he agreed, and admitted, "The Amazon's more of a challenge than I expected. I can't tell north from south or east from west since we got here, and I've always had an excellent sense of direction." The ground was thick with layers of deadfall comprised of downed trees, branches, leaves and a lot of detritus he plain didn't recognize. The path they'd been following was bouncy yet firm in some places, uneven in others and spongy or flat-out treacherous in yet others. Even only having a pole apiece provided a lot of stability.

"I'll teach you the way I learned to find north in the Amazon. Meanwhile I'm diggin' the pole."

Smiling at her with genuine delight, he admitted cheerfully, "I thought hiking poles were for sissies. My brother David had the first set I saw and the rest of us gave him a rash over it. I think 'girlie' might have come up in that conversation." More likely pussy...but as his ma used to tell him when he was a kid, he really didn't have to say everything that popped into his mind.

As it was, Mags scooped up a clump of he-couldn't-say-what and threw it at him.

He dodged the missile handily. "Bren was next to get bit by the HP bug when he bit off more than he could chew on a short hike with too much elevation gain for someone who'd only gotten a clean bill of health three months before. Big Brother went right out the day after we got home and bought his own pair." He shrugged. "But, c'mon, that's hardly a definitive vote, right? I mean, the guy had cancer."

She gave him a knowing look. "So, what made you a believer?"

"I strained a muscle. It wasn't bad and luckily it was at the tail end of a weeklong backpacking trip, but we were still a long way from the trailhead. David insisted I take his poles. And they were effin' amazing." He grinned.

"Thus sending you out to buy your own pair the next day as well."

"Hell, no," he said with faux affront. But he couldn't keep his mouth from crooking up. "I held out damn near an entire week."

She laughed and set off once again. Twenty minutes later she swore and came to a stop.

He stopped as well. "What's up?"

"We've gone in a circle." She indicated a leaf that

had been bent in half, showcasing its duller underside. Finn looked behind him and saw a noticeable number of similar ones standing out amidst the dense growth of brilliant green and realized she'd been doing that all along. "We need to backtrack to find where the trail branched off."

They found it about a hundred yards away, a narrow path that angled away from the one they were on and plunged into even deeper woods than those surrounding them now. They likely wouldn't have spotted it had they not been specifically searching for it.

The good news was that, within fifteen minutes of turning onto the new path, they came across a fast-flowing stream. It turned out to be a twofer since it was on the map the old guy had drawn them last night and it provided a much-needed source of drinking water. The thick, killer humidity had made them even thirstier than usual, but aside from the occasional leaf that had caught a tablespoon or so of pooled rainwater—only the clearest of which they'd dared drink—they hadn't seen much in the way of a water source since leaving their room this morning. He'd started rationing their portions for fear they'd run through all they'd brought with them and have no way of replenishing their supply.

Finn signaled Mags to hold up. "We need to refill our water containers."

They killed off the water left in his filtration water bottle, then he took it to the deepest part of the creek and filled it up. Next, he filled his backup storage bottle. "If we need the unfiltered water before we can make camp and boil it, I have some water-purifying pills that are the next best thing."

He peered up at the light filtering through the profuse, leafy canopy far overhead, then glanced at his watch. It wasn't yet five o'clock, but he'd read somewhere when he'd researched the area that in the more densely vegetated areas—which they definitely appeared to be in—5 percent or less sunlight made it all the way to the floor of the Amazon. Given how he'd felt as though they were hiking under a green glass dome, he'd say that was true. "And speaking of making camp, you think we oughta start looking for a spot?"

She, too, peered up at the vast canopy. "It's probably a good idea. I forgot how dim it can get down here." She glanced at the creek. "We need to hike to a higher place, though, away from the water."

"You sure? That seems counterintuitive."

"I know, but it was always the rule the few times I camped out as a kid. Higher ground was best. It had something to do with malaria and typhoid fever. Malaria is caused by mosquitoes, so staying away from stagnant puddles and ponds that are by-products of the creek makes sense. My knowledge is a lot sketchier when it comes to typhoid."

"Neither of us wants to risk exposure to either disease, though, so camping away from water it is."

They jumped the creek and climbed an increasingly steep slope on the other side, digging in their poles for balance where necessary and using the more vine-like vegetation to pull themselves up when the poles weren't enough. Finn carefully tested every patch of ground he managed to clear with the machete they'd picked up last night before he'd let Magdalene attempt it. They arrived at a small plateau just as it began to rain.

Dropping his pack by his feet, he pulled out the tent, separated out its fly and hung it from overhead branches for a shelter while he set up the tent. He squatted beneath the tarp to clear a spot but when he reached out to level the area by sweeping away part of the first stratum with his hands, Mags stopped him.

"Use a stick or your hiking pole to do that," she said. "Snakes tend to stake out spots beneath or in the lee of downed branches. Add a nest of leaves to that and they think it's the Four Seasons."

He managed to suppress a shudder, but *man*, he hated snakes. He hoped to hell she couldn't tell, because she seemed pretty copacetic with the whole hidden-carnivorous-reptiles thing, and he wasn't about to admit he was scared of something she wasn't. "You gotta be the first chick I've ever met who can speak neutrally about snakes."

"I hate the startle factor of them, but if I know they're there they don't bother me much. Spiders, now, that's a whole different story." She shivered. "Spiders are my kryptonite. Just talking about them gives me goose bumps down to my ankles."

"Hey, I'll kill your spiders if you kill my snakes."

"Deal. I'll even skin them out and roast them over a fire for dinner."

He gaped at her. "Tell me you're just screwing with my head."

She snorted. "Well, *yeah*." She let loose a huge belly

laugh. "God, you should see your face." Even as she messed with him, however, he noted the way she bent to give his hair a consoling little stroke.

"I might not be terrified of reptiles," she continued as she straightened once again, "but I'm sure as heck not getting within touching distance of one. Especially not one of those boas that can pretty much match a pickup for length, headlights to a freaking open tailgate."

Christ. "*There's* an image I could have lived without you planting in my brain."

She just grinned at him and he found himself smiling right back at her.

He was almost finished setting up camp when a troupe of howler monkeys swung through the treetops, heading in their direction. A couple of the smallest scrambled from branch to branch partway down a nearby tree to check them out. They stared silently and Finn pulled his camera out of the pack and zoomed in on them. He snapped a couple photos before one noticed him looking back at them through the viewfinder. The monkey threw back his head and, mouth open wide to display an impressive set of sharp teeth, let loose with the guttural, barking noise that was the breed's trademark. The other monkey simply stared at them as he placidly chewed a leaf. A few moments later both grew bored and chased off after the adults, who were now several trees ahead of them. Finn put his camera back in the pack and refocused on setting up the remainder of their camp.

Half an hour later, he and Magdalene sat in the tent with their feet outside, eating their newly heated meal and passing a bottle of red back and forth as they took turns drinking directly from it.

"We're only a day or so from where we think Munoz's grow farm is," he said. "We should probably talk about how we intend to spring your folks without getting captured ourselves." If the place was as tightly secured as he imagined it must be, their chances of actually freeing her parents without getting the Delucas and themselves killed were…well, not real good.

"Yeah," she agreed gloomily and knocked back another gulp from the neck she'd just wiped with her hand in preparation to sharing it with him. Lowering the bottle, she knuckled her bottom lip, where a drop of wine had nestled, looked at the smear it left on her finger, then licked it away. "Truth is," she said to her feet, "I've been kind of avoiding that."

Then she turned her head to look him directly in the eye. "Because after dragging you into my mess and coming up with my big plan to bust my parents out of Munoz's grow farm, I don't have the first idea how we're supposed to manage that."

"We need a diversion." He gave her a big, feral grin. "And for that we have Joaquin's gun."

"Omigawd," she said faintly. "We're going in guns—gun—blazing?" Her horrified eyes told him what she thought of that idea.

"Hell, no. The big problem, as I see it, is that Munoz probably has the perimeters of the grow farm rigorously patrolled. That's what I'd do, have a lot of men out there to make sure no one got in or out. So we'll watch them - until we know what the routine is, then set some traps.

If we can thin the ranks without getting caught, we'll set the traps again, build us the smallest smokeless fire we can get away with. Then, when it's nice and hot, we're tossing the J-man's bullets into it and getting the hell away from the area, because, darlin' that's gonna bring soldiers on the double. And while they're checking out the disturbance we'll try our damnedest to locate and extricate your folks."

Mags merely stared at him openmouthed and he shrugged apologetically. "I know," he said. "It's a far from awesome plan. But it's the best I can come up with without more in our arsenal than a handful of bullets, a decent amount of rope, the machete and my two flares, which we'll also utilize."

"Oh, God, are you kidding me?" She threw herself in his arms and smacked little soft-lipped kisses all over his face. "At least you have a plan. I had *nothing*. *Nada*—not a single freaking idea in my head. With my skill sets, what was I going to do, give them a makeover?"

"That's actually part of my plan."

She blinked, then stared at him as if he'd lost his mind. "Giving them a makeover?"

"No, camouflaging us. Truth is, we won't know what we're dealing with until we get there, but don't you imagine the farm's likely been reclaimed from the rain forest?"

She nodded. "Makes the most sense."

"It does, and the better we blend into our surround-ings—the forest that hopefully comes right up to it—

the safer we'll be. So, your makeup skills are important. You'll need to make us one with our surroundings."

She gave him a delighted smile. "I can do that!"

"Damn straight you can. In the dead of night, blindfolded."

She stilled. "Da-a-amn, Finn. You are probably the nicest guy I've ever met."

He bit back a grimace. But, please…again with the nice? Even knowing she considered it a bona fide compliment, he couldn't help but think that *nice* from the mouth of a pretty girl was usually the kiss of death. It meant they wanted to be friends with a guy.

Which was Kiss of Death II, The Overkill.

And didn't his timing just suck the atom bomb? Because after all his do-I-or-don't-I's, he'd solved his dilemma about whether to seek a monogamous relationship or to carry on with his long-standing, comfortable man-ho ways.

He wanted a relationship. With Magdalene.

What a kick in the pants. It felt like a revelation, yet it wasn't out of the blue. From the moment he'd clamped eyes on her, he'd been drawn like he was the magnetic needle and she true north. Still, whenever he'd found himself hung up on her smile, her fit body, her eyes when the sun hit them or her uncomplaining way of getting things done—even the curve of her *cheek*, for God's sake—he'd assured himself he'd known her for a couple of *days* and the way she made him feel was likely simple lust or part of the adrenaline rush of their mad scramble across El Tigre.

And, shit, who was to say that wouldn't turn out to

be the case? Maybe his feelings wouldn't carry over to real life when things went back to normal and they left this country behind.

But he didn't believe that. Because he got it now, why people committed to just one person—he totally did. He'd never known he could feel about a woman the way he did about Magdalene. Yet suddenly he could visualize something he'd never even imagined. He could truly see them settling into a regular everyday life—hold the big adventure—and still couldn't imagine himself not wanting to commit to her alone for the long haul. And where the mere thought should have been enough to make him break out in a cold sweat, it instead made him feel…great. Shockingly, amazingly great.

Except for that part where she thought he was fucking *nice*.

So, that's it? his subconscious demanded. *You just pack up your toys and go home?*

Oh, hell no. He squared his shoulders. He had the woman he—holy shit—just might *love* on his lap with her arms around his neck and her legs around his waist. A guy would have to be a much less strategic planner than he was to let that opportunity pass him by. Bending his head, he kissed Mags's neck.

She shivered and tipped her head to give him wider access.

He licked the hollow at the base of her throat, then lowered his head farther to graze her collarbone with his teeth. "I'm not *nice*, Magdalene—get that through your head once and for all."

"Not nice," she murmured agreeably. "Even if it's not a *bad* thing. Got it."

"Would a nice guy do *this*?" Both of them were covered from head to toe to avoid the lively insect life in the rain forest, but he slid his hands up her back beneath her long-sleeved T-shirt and popped her bra. Before he could bring his hands around to cup her breasts, however, he heard a rustling in the woods.

Ardor promptly sidelined, he lifted her off his lap, held a finger to his lips in the universal "don't say a word" as he set her back down, then moved to put himself between her and the trail, from which he was 99 percent certain the sound was originating.

"Finn," she breathed in protest, but he shot her a steely-eyed don't-even-think-about-arguing look over his shoulder. And, wonder of wonders, it was actually effective, since she settled behind his back without further argument. Finn reached into his backpack and pulled out Joaquin's gun. He'd never imagined himself actually using it except in the diversionary way he'd described to Mags, but his aversion to the weapon paled in comparison to his fear for her, so he checked the clip, removed the safety and steadied his grip on an up-drawn kneecap to take aim at the point where the path opened to their camp. The continuing muffled noises were definitely coming from that direction. Sweat trickled between his shoulder blades at the thought of a troupe of cartel soldiers stepping into view.

It was an older man and woman, however, who rounded the bend, and they looked the worse for wear.

"Hold it right there," he said in a flat voice and they stumbled to a stop.

The woman had a graying blond braid and wasn't dressed for the rain forest. Instead of being covered up the way Mags had decreed they must, she was dressed only in a lightweight dress. It was made of dark material and had a modest cut, but her arms, exposed from elbow to fingertips, and her legs, exposed from calf to her bare feet, were swollen with insect bites. The man also wore no shoes, but he looked in better shape than she.

"You're American," the woman said in a dazed, yet somehow no-nonsense, voice. In English.

Mags gave his back a shove, but until he was positive these two weren't armed he wasn't about to expose her, so he merely tightened his back muscles and refused to move.

"Dammit, Finn," she said and shoved to her feet behind him.

The woman looked shell-shocked as she said, "Magdalene?"

At the same time that Mags blurted, "Nancy? *Brian?*"

CHAPTER TWENTY-TWO

ON THE HEELS of her shocked outburst, Mags felt as though someone had nail gunned her feet to the ground. For the space of several long heartbeats she could only stand there and gawk at her parents.

Ever since Joaquin let slip that Munoz had Nancy and Brian, she'd been operating with tunnel vision, her sights firmly set on one goal alone: to locate the farm where her parents were being held and get them away from it. It was an eye-opening shocker when Finn asked how she planned to do that once they found the grow farm and she'd realized she didn't have the sketchiest of strategies. And worse, that she had dragged him into something with a very real potential for getting them both killed.

She knew their run-ins with Munoz's goons should have drummed that into her head from the get-go— knew it, knew it, knew it. Instead, even as it had scared the pants off her, she'd found it kind of exciting. God knew she hadn't taken the threat to their lives seriously enough.

Now here her folks stood, alive, relatively unharmed and close enough to touch if she could get her feet to move. So aside from keeping the heck away from anyone connected to Victor Munoz, it slowly sank past the muzziness in her brain that a game plan was no longer needed. And it was a relief—God, such a relief.

So, why, at the same time, did it feel kind of... anticlimactic?

She shook her head to shoo the thought away. "We heard Munoz had you stashed on his grow farm."

"And you were coming to get us?" Nancy demanded incredulously. "Oh, Magdalene. Don't you know how dangerous that is?"

She was beginning to. But in an admittedly knee-jerk reaction toward her mother in particular—since Nancy was the more iron-willed of her parents and in Mags's mind Brian had always done as she wished—she shrugged. Sulkily, God help her, as if she'd taken a page straight out of her angry-adolescent playbook.

"What were you thinking?" Nancy continued with crisp schoolmarm-to-student use-the-brain-the-good-Lord-gave-you diction. "Munoz wanted nothing more than to get his hands on you so he could use you as a bargaining chip to control us. He knew—"

"Is this really the way you want your reunion with your daughter to go?" Finn demanded in his most clipped, authoritarian voice, and Mags watched as her mother's mouth first dropped open, then snapped closed as the older woman turned to face him, chin elevated and her expression loaded with a steely authority of her own.

Which clearly didn't affect Finn in the least. "You honest to God want to treat her like the irresponsible thirteen-year-old you shipped off to the States?" He met her mother's gaze with level-eyed disinterest in her umbrage. "Except, wait. She wasn't actually irresponsible then, either, was she?"

His voice went hard. "She knocked herself out and, yes, put herself in danger, all in order to save your ass—and all you can do is stand there and tell her how wrong that makes her?" Without awaiting a reply, he turned his attention to Mags and his tone gentled. "Grab the first-aid kit. Let's see if we can't make your folks more comfortable."

She turned numbly to follow his instructions. Holy crap, he'd said "ass" to her mother. Her *mother*! And he'd stood up for her. She smiled slightly as she unzipped the backpack to find the medical kit.

Behind her Nancy demanded, "Who are you, young man?"

"My name is Finn Kavanagh. Finnegan, if you feel the need to be formal."

"Really?" Mags craned to look at him over her shoulder. "Finnegan? I never knew that."

He hitched a muscular shoulder. "Why would you? It's not like anyone in the known universe ever calls me that except for Ma when she's mad at me. And then it's all—" his voice went vaguely falsetto *"—Finnegan Declan Kavanagh!"*

Clearly impatient with what she deemed nonessential chitchat, Nancy firmly inserted herself between them, blocking their line of sight to each other. Hands on her hips, she glared up at Finn. "Are you a mercenary?"

Mags snorted and Finn threw back his head and laughed with uninhibited amusement. He quickly got himself under control, however, and said politely to Nancy, "No, ma'am. I'm a contractor. My brothers and I own a construction company in Seattle."

"Finn came to El Tigre to hike the Andes and got caught up in my problems when he came across one of Munoz's soldiers threatening me. He intervened and we've been on the run from them ever since." Mags gave her head an impatient shake. "But that's not the important thing here. How on earth did you and Brian get away from the farm?"

"That would be your mother." Her father spoke for the first time, then smiled wryly. "Well, in a backward sort of way." He crossed to Mags to carefully gather her to his chest and give her a gentle hug. "It's good to see you, kiddo. You're so grown up." He stroked her hair. "And even more beautiful than I imagined."

Mags closed her eyes against the rush of warmth of being in his arms, and at his scent, which, although faint beneath a bitter, masking aroma of whatever he had smeared on his skin, was still familiar even after all these years. Cautiously, she slid her arms around his waist and hugged him back.

They stood thus for a moment before he stepped back to hold her at arm's length. Brushing a tendril away from her temple, he looked down at her. "She finally drove Munoz's cousin to the breaking point."

"I merely pointed out that the prostitutes should have access to medical care and frequent checks for STDs," Nancy said hotly. "It was in his own best interest, and the way they treat those women is *criminal*!"

"Yes, it's a worthy cause, as was your agitating for

the crop workers to strike for more money. But even you realize that you have a way of ordering people around that puts their backs up."

She sniffed indignantly, but admitted, "Perhaps I could have been more diplomatic."

"That's like saying perhaps Genghis Khan could be a tad ruthless in his drive to create an empire," Mags interjected, and stood her ground when her mother whirled on her.

"These injustices need to be addressed," the older woman said coldly.

"No one knows that better than I, Nancy," she replied with equal chilliness.

"Mother! Not Nancy, I'm your *mother*!"

She shrugged and agreed in a tone that leaned to the left of agreeable, "No one knows that better than I, *Mother*. After all, it's the reason you sent me away from home when I was thirteen—to have more time for your causes."

She saw her mother open her mouth and jumped in before Nancy could climb on her political high horse. "I was under the impression the reason they kidnapped you in the first place was because you kicked up a fuss against Munoz's conscription of the neighborhood kids into his organization. I'm kind of surprised you weren't murdered outright. No, no!" she hastened to add when she saw the look of horror on her mother's face, as if she'd actually believed Mags would be *okay* with that. "I'm gratified beyond words that you weren't hurt! I just meant that drug lords aren't exactly known for their mercy."

"For reasons that nobody truly understands, Munoz's mother decreed that Nancy was not to be harmed," her father explained. "And since everyone's terrified of Senora Munoz, Victor sent us to Juan Carlos, the cousin who manages his farm for him."

"So, I don't get it. This cousin was holding you both prisoner, then he just suddenly let you go?"

"You know your mother is constitutionally incapable of *not* stumping for socioeconomic reform, and as we said, she fomented one rebellion after another. The health check for hookers was apparently the last straw for Juan Carlos. He had a couple of his men drive us into the rain forest about an hour's distance from the farm and they turned us loose without water, food or proper clothing."

A chill chased down Mags's spine. "Therefore being able to tell Victor Munoz that while he hadn't killed you as ordered, you had still somehow managed to escape. But that, sadly, you hadn't taken anything with you to aid in your continued well-being, so your chances of survival were virtually nonexistent."

She couldn't help her sense of pride when she looked at her parents. They'd definitely taken a beating, so were in less than tip-top condition. But for a man and woman in their late sixties who'd been in the Amazon without proper equipment and zero supplies, they were still much healthier than they likely had any right to be. Certainly more so, she'd wager, than Juan Carlos had anticipated when he'd tossed them out like a couple of unwanted mongrels. "How long since they dumped you in the rain forest?"

"Two days, maybe three," her mother said, still sounding stiff.

"It was two, dear." Brian's voice came from directly overhead and Mags looked up to see her father had drifted across the clearing to stand next to her.

Mags handed him the water bottle and rose to her feet. "Sip that slowly," she instructed and, seeing that Finn was keeping an eye on him, she took the tube of cortisone cream over to her mother, whose insect bites appeared in most need of attention.

For a while, as she gently treated the worst of them, she maintained her silence. Ultimately, however, she said, "I take it this Juan Carlos guy didn't know you and Brian spent years ministering not far from this very area and actually know your way around it quite well."

She noticed how much less plump and pliable her mother's skin was than it'd been the last time Mags had seen her. Observed as well that veins snaked beneath the thin flesh on the backs of Nancy's spotted hands. These were the first signs of aging Mags had ever noticed in her, and something about viewing them now made her heart hurt.

For a brief moment, she thought she felt her mother stroke her hair. Then Nancy made an un-Nancy-like rude noise, and she nearly snorted as well at how active her own imagination was.

"He cares for and knows nothing beyond that godforsaken coca farm," the older woman scoffed. "He is a city boy at heart. And since *he* wouldn't have a snowball's chance of surviving the rain forest without every amenity known to man at his disposal, he clearly believed the chances of old coots like your father and me were even bleaker."

Finn came over and squeezed some of the cortisone from Mags's tube onto the back of his hand. "For your dad," he said as he handed it back and flashed Nancy a small smile of approval. "Guess you proved him wrong, didn't you?"

"Yes, we did," she said with grim satisfaction at the same time that Brian murmured, "Oh, she determined we'd do that within minutes of being pushed from the car onto an old defunct road in the rain forest."

She turned to him. "They tied you up like a roped heifer—you with your bad hip!—and just tossed you out like so much garbage!"

"They did the same to you, dear."

"Indeed. But I don't have a tricky sciatica." She made an impatient erasing motion as if that were hardly the point, when patently it was. "We couldn't let them get away with that, could we?"

Mags was surprised at the depth of her fury. She had to unclench her teeth before she asked, "How did you untie yourselves?"

"Fortunately, when they trussed our hands, they did so in front rather than behind us. They obviously didn't expect us to get loose either way, so being senior citizens in this instance worked in our favor."

"The fact they weren't particularly skilled at knots didn't hurt, either," Brian said.

Nancy's lips curved up in a slight smile.

Mags concentrated on doctoring her mother's bites while she wrestled her anger under control. "A couple

of these are infected," she observed with laudable brisk-
ness to disguise the emotions roiling inside her. "But
most of them aren't too bad."

"The infected ones are bites we got before we found
the andiroba tree."

It took her a second to remember the significance of
the andiroba. Then the bitter smell she'd caught on her
father's skin kicked up memories of her youth and her
mother concocting remedies from the local flora. "You
managed to make oil from the seeds?"

Nancy nodded. "It's supposed to ferment for a week
or two but obviously we didn't have that kind of time.
Luckily, even fairly raw it was beneficial. As you can
see, as an insect repellant it didn't work as effectively
as a properly made batch would have. But none of the
bites we got while wearing it are infected."

She and Finn finished doctoring her parents and
fetched warm tops and socks from their supplies for
the older couple to put on. And not a moment too soon.
They had barely finished donning the garments when
the sun went down and the temperature dropped what
felt like—and likely was—a good forty degrees.

As Finn built a fire and cooked them dinner he asked
Brian and Nancy whether they'd be able to give directions to the grow farm to the Santa Rosa authorities.

"We can't go to the police there!" Nancy said in
alarm.

"I know," he agreed in his most soothing voice and
Mags watched his deep tones calm them the same way
they always did her. "Mags told me Munoz's cousin is
a high-ranking officer there. I was thinking more along

the lines of the US consulate. Do you think you can remember well enough to make them a map?"

Her parents claimed emphatically that they could, but as they both showed signs of nodding off during the meal, Finn declared tomorrow soon enough to pursue that avenue and ushered them into the tent. He was back out a moment later with a handful of items he'd fetched to set up a rudimentary bed for the two of them.

As soon as they were settled, he wrapped her in his arms. "You okay?"

She nodded, although she wasn't sure she truly was. "We dodged a bullet having them thrown out in the wild," she admitted. "But I'm furious over the way they were treated." She hesitated, then admitted, "At the same time—and I know this is juvenile and petty beyond belief—I'm struggling with my same old anger at *them*. And feeling guilty about putting you in danger. God." She rubbed at her temples. "My thoughts keep twisting in so many different directions my head feels like it's about to explode."

"Hey, don't waste your guilt on me," he said and dug his strong fingers and thumbs into the knots in her neck and shoulders, an action that probably did more to alleviate her headache than the two pain relievers she'd taken before crawling into their makeshift bed. "I've had fun."

"Oh, God, really? I thought it was only me! I kind of enjoyed the adrenaline rush of it all. I've been feeling guilty about that, too."

"You'd make a good Catholic girl with all that guilt," he said with a grin.

"You better hope my mother didn't hear you say that," she muttered. But she realized, as Finn drifted off, that he'd made her feel less blameworthy.

She still didn't sleep for beans. She was cold everywhere Finn's body heat didn't reach, and it was far less comfortable lying with only their dirty laundry between them and the ground than she'd grown accustomed to in his snug little tent.

The physical discomforts, however, she could deal with. It was her folks' unexpected appearance that had her brain spinning with what-ifs, an anger she knew she had to grow up and get beyond, and relief and regrets that intertwined in one long, no-resolution loop after another.

She stumbled out of her nest at dawn and, to the accompaniment of birds and monkeys screeching overhead, trotted knock-kneed a short way down the path until she selected an out-of-the-way, hopefully critter-free tree to do her business behind. Black beetles the size of her palm lumbered along the forest floor as she squatted, and she engaged a bright green frog with red eyes and a blue-and-white striped stomach in a stare-down.

When she got back to camp, she was a bit disappointed to find everyone else already up. She wouldn't have minded a few more minutes' solitude to get her Zen on.

Nancy and Brian looked stronger this morning and after discussing strategy over breakfast they broke camp and started back in the direction she and Finn had come from yesterday. Her parents were still recovering from their stint in the rain forest without proper gear and nutrition, however, so despite earlier appearances the going was a good deal slower. Mags spent part of it wondering how far the train she and Finn had come in on went on its return trip. She hadn't paid attention to its originating city when they were looking into tickets to take them toward the Amazon.

With luck, perhaps it would take them a good part of the way toward Santa Rosa.

Four days later
Around 10:00 p.m.

MAGS WAS FLATTENED by exhaustion by the time Finn parked the car that they'd rented in La Plata near the front of their capital-city hotel. She knew it, in turn, was near the American embassy where they had an appointment with the ambassador late the following morning. At the moment, however, she didn't really care.

All she wanted when she climbed from the automobile was to go up to her room and sleep for a week. Since her reunion with her parents she hadn't managed more than a catnap here or there. So if she'd been rather uncommunicative during their trip back to Santa Rosa—well, it was better to say too little than too much. That was the only way she knew to avoid torching the few tenuous bridges she still shared with Brian and Nancy. Her temper was far too close to the surface, lurking like a troll beneath one of those bridges just waiting for someone to take a single unwary misstep.

On autopilot, she followed her folks and Finn into

the hotel. It was much larger and worlds grander than any other place they'd stayed on this journey. Her eyes kept drifting closed as they waited in a short line to check in. Giving in to the urge, she leaned against Finn and let her eyelids fall shut the instant she felt his arm slide around her.

They were next in line when she heard Nancy say in her you-will-obey voice, "I bit my tongue and said nothing when you shared a room with my daughter in that small-town inn on our way up here—even when I failed to see why she couldn't share a room with me, and you with Brian. But now that we're in a big-city hotel with ample vacancies, I assume you will get Magdalene her own room, yes?"

"No," Finn said and stepped up when the clerk signaled. Hearing her mother sputter, Mags cracked a heavy-lidded eye open just enough to see where he was navigating them.

And smiled to herself.

Moments later Finn gave her folks their room card and ushered all of them onto an elevator across the lobby. Outside the doors to their across-the-hall rooms moments later, he said to her parents, "Get a good night's sleep and meet us in the lobby at eight. We'll get breakfast, then buy some clothes to wear to the embassy appointment."

"We don't need fancy clothing to be credible!" Nancy protested.

"We need to be taken seriously so we can shut that grow farm down, and looking like a bunch of refugees won't aid in that. We're getting some decent clothing.

Deal with it." He opened the door to their room. "Come on, darlin'. Let's get you to bed."

"'Kay." Mags yawned and fought to pry her eyes open once again. "Good night, Nancy," she murmured. "Night, Daddy." She staggered into the room ahead of Finn, barely making it through the door before her grip on her tote went lax and her big purse tumbled to the floor. Stumbling around it, she navigated past a desk and a chair toward the most luxurious-looking bed she'd seen in ages.

The last thing she remembered was falling face-first on top of it.

CHAPTER TWENTY-THREE

IN A NEARBY café the following morning, over *café con leche*, eggs and sweet croissant-type pastries called *medialunas*, Finn spent most of breakfast trying to strategize with Mags and her folks about their upcoming meeting. It was like herding cats.

It took no time at all for him to realize that, of the four of them, he was the only one with real business sense. Mags had that artist's mind-set that made her so good at spontaneous disguises and role-playing. But when it came to the type of protocol they'd likely be smart to follow at their upcoming meeting, she kept losing focus, most of her attention spent on sneaking peeks at her mother while pretending she was above that sort of thing. Brian's attention span was equally brief and Nancy kept wanting to sidetrack everyone with the social injustices she felt should be included in the discussion with the ambassador.

"No," he finally said flatly, the third time she tried to take them in that direction. "Today is about telling how you were kidnapped and held, how Mags twice escaped an attempted kidnapping, and how she and I were repeatedly threatened by armed men. It's about pointing the authorities to the grow farm—and nothing else." He leveled her with a stern look.

Then blinked. *Holy shit. You channeling Ma now?* That was kind of embarrassing.

Still, if it was what it took to make the Delucas see they might only have a finite number of minutes to state their case and they damn well better make the most of them if they wanted to see Munoz put out of business, so be it. They had a good map, made by all of them first thing this morning. The senior Delucas had given them detailed directions, he'd figured them to scale and Mags had drawn it. The more facts they had at their fingertips to help the authorities see ways in which they could facilitate *their* end of the operation, the better.

But that meant staying on track and relating their experiences briefly and concisely, not wandering off on unrelated tangents.

He would give them props for the way all three were briskly respectful of each other. Hell, if anything they were too respectful, working overtime to ignore their checkered family relationship. As if there really weren't a two-ton elephant in the room.

Until, in the midst of another rehearsal he'd forced upon them, Mags's mom leaned into the table. She pinned an uncompromising gaze on her daughter, who sat across from her, desultorily pushing food around her plate with her fork, and suddenly turned things very personal, indeed. "Why did you call me Nancy when you said good-night last night but called your father Daddy?"

Finally! Finn felt like pumping a fist in the air. He'd

been watching the Delucas' interaction with Magdalene ever since they'd stumbled into camp five days ago. Brian was pretty much an open book. The man was good-natured, easygoing and slightly vague, and it was plain to see he was perfectly happy letting his wife rule the roost. Unlike Nancy, however, he had no problem demonstrating his love for Magdalene. Given the slightest opportunity, he touched and hugged her. And he kissed her every chance he got. On her forehead, or her cheek or her temples. Or on—Finn's personal favorite—the little dent in her chin.

Nancy did none of those things. But even as Finn winced to watch her shoot herself in the foot time and again by letting all that stiff-necked pride get in her way—not hard to see from whom Mags inherited hers—he recognized the longing with which she looked at her daughter whenever Mags's attention was elsewhere. He saw the covert touches that skimmed Magdalene's hair or brushed against a fold of her clothing.

And he thought it was about time she actually said something.

Mags's chin shot up. "Maybe I call him Daddy because I know it was your idea to exile me when I was just a kid."

"Oh, no, sweetheart," her father protested, but Nancy reached for his hand and gave it a squeeze. He fell silent.

He did not, however, look happy about it.

"She's right, dear," she admitted. "That was my idea."

Brian scooted his chair a little closer to his wife's

and said, "But not for the reasons she believes. And at the time, I totally agreed."

"What?" Mags looked as though he'd just kicked her kitten. "No." Then her eyes hardened. "So tell me, for what other reason was I *supposed* to believe I'd been banished from my home?" she demanded. "You just wanted more time to improve the lives of other people's kids."

"Ah, Magdalene, *no*." Nancy leaned even farther into the table and for once didn't retreat behind the imperious silent disapproval she occasionally wielded to great effect. She reached for her daughter's hand, but Mags slid hers from the table and onto her lap.

Nancy sighed but straightened her shoulders, which had momentarily slumped. "Our decision had nothing to do with having more time to work with other people's children and everything to do with the way you suddenly developed overnight and the explosion of interest it brought from the local boys."

"What?" Finn watched as Mags finally quit pretending she was just too, too disinterested in her mother's explanation and leaned into the table as well. "What are you talking about? What boys?"

"You know." Her mom twirled a hand. "The boys you played with in the jungles and on the streets of every small township or larger city we lived in," she said earnestly. "I have to stop and think to recall we were living in Onoato at the time. But, Magdalene, I will never forget the way those boys started looking at you."

She thrust her fingers in her hair and held it off her

forehead as she stared at Mags. "I admit we could have handled things so much better than we did, beginning with telling you our reasons for sending you to school in the States in the first place and continuing right through all the rebellious years that followed. But the truth is, I saw those boys beginning to...what do the American kids call it? Check you out? And I panicked. Lord above, Magdalene, I was terrified right down to my bones. We wanted so much more for you than marrying young and living too short a life having too many kids in too much poverty. We wanted you to have a good education and a chance at whatever your dream turned out to be."

"So you screwed me up for life when a single conversation might have made things so much easier?"

"Honey, I'm sorry. I am genuinely, deeply sorry. We didn't know how to connect with the new you when you came home on holidays, but we should have—*I* should have—tried harder. I know I did everything wrong." Then she added fiercely, "But you are not screwed up. You turned out to be such a strong, capable woman."

Mags opened her mouth and Finn held his breath, waiting for her to tell her folks about sleeping with half the lacrosse team before she turned fifteen. He was pretty sure it would kill them to learn what their lack of a simple explanation had cost.

His gut clenched when he looked at her. Jesus. Except for exhaustion-generated dark shadows beneath her eyes, she was pale as rice paper. He knew damn well she'd hardly slept since her parents' return into her life.

And despite the way she'd fallen into what had looked scarily close to a coma last night, he knew she was still sleep-deprived. One good night didn't make up for the other four spent tossing and turning. And that wasn't even taking into consideration the sketchy sleep they'd gotten before that.

But with so many years of being furious with her parents, that made keeping her own counsel even iffier.

At the tail end of a moment's hesitation, however, she merely said, "You'd be heartsick if you knew the many ways I've messed up."

"Well, of course you made bad decisions," her father said with beatific acceptance. "You were an angry kid. But that's not your fault, kiddo—that's your mom's and my burden to carry for making you feel abandoned." He met her unhappy gaze squarely and said with a firmness Finn hadn't before heard from him, "We can't undo the past, Magdalene. But we can take responsibility for it, and we'd sure like it if we could build a better relationship with you going forward. Do you think you could open your heart to that?"

Finn doubted anyone drew a breath while Mags pondered the question. Then she slowly nodded. "I guess I could try."

Her parents audibly exhaled. Then Nancy actually laughed, and it transformed her, making her look years younger and worlds more approachable. He was helpless against smiling at her in return. Then he glanced at his watch.

And swore under his breath. "I hate to break this up," he said, "but the clock is ticking down and we still need to find something to wear and get ready for our appointment."

He decided to count it as a corner turned when Nancy didn't argue.

JOAQUIN WAS ON the outskirts of Santa Rosa when his cell phone rang. Glancing at the screen, he saw the mercenary Palmer's name and hovered his thumb over the red phone icon with its slashed-circle international No symbol. He'd failed in his mission and Munoz had ordered him back to the capital city. All the way back here he'd been fighting the urge to run in the other direction, fearful of what lay ahead for him.

Did he really want to further burden his day listening to the moron *yanqui* as well?

No. Yet he thumbed the green button all the same. "Palmer," he said with admirable neutrality.

"Boss, Boss, I got me a bead on the woman and her American boy toy!"

"What?" He sat straighter in his seat, a rare joy suffusing him. He was saved? When Munoz had spent only the few seconds it took to bark at him over the phone to return to Santa Rosa *now*, he'd thought he was a dead man for sure for failing to complete the task he'd been assigned. But he had another chance! "Where?"

"I saw them entering the Hotel Almerante with shopping bags. Some older people who also had store bags went into the hotel in front of them but I couldn't tell if they were together or just hitting the door at the same time. Unfortunately, I couldn't stay to keep an eye on the joint—it's sum-bitchin' upscale, and first the door-

man, then a *guardia*, rousted me. But I'm driving past
as often as I dare, because that doorman's got, like,
fucking eagle eyes. With this bum leg, I won't be much
good to you for the takedown, but I can call up an associate if you'd like."

"Do that. And, Palmer, excellent work. I will see that
you're paid a bonus if all goes well." Disconnecting, he
tossed the phone on the seat next to him.

And pushed the gas pedal to the floor.

"I very much dislike not being able to see for myself
what, if anything, is being done," Nancy said as they
returned to the hotel after their appointment with the
consulate. "And while I understand the reasoning behind not yet being able to go back to our apartment, protective custody for your father and me by those United
States drug people seems extreme. I don't understand
why they're even involved in El Tigre business in the
first place."

Mags was running on a real lean mix but she dug
deep for patience. Because contrary to Finn's warnings
regarding the need to make their case quickly and concisely, they'd been met by not only a very accommo-
dating ambassador, but also representatives of the US
Drug Enforcement Administration eager to hear their
stories. "Special Agent Morgan explained it to us," she
said to her mother. "The DEA works closely with coun-
tries who ask for their help. And because corruption in
El Tigre's police departments is fairly widespread, this
country did precisely that. Your testimony may well put
a good part of Munoz's operations out of business—if

not shut down them down entirely. So of course they want you someplace safe."

"I'm so disappointed, though, that you're going home when we've only now gotten you back."

"I know, Mom," she said gently, "but my bank account is running on fumes and I need to get my career back on track so I can pay my bills."

Because she and Finn had no firsthand information from Munoz that he'd held her parents on his grow farm, the DEA had given them permission to go home. If Joaquin wasn't brought down by the case against Munoz, they'd be brought back for a separate trial, but no one honestly expected that to happen. Seeing her mother's disappointment now, however, she said, "I promise not to let so much time go by between visits—I'll come down as often as I can afford. Plus you and Dad still get sabbaticals, right?"

Nancy nodded.

"Then you need to come up whenever you can and see what my life is like."

She was still reeling from the knowledge that everything she'd believed about her parents' reasons for sending her away had been wrong. The upside-down and inside-out kind of wrong. A wound she'd carried deep inside for what seemed like forever felt as if it might finally heal once and for all.

Yet she also felt guilty, because even accepting they'd tried to protect her, a bitter-edged resentment still lingered. They'd have better protected her by telling her their reasons, and should have done precisely that. She'd spent all these years guarding herself against further rejection because they'd kept silent over something that, had she known, would have spared her that—as well as saved her years of heartache. At the very least, knowing might have made her less stingy with her emotions over the years, perhaps even to a point where she'd have been open to the kind of genuine relationships other people shared.

Oh, please. Her shoulders twitched impatiently. *Pity party much?* She was fully accountable for her actions and certainly usually more stoic. But all the same—

"Why didn't you tell me until now the things you said at breakfast?" she demanded. "I understand not trying to get through to me when I was a teen—I was too angry then to give you an honest shot at an explanation." Only barely conscious of crossing her arms over her breasts, she leveled a look on Nancy. "But I've been an adult for a long time now, Mom. How many years have you been writing to me? I've heard all about the problems in the neighborhood and the ups and downs of the kids you work with. Why did you never once say anything meaningful about *our* relationship?"

Her mother abruptly sat on the edge of the bed and stared down at the work-worn hands she'd folded in her lap. For several moments Mags didn't think she intended to reply.

But then Nancy looked up. "Oh, Magdalene," she said, "I have no defensible explanation. I intended to tell you once you turned twenty-one, but you quit coming home for even those uncomfortable short visits when you were nineteen. When you started writing to me I told myself I'd explain in a letter, but I kept putting it off. I've never been good at talking about my feelings." Looking miserable, she met Mags's gaze. "I know that's no excuse."

"Actually, it's not too shabby," Mags admitted. Surprisingly, the simple act of demanding an answer had mitigated some of her anger. Her mother's words abated yet another portion. It might take a while before her anger went away entirely, but this was a start. "I'm not all that great about opening up to people, either. So how about you and I make a deal? Let's both try to do better in that area."

Her mother nodded, her eyes lighting up. "I'd like to try that. I would *very* much like that."

Mags abruptly realized how tired she was. And hungry—she hadn't had much of an appetite the past several days, but it appeared it was back with a vengeance. "I'm sorry," she said, "but I need to lie down. Let me grab a nap, then we'll talk some more."

"All right." Nancy stroked her work-worn fingers down Mags's cheek. "I'm so glad to have you back in our lives," she said and tears rose in her eyes, shocking Mags to the core. The older woman leaned in and pressed her damp cheek against Mags's.

Then, with a kiss to her forehead, her mother stepped back, but maintained contact by lightly grasping her upper arms. She gave them a squeeze. "I love you, dear. You go get some rest. We'll be right here when you wake up."

"I will." She started to turn away, but paused to face her mother again. "And, Mom? I meant to tell you, you look really pretty in that dress."

A pleased smile curved her mother's lips and she ran a reverent hand down the front of her garb. "I think this might be the most beautiful garment I've ever owned," she admitted.

"It suits you." Mags had searched for something that met all her mother's requirements, the most important of which in Nancy's eyes was a sales tag, as she hated to waste valuable resources on anything so frivolous as her appearance. Mags had found this dress at a deep discount, *plus* it was modestly cut and had white piping around the slightly scooped neckline and hemline that gave it the neat appearance her mother preferred. But the polished cotton was a beautiful blue-and-white delft print that made Nancy's faded eyes regain the more vibrant blue Mags recalled from her childhood.

Or perhaps it was the makeup Mags had applied. Her mother had pooh-poohed the idea of fussing with lipsticks and blushes, but Mags had persisted. Not until she'd asserted rather acerbically that she was a trained professional and the last thing she would ever do was make Nancy look like a tart had her mom reluctantly agreed. But Mags had watched her check herself out in the ladies room mirror at the embassy.

Had seen the tiny smile and the way she'd stood a little taller after that.

"I'll see you in a bit." She turned away and let herself out of their hotel room, blinking when Finn stepped around her to open the door to theirs.

"I thought you'd already gone back to our room." And had been afraid that even as she talked to her parents, he might be packing up to get back to his hiking trip.

"Nah. I like watching you with your ma and da." He grinned and escorted her into their room. "Especially your mom. It's kind of like watching the mating dance of the cacti."

She snorted. "I know, right? But you know what? We used to have a wonderful relationship and I think, given time, we might get back to a good place." It felt good to give voice to the thought and she whirled back to him.

"You know what else? I'm starving. And since I'm still mourning the loss of the *ajiaco* soup we had to leave in La Plata, I'm going to run to the bodega on the next block and see if they have any." She grabbed her wallet out of her tote and, rising onto her toes, planted a quick kiss on his lips. "I'll be right back."

Then without giving him a chance to respond, she whirled away and headed for the elevator. When she caught herself darn near dancing, she realized she felt lighthearted—and freer than she had in ages.

THAT'S RIGHT, Joaquin silently urged the woman walking in his direction, *come nearer*. Just. A. Few. Steps. Nearer.

He was close—so very, very close—to getting his hands on Magdalene Deluca. When he'd seen her striding up the street a few minutes ago, he'd thought for an instant he'd summoned an image of her through sheer wishful thinking. When it sank in that she was very real, he'd had to concentrate on not making an abrupt jump back from the mouth of the alley he'd been using as his lookout post.

Then promptly chided himself even as he inched

away. Because, would his imagination have conjured her in a dress and high-heeled shoes when he'd only ever seen her in shorts and those undershirts the *yanqui* mercenaries so colorfully termed wifebeaters?

The timing of her appearance was fortuitous, as he'd been on the verge of relinquishing all hope she was still at the Hotel Almerante. Even as he'd made this alley his headquarters, his first thought had been that he'd missed his opportunity to grab her. In the wake of Palmer's phone call it had taken more than an hour to make his way through the city's congestion from the south, where he'd entered Santa Rosa, to this neighborhood occupying the far northwest end of town. In that amount of time she and the interfering man she traveled with could have left Santa Rosa entirely or gone anywhere in the city—including the airport. He couldn't guess why she'd given up looking for her parents when she'd seemed so determined to find them, but maybe she'd finally realized the futility of her plan to rescue them.

And it wasn't as if he had other options. Palmer's sighting was his only lead. So he'd taken up position here for the simple reason it allowed him to keep an eye on the hotel entrance without being conspicuous. Unlike the American mercenary, he knew better than to parade back and forth in front of the hotel, so he melted behind the large garbage bins at the rear of the alley anytime he spotted a *policía* swaggering in his direction.

But Magdalene was here now and he fumbled for his phone, called up the number he'd entered for Palmer's contact and placed his call.

"Yo," the *yanqui* who answered said. "Wolkowski

here." Palmer had evidently delivered on his promise to bring in an associate.

"The woman is almost in my grasp. Bring the car."

"Uh, about that," the man rumbled and Joaquin stiffened. Those were not the words and tone that usually accompanied good news.

"Turns out this 'hood is lousy with embassies," the man said, "so it's crawling with cops and feds. I was rousted twice. Since I know how this game is played, I quietly moved along as instructed. But when the same fed rousted me a third time he called someone to put a boot on my car."

What was this boot? Cars didn't wear boots. Joaquin knew, however, it couldn't be a good thing. "Can you take this boot off?"

"Not without the proper tools. I have a friend coming to do just that. He'll be here any minute, and the second he arrives I'll trade cars with him. I should be there very soon."

If anyone ever suggested he work with an *americano* again Joaquin would stab them in the eye. And he'd do so cheerfully.

No. Not merely cheerfully. By all that was sacred, he'd sing like Carlos Vives even as he popped that eye like a grape. "I will trail the Deluca woman as long as I can to give you more time," he said through his teeth. "But when I call again, you had better be ready to pick us up."

He'd barely disconnected when Magdalene sashayed by. He gave her a second, then slipped out to follow a short way behind her. He had to whirl and feign inter-

322   RUNNING WILD

est in a window display of expensive-looking women's clothing when she suddenly turned into the bodega next door.

As soon as the door closed behind her he edged over to the store's window and craned to peer through the glass. He watched as she strode straight up to the counter and said something to the clerk. The man behind the counter turned away and selected a takeaway container.

"Ah." She was only there to get something to eat. He failed to comprehend why she hadn't simply ordered room service from her fancy hotel, but it was fairly evident she meant to take her purchase back to the hotel.

Joaquin walked back to the alley, where he slipped into the shadow thrown by the west wall. He stood motionless near the sidewalk. This wasn't an ideal situation, but it was one he thought he could work with—as long as the new mercenary arrived with the replacement car quickly. He glanced around, then had to jerk back when he saw she had almost reached the alley. He sidled back into the shadow.

It all hinged on this moment. If anyone was nearby and witnessed him grabbing her, there would likely be trouble. Yet it was either this or allow her to go back to her hotel—and what were the chances that the next time she came out she'd be alone?

She strolled past and he stepped out behind her, sending a quick glance up and down the sidewalk. A smile tugged his lips, for the gods were finally smiling down on him. Hooking an arm around her waist, he yanked her back against his front and hauled her into the alley, slapping his free hand over her mouth. The container in her hand hit the alley pavement and broke open, splashing hot soup.

She made a wild noise, but what would likely have clarioned to the heavens was an inconsequential sound muffled by his palm. Smiling even more widely, he turned her loose and shoved her up against the wall, pulling his knife from its sheath and holding it up for her to see its gleaming blade. "Hello, Magdalene. I had a feeling we would see each other again. Do not make a sound."

"WHAT THE HELL were you thinking?" Finn suddenly demanded of the empty hotel room and reached for the backpack he'd dumped on the bed just minutes ago. He headed for the door. He'd had no business letting Mags go to the store on her own. Yes, plans were in the works to clean up Munoz's cartel. At this moment, however, not a single bad guy was in custody.

Which meant they were all still in danger.

Granted, he thought as he exited the elevator and strode across the lobby to the exit, the odds of one of those bad guys just happening across Magdalene during the ten minutes—if that—it would take her to run to the bódega for her soup were probably a million to one. Hell, a trillion to one. Still, better safe than sorry.

He wasn't genuinely worried about that happening… until the moment he made it to the store without running into Mags on her way back and discovered the bodega empty of anyone but the guy at the counter. Then fear sank poison-tipped claws into him, but he forced himself to take a deep breath and look more closely down the aisles between the shelves to make sure he hadn't merely overlooked her. When he saw that he had not, he strode up to the man at the counter.

"Blonda senorita—" he waved his fingers over his own hair *"—adquisición ajiaco?"*

"Sí, marchado momento—" The man was still replying with the cheerful smile of reminiscence Mags seemed to inspire in people when Finn turned on his heel and ran out the door again.

"Oh, fuck," he muttered sotto voce. "Fuckfuckfuck-*fuck*!" Ordinarily he didn't possess a hair-trigger panic button and might have believed she'd simply ducked into another store. But she'd shopped today already, had professed herself starving and they had just spent a week being chased the length of this hell-bit country by goons with guns and knives. Pacing from the store entrance to the alley and back, he carefully checked out the cars driving down the avenue.

And choked back a bitter laugh.

Because if whoever snatched her had thrown her in a car, it didn't matter if he were two lousy minutes behind her or an hour. She could be goddam *anywhere*.

To add insult to injury, he swore he could smell the soup she'd gone to pick up and a sour acidity churned in his stomach. Why hadn't he—he should have—

Wait. That wasn't his imagination; he *did* smell it. He began examining the sidewalk and just inside the alley saw a pool of still-steaming liquid. A little farther in, the container lay on its side. His gut promptly tried to twist itself into a pretzel.

The alley appeared deserted at first glance but there was the El Tigre version of a Dumpster with cardboard boxes heaped atop it down near the alley's dead end. The shade cast by the container on the far side was deep enough to disguise a person or two.

Finn moved into the shadow thrown by the wall, slid his pack off his back and squatted to open it. He pulled out the gun and checked its clip. He had almost zero experience with guns and had shied away from the idea of using this one ever since he'd appropriated it from Joaquin.

But this pretty much answered once and for all the question of whether his feelings for Magdalene were merely a momentary lust for ownership fueled by the high-octane adrenaline rush of their adventures across El Tigre or the real deal. Because if it meant getting her back, he would shoot whoever held her without a second's remorse.

And he was damned sure that only for someone he loved with all his heart and soul could he ever bring himself to put a bullet in—let alone kill, if necessary— another human.

HEART POUNDING, Mags watched Joaquin disconnect his call. Lord have mercy, how had she ended up in this situation? She could barely breathe she was so…well, scared, of course.

But also more than a little pissed. *Are you freaking kidding me, God? We managed to get through all the shit of the past ten days, finally got my folks here safe and sound, and did the right thing by reporting Mu-*

noz's activities to the feds and you're allowing the bad guys to win, anyhow?

Joaquin suddenly pinned her in his sights. "We are going to wait here for our transportation. If you know what is good for you, you will remain very, very quiet."

"Why do you keep threatening to hurt me?" she asked, keeping her voice equally low and carefully neutral. "I've never done anything to you or your Senor Munoz."

"He doesn't want to harm you, imbecile. He wants you as a bargaining chip to keep your mother in line at the coca farm."

That would have been nice to know while they were dodging armed men. But she shook it off and concentrated on how she could use it to her advantage now if words didn't do the trick. "That won't succeed."

"You know nothing of the matters of men."

Okay. Swallow it down. Swa-a-a-llow it down. "I know that my parents are no longer at the grow farm, no longer in any territory that Munoz controls. Are you at all curious why I'm in this neighborhood?"

She could see he very much wanted to say no. But curiosity won out. "Perhaps." She remained silent and he gave her arm a shake. "Very well, why?"

"Because my parents escaped and were put into protective custody by the United States Drug Enforcement Agency in return for their testimony against your boss." She was taking a huge risk divulging this before they rounded up Munoz and his people. But saving her own butt was kind of imperative at the moment, so she'd simply have to hope she didn't screw everything up as she attempted to do so. "If I were you, Joaquin, I'd get out of town while you still can. Your boss is going down."

His brows furrowed. "Going down where?"

"It's an expression for the certainty of him going to prison for all the crimes he's committed. They wire-tapped his phone, you know. You actually saved your-self when you failed to tell him that you'd accidentally let me know where my parents were. But what do you think will happen to you when it comes out that you had information that would've given him the opportu-nity to kill my folks before they could use the things they observed on the farm against him? If El Tigre jails are anything like American ones, he'll likely still have a power base."

He turned a little green but said, "I could just slit your throat now and be done with it."

"Yeah, you could do that," she agreed even though she was this close to wetting her pants where she stood. "But when they find my body—and they *will* find my body, sooner, rather than later given this heat." Only by sheer force of will did she calm the gag reflex urging her to vomit. "Guess who will be the first person they look for? It's not like they don't know you've been hunt-ing me." She met his narrowed gaze. "Be smart, Joa-quin, and just walk away. Save yourself while you can."

Joaquin suddenly froze and she started when the heavenly sound of Finn's voice said, "Or I could shoot you where you stand."

Tearing her gaze from Joaquin's face, all she saw at first was Finn's long, competent hand—and the barrel of the gun he'd gotten off Joaquin that first night pressed against the thug's temple.

Then he stepped into sight from around the corner of the Dumpster. "Drop your knife," he snapped in a tone she'd never heard from him before. "Or I will pull the trigger."

Joaquin's knife clattered to the ground and Finn hooked him by the collar of his shirt and hauled him away from her. His hand didn't have so much as a tremor as he pressed the muzzle of the pistol against the base of Joaquin's skull. Then he looked at her where she'd scooted several feet down the wall from her former captor. "Are you okay?"

"Yes." She wanted to run to him but feared any distraction might put them back at square one. "I'm sure glad to see you, though."

"The feeling's mutual, darlin'. I called the feds. They should be here any second now."

THE WORDS HAD barely left Finn's lips when a black sedan roared into the alley and rocked to a halt. A tough-looking man stuck his head out the driver's window and said in American-accented English, "You Joaquin?"

"Shit," he whispered. The only saving grace here was that Joaquin and Mags were out of the new guy's line of sight behind the Dumpster. But feeling the indrawn breath that told him his captive was about to yell the truth, he quickly reversed his pistol and coldcocked Joaquin, thrusting his hand between the thug's shoulder blades to keep his suddenly inert body pressed against the wall. *"Sí,"* he said as he bent to lower the kid's dead-

SUSAN ANDERSEN

329

weight to the ground. "She was getting ready to yell so I...how you *americanos* say? Knocked her lights out. Open the trunk, then come give me a hand with her."

He was estimating his chances of taking the mercenary while his back was turned when another car wheeled into the alleyway and four men in black with DEA printed on their flak vests jumped out, guns drawn. "Drop your weapon on the ground and kick it over here," one yelled and, when after a brief hesitation the mercenary used two fingers to extract it from his holster and do as he was instructed, they tackled him to the ground and cuffed him.

An agent Finn had met earlier whose name escaped him at the moment approached him and looked from him to Mags. "You two okay?"

"We are now," she said and came over to stand close to Finn. He wrapped an arm around her and hugged her tightly to his side. He had a feeling it was going to be a while before he could make himself let her go.

They both gave accounts of what had happened, then watched as the two cartel soldiers were bundled into the DEA's car. One of the agents climbed into the sedan the mercenary had arrived in and followed the agency car from the alley.

He looked down at Mags. "You ready to go back to our room?"

"God, yes," she said fervently. Then her eyes narrowed. "Just as soon as I get another container of soup."

"You must think I'm a total idiot to make such a big deal over *ajiaco*," Magdalene said a short while later as she dropped the empty replacement carton of soup they'd just finished sharing into the wastebasket. She felt euphoric to be alive and fed and safely in the hotel room with Finn.

"Not now that I've tasted it," Finn said. "Besides, if I've learned nothing else about you, Deluca, I've learned that you never give up." He stepped close as she turned to face him. "It's one of the things I love about you."

Caught unprepared, she stepped back. "Wh-what?"

"You heard me. I love you."

"We've only known each other—"

"Ten days," he said easily. "During which time we've dealt with more situations than most people might in a lifetime. But like your mother said, you're a strong, capable woman, not to mention beautiful, brave and resourceful." He looked at her with those dark, intense eyes. "I love you with everything I've got, Magdalene, and want you to come back to Seattle with me."

"I can't, Finn. My work—"

"We have a film community in Seattle. Granted, it's nowhere as big as Hollywood, but it's very active. They must need a good makeup woman." He shoved his hands in his pockets and rocked back on his heels. "Or, hey, get a job on a Hollywood movie. We don't have to live in each other's pockets 24/7. I just want you there whenever I can getcha." He tilted his head to bestow a slight smile upon her. "And as an added bonus, if you take me you get my family as well."

Oh, God. It was everything she wanted—too much so, and she just knew she'd screw it up and his family wouldn't like her. And then he wouldn't want her anymore, either.

Okay, that was probably irrational and opening her mouth to try to explain some of her fears to him, she felt them instead all coalesce into one big burning ball of panic. "I can't." She couldn't quite catch her breath and she took another step back to put more distance between them. "I can't just upend my entire life!"

"Darlin'—" Eyes full of concern, he moved forward for every step she took back and reached out a long-fingered hand to touch her face, or hair, or she didn't know what. She only knew that if he made contact, something inside of her might rip irreparably. She slapped it away.

Finn froze. Then he, too, stepped back, all expression wiped clean. "Can't," he said in a cool, disinterested voice. "Won't try. Got it." He turned away and walked over to his backpack. Scooping it off the floor, he dumped it on the bed and started hurling stuff into it.

People left, that had been a given most of her life. *So this just proves my point, right?*

Except…

More often *she* had been the one to leave and Finn—

Finn had stuck by her. From the first encounter when he'd inserted himself in a total stranger's situation against an armed man he'd stuck by her. He had put everything on the line again and again.

For her.

He could have walked away at any time and no one would have blamed him. But he hadn't. He'd taken risks

at every turn and she was too chickenshit to risk anything. She'd once thought him an idiot.

*But who's the real idiot here, Deluca, if you let him
walk out that door?*

She watched as he buckled the fastenings on his pack
and straightened, slinging the bag around to hook it by
one strap over his left shoulder. He looked at her with
unreadable eyes. "Well, hey," he said, and shrugged.
"Can't say it hasn't been real."

Then he headed for the door.

Her heart pounded so hard and her throat clogged
with so much emotion, she was afraid she couldn't say
a word. But when she saw him reach for the doorknob,
she took a lurching step forward. "Don't go!"

Slowly, he turned to face her, his black brows gathered over his long, strong nose, his arms folded across
his chest. "Why the hell should I stay?"

"Because, if you leave me—" She licked her desert-
dry lips. "If you allow my fear to get between us, I'm
afraid I'll never change, that I'll just keep going through
life closed to all the possibilities I've felt since meeting
you." She wrapped her arms around herself, but took a
tiny step toward him. "God, Finn, I've felt more alive
in these past days with you than at any time since I was
sent away from El Tigre." She took another little step.
"I'm so tired of being lonely and too damn afraid to do
anything about it."

"And you love me," he said in a flat voice.

It was true. She could pretend otherwise but he knew
it and so did she. She nodded.

"Say it."

"I—" She cleared her throat "I…love you, Finnegan Kavanagh."

His backpack hit the floor with a thud, but he didn't otherwise move. "You love me madly."

"I do. *Beyond* madly."

"And you'll be my sex slave for life." It wasn't a question.

"And I'll be your sex slave for life," she agreed. Then hitched a shoulder. "When I'm not busy making you mine."

"Fair enough. But you'll wash my socks and fetch me beer and pick up after me until the end of time, right?"

"Not in this lifetime, Kavanagh."

"Thank you, Jesus," he said, casting a glance ceiling-ward before turning the full focus of those mesmerizing eyes back on her. "You were so damn agreeable, I thought for a minute there the body snatchers had gotten their hands on you. Most bullheaded woman on the planet, my Magdalene is—and that's the way I like her." He opened his arms to her. "Get over here, you stubborn wench."

She raced to throw herself into his strong embrace, clinging to him for a moment with her nose tucked into the curve where his neck flowed into his shoulder, simply breathing in the comforting scent of him.

He tipped his chin in to look down at her. "This— you in my arms and me in yours—this is home base for both of us from here on out, got it?"

She nodded. Lord, yes, this was home. She couldn't think of a single place safer. Better. Sweeter. "Got it."

"Then life is good, darlin'." He waltzed her over to the bed, where he lowered her onto the mattress. "Now. About that sex-slave thing..."

EPILOGUE

Seattle
Two and a half weeks later

MAGS WAS EXCITED about Finn's welcome-home party and when they arrived at the pretty medium-sized house where he'd grown up, she found it all but bursting at the seams. A tsunami of sound hit them as they pushed through the front door and she blinked, trying to take in everything at once.

The sheer number of people, all of whom appeared to be balancing drinks and plates of food, crowded the rooms to SRO capacity. A gang of kids, aged from maybe four to what looked like preteens, spilled past them into the yard, the girls in the group squealing. Even when the door closed behind them, the house rang with voices raised in conversations, laughter and song, and—in one case—a not particularly heated argument.

Her energy level revved up as if she were just hitting a night out at the hottest club in town. Who knew she could feel like this at a party held in broad daylight in a private residence, with children present?

She'd met a lot of Finn's family Tuesday evening when they arrived in Seattle in her old beater after

spending several days packing up her apartment. That
at least gave her a working knowledge of who was who,
starting with his mom and dad, his brothers and sisters and their respective wives, husbands and assorted
kids—although, in truth, she only had the siblings and
spouses figured out. She was still working to match all
the kids' names to their faces.

She was suddenly swept into a warm, fragrant hug
and emitted a surprised "Oh!" Then, connecting the
vanilla scent to Finn's mother, Erin, she laughed and
hugged her in return, trying not to poke her in the back
with the mixed-color gerbera daisies she'd bought on
the way here. When they pulled apart, she handed the
plump older woman the bouquet. "For you."

"Oh, darling, you shouldn't have." She grinned and
gave her lovely, slightly faded red hair a little toss as
she hugged them to her breast. "But they're simply gorgeous and I'm glad you did."

"This is quite the party."

"I know, it's a crush." Erin's quick one-shouldered
bump-and-drop was good-natured. "I'm sure Finn tried
to warn you, but no one can quite visualize a Kavanagh
family get-together until they see one for themselves.
Welcome to your first of many."

Finn's mom had no idea how that struck to the very
heart of her, and Mags's entire being filled with warmth.
"I'm so happy to be here."

"Aw. You're definitely a keeper."

"No fooling," Finn said. "Because that's not just good
manners, Ma. She's happy to the *bone* to be here."

With a smile that lit up the room, Erin hauled her

in for another hug and planted a smacking kiss on her temple. Turning her loose, she reached up to pat Finn's cheek. "God bless my boys for picking smart women."

Then she hefted the bouquet. "I'll go find a vase for these. You kids get a drink. Have some food." She gave her son a knowing look. "I'm sure you'll be shocked to hear that the usual suspects have taken over the basement."

He bent to give her a kiss, then turned to Mags. "You ready to meet more people?"

She gave him a brilliant smile. "Yes, please."

FINN GRINNED. Of course she was—his Magdalene had been *born* ready. Hell, he'd watched her careful preparations in front of the bathroom mirror before coming here. He'd seen women put on makeup before but had no idea one could take such care and use so many products, only to look like that glow was completely natural. And, face it, were the name Mags Deluca to be bruited about, shyness wouldn't be the first word that popped to anyone's mind.

Hooking her neck in the inner bend of his elbow, he hauled her to his side, then carved a path for them through the crowd. They were stopped several times and he dutifully introduced her. But his goal remained front and center in his mind: to gain the escape hatch in the kitchen, otherwise known as the door to the basement.

He spotted his aunt Eileen as they made their way through the dining room, but he whirled Mags in the opposite direction toward the long table that all but groaned beneath the weight of the food upon it. "Grab a plate, darlin', and we'll take it downstairs."

"Ooh. Great idea." She plucked two sturdy paper plates off a stack and handed one to him. They selected an assortment from the multitudinous offerings, then, with a promise to come back to fetch them something to drink, he steered her though the kitchen and headed for the door. He had his hand on the knob when a voice barked, "Not so fast, boyo. Hold it right there."

"Crap." Balancing his plate in one hand, he tugged Mags nearer with his other and murmured, "I love my aunt, but I gotta warn you she's a world-class busybody."

She beamed up at him. "I'm sure she's curious. You can't blame her for that."

He bent down to plant a kiss on lips he wished he could savor for more than a here-and-gone peck. "I love you, girl. But don't say I didn't warn ya." Swinging her around, he pulled her against his side and slapped on a smile that became genuine as he watched his aunt stride toward them with her usual flame-haired, proud-postured presence. "Hey, Auntie Eileen. Meet my Magdalene."

She came to a halt in front of them. "How do you do," she said to Mags, then added before she could reply, "You've only known my nephew for a few weeks. What can you possibly *actually* know about him in such a short a time?"

"Aunt Eileen," he said warningly, but Mags squeezed his side with the hand she'd slipped around his waist.

"It's a fair question," she told him, then turned to Eileen. "Finn jumped in to help a total stranger in trouble, so I knew from the minute I laid eyes on him that he had a good heart. Or was an adrenaline junkie," she added with a little smile and a nudge of her shoulder against his side, making him snort.

Then she sobered and looked Aunt Eileen straight in the eye. "I know he can fix just about anything and is the most competent man I've ever met. I know he's smart and his word is gold. And I know he thinks *nice* is a dirty word and isn't to be used in compliments."

"Why on God's green earth not?" his aunt demanded. "It's a perfectly good word."

"Right?" Mags looked at Eileen as if genius had rolled like pearls from her lips.

Eileen turned to Finn. "How about you, boyo?"

"I know that she's talented and inventive and that she never complains no matter how tough things get. I know she gets things done. Oh, and that she doesn't have a bladder, just a wide spot in the tube," he added and it was Mags's turn to snort her amusement. Then he looked his aunt in the eye. "But most importantly? I know she loves family above all else. And that I love *her* above all else."

"You're wrong about one thing." Magdalene tilted her head to look up at him. "I love you above family."

"Yeah?" His heart just might explode, it felt so full.

Without taking her gaze off him, she stroked her cheek against his chest. "Absolutely."

Aunt Eileen cleared her throat. "So, have you two set a date?"

"A date?" Mags blinked. "Like, for a wedding, you mean?"

"Of course."

"No. As you said, we've only known each other a short while and we're taking some time to simply be together and grow our relationship without worrying about men with guns chasing us across El Tigre." She shot Aunt Eileen a glance. "Although I know Finn's good at dealing with them as well."

"As is Mags," he said and gathered her closer. "We'll catch up longer next time, Auntie, but for now, we're grabbing something to drink and taking our food downstairs."

"Give me a kiss," she said and, after he leaned in to comply, patted his cheek like his mother had. "You're a good boy and it looks like you finally hooked yourself a good woman." Turning away, she strode over to a boy trying to sneak a beer from the tub of drinks. "Pull that bottle out, Aiden," she said in a voice that snapped with menace despite its pleasant tone, "and I'll tan your hide."

Finn laughed and opened the door, gesturing for Mags to precede him down the stairs.

THERE WAS CONVERSATION and music down there as well, but not at the burst-your-eardrums decibels of upstairs. The first person Mags saw was Finn's sister Hannah. The pretty brunette strode over to them the moment they stepped onto the Berber wall-to-wall and gave Mags a quick hug.

"Welcome to the real party," she said as she released

Magdalene and stepped back. "Sit down and eat your food. Did you see your Welcome Home sign?" She gestured at the homemade banner strung horizontally above the fireplace mantel.

Mags shot Finn a delighted smile. "Look, it has my name on it, too!"

"Well, of course it does," Hannah said. "Finn's told us all the things you did—like distracting that armed cartel thug while he dismantled the guy's car."

"Yeah?" She shot him a look. "I'm surprised he mentioned that one, since he was sure pissed off at my methods at the time. He thought I was offering the guy a bl—"

"Hey," Finn hastily interrupted, "let me introduce you to everyone. You know Dev and Jane." He flicked a finger toward where they were shooting a game of pool and they both looked over and waved. "But these are Jane's best friends—" he indicated the two women seated on a comfy-looking old beat-up leather couch "—Poppy and Ava."

She stilled as an old insecurity over women with inner circles she'd never belong to reared its ugly head. It was a complete flip-flop of her fear of intimacy, but, hey, when had *any* of her issues made sense?

In any case, she shook it off and handed Finn her plate before stepping forward with squared shoulders and a smile. "Hi. I'm Mags." She thrust out a hand to Ava, the voluptuous redhead who was first off the couch.

"Oh, screw that," Ava said and pulled her in for a warm hug. When she turned her loose, she said, "Janie's been telling us since Tuesday night about how you and Finn set off to rescue your folks and ended up bringing down an entire cartel. We've been dying to meet you, haven't we, Poppy?"

"We have," her blonde friend agreed and also gave her a hug. She pulled her over to the couch. "Sit down and tell us how you plan to follow up all that excitement. Jane says you're a makeup artist and a street performer?"

"I am." Mags sat where Poppy indicated, next to her on the couch. "I'd just gotten my foot in the door to do a Hollywood space epic when my folks disappeared, so I have to restart from scratch. That could take forever, though, so I picked up a job yesterday with a photographer in Belltown whose rep for his author photos in the writing community is exploding."

"So you're pretty good at it?" Ava asked and Mags had barely gotten "I am" out of her mouth before Finn squatted down in front of them.

"That artist part of makeup artist?" he said. "It's no exaggeration." Turning on his camera, he flipped open the view screen and clicked through his thumbnails. Finding what he wanted, he handed the camera to Ava. "This is what she did with her travel kit in about ten minutes in a four-by-four bathroom while goons were searching for us at a festival. You can click the right arrow to see more."

The women leaned in. "Holy shitskis," Poppy breathed. "Look at… Is that *you*, Finn?"

"Yep."

"Omigawd, look at this one!" Ava said and leaned

around Poppy to look at Mags. "I didn't realize that was you at first. You look like a statue."

She gave her a delighted smile. "Living statues is what I do. That's my performance art." She smiled wryly. "If you can call staying perfectly still performance."

"Having seen it for myself," Finn said, "I'm here to tell ya you can."

"Where's Cade? He's gotta see these." Ava looked around, then raised her voice. "Cade!"

"I'm right here." A man with sun-streaked brown hair and Paul Newman blue eyes strolled into the room from another part of the basement and leaned over the back of the couch to kiss the top of Ava's head. "What's all the racket, baby?"

"This is Finn's Magdalene," Ava said and Mags realized she'd quit minding that people called her that. "Mags, my husband, Cade. She's a makeup artist." Ava tipped her head back to look up at her husband. "Look what she did when they were in El Tigre."

She started to hand him the camera, but Finn's deep auburn-haired, dark-browed brother Dev reached over the back of the couch to intercept it. "Beauty before the feebly aged," he said with a cocky grin at his brother-in-law.

"Correct me if I'm wrong, Kavanagh," Cade said drily, "but aren't you older than me by a couple years?"

Dev hitched a shoulder. "Details." He looked down at the camera's screen.

And stilled. "Holy shit," he breathed as he clicked through the photos. He passed the camera to Cade. "You do have to take a look at these." Then he sent a sly look Finn's way. "Gotta say, bro, tiger stripes and furry forearms are a real good look on you. Big improvement over your usual ugly mug."

Cade seemed to tune out the byplay as he stared down at the screen for what seemed like an age before looking up to meet Mags's gaze. "This is good. How long did it take you to achieve each look?"

"I did both in about ten, fifteen minutes."

"With her small makeup kit in a tiny bathroom, Finn said," Poppy chimed in. "With thugs looking for them."

"Thus the quick job," Mags told Cade. "Ordinarily I like to take a little more time than that."

"Jesus, you did this in fifteen minutes? Do you have a portfolio?"

"Yeah." She wasn't sure why he'd care, but everyone was being really nice, so what the heck.

He proffered his hand across the back of the couch. "I'm Cade Gallari. I do—"

"Omigosh, I know you!" She shook her head along with his hand, trying her best not to squeal like a fangirl at meeting an honest-to-goodness famous documentary filmmaker. "Obviously, I don't *know* you, know you. But I know your work. It's *excellent*." She turned to Ava. "This is your husband?"

"Yep. Isn't he cute?"

Cade rolled his eyes but the look he gave his wife brimmed with love. Then he turned his attention back to her. "I'd like to talk to you about your work. Maybe I could give you a call this week?"

Yes, yes, yes! "I'd like that," she managed to say as

if she wasn't twirling in circles inside. "The only problem is my phone's new to me, so I don't have the number memorized yet."

"Here," Finn said, pulling his cell phone out of his pocket. "Take it off mine." Cade produced his own and the three men wandered into the other room.

Mags stared at the other two women on the couch. "Wow," she said and nudged Poppy, who sat next to her. "Are you married to a famous guy, too?"

"Nah." The blonde laughed. "My husband's a detective in the SPD. Our little girl still has the tail end of a cold, so he volunteered to stay home with her so I could come meet you. We'll have a dinner at our place soon so you can meet him and Bella."

"Poppy makes the best Stroganoff," Jane said.

Mags was in a happy daze when she came out of the bathroom a short while later and found Finn lounging against the wall. "Having a good time?" he asked.

"Oh, God, Finn." She walked into his arms and laid her head on his chest. "Everyone's been so *nice*. They treat me like I'm some big deal."

"You're sure as hell *my* big deal. And I don't think you appreciate how interesting you are."

"Awww." Pleasure suffused her. Yet at the same time— "I feel kind of guilty being so happy when my folks are stuck in protective custody."

"Hey, the El Tigre government busted Munoz's operation and are cleaning up the corruption in their police department. Your parents will soon be back doing what they do best—converting hearts and minds."

"Yeah." She smiled against his shirt. "And they

promised to come visit during their next sabbatical. By then living in your place will be old hat."

"Our place," he corrected. "But I know it was hard to give up your apartment. You lived there a long time."

"I admit it pinched a bit to leave it. But moving up here with you, Finn? I never knew this kind of happy even existed."

"Me, either, darlin'." He stroked his hand down the fall of her hair. "And you know what the best part is?"

"That we're just gonna keep getting better and better?" He'd said that more than once—and she was a believer. Because she had faith in relationships now and both of them were prepared to work hard on theirs.

"Damn straight, darlin'." He smiled down at her. "Better and better yet."

* * * * *

If you enjoyed Finn and Mags's story, be sure to check out the rest of the books in this series, available now from Susan Andersen and HQN Books!

CUTTING LOOSE (Jane and Dev's story)
BENDING THE RULES (Poppy and Jase's story)
PLAYING DIRTY (Ava and Cade's story)

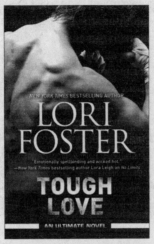

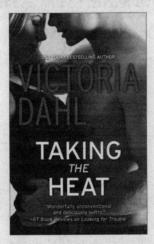

Susan Andersen

77887	NO STRINGS ATTACHED	___ $7.99 U.S.	___ $8.99 CAN.
77776	SOME LIKE IT HOT	___ $7.99 U.S.	___ $8.99 CAN.
77691	THAT THING CALLED LOVE	___ $7.99 U.S.	___ $9.99 CAN.
77589	PLAYING DIRTY	___ $7.99 U.S.	___ $9.99 CAN.

(limited quantities available)

TOTAL AMOUNT	$ _____
POSTAGE & HANDLING	$ _____
($1.00 FOR 1 BOOK, 50¢ for each additional)	
APPLICABLE TAXES*	$ _____
TOTAL PAYABLE	$ _____

(check or money order—please do not send cash)

To order, complete this form and send it, along with a check or money order for the total above, payable to HQN Books, to: **In the U.S.:** 3010 Walden Avenue, P.O. Box 9077, Buffalo, NY 14269-9077; **In Canada:** P.O. Box 636, Fort Erie, Ontario, L2A 5X3.

Name: _____

Address: _____ City: _____

State/Prov.: _____ Zip/Postal Code: _____

Account Number (if applicable): _____

075 CSAS

*New York residents remit applicable sales taxes.
*Canadian residents remit applicable GST and provincial taxes.

HQN™

www.HQNBooks.com

PHSA0915BL